The
TEDDY BEAR
BOOK
of Bedtime Stories

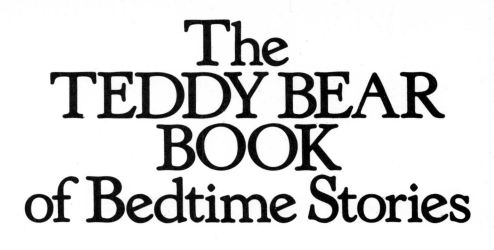

The TEDDY BEAR BOOK of Bedtime Stories

Written by Barbara Hayes

Illustrated by John Astrop

Derrydale Books
New York

First published in Great Britain by
Beehive Books, an imprint of Macdonald & Co (Publishers) Ltd.

1986 edition published by Derrydale Books,
distributed by Crown Publishers, Inc.

Printed in Yugoslavia.
ISBN 0-517-61770-6

January

1
January

Happy New Year

It was January the first, New Year's Day. Teddy Bear looked across at New Dolly.

'Happy New Year!' he said.

'Thank you,' replied New Dolly. 'Happy New Year to you, too.'

Just then a flurry of snowflakes blew against the window.

New Dolly did not know what it was. She had arrived only a week ago on Christmas Day and she was not very old.

'What is that funny white stuff falling from the sky?' she asked.

Teddy Bear was several years old and he knew everything – well, almost everything.

'That white stuff is snow,' explained Teddy Bear. 'It is cold and wet and really not very nice, but it is pretty to look at.'

New Dolly peered up into the sky.

'Where does the snow come from?' she asked.

'It falls from the chariot of the Snow Queen as she drives across the sky,' said Teddy Bear.

New Dolly peered up into the sky again.

'I can't see the Snow Queen,' she said.

'Ah well,' said Teddy, 'you need sharp eyes to see magical things like the Snow Queen. I can see her, of course, but then we teddy bears are clever little fellows.'

He leaned close to the window and called:

'Happy New Year, Snow Queen. I hope you are keeping well. Remember me to the polar bears when you get back to the North Pole.'

Up in the sky the Snow Queen drove on her way.

'How that Teddy Bear does like to show off!' she smiled.

2
January

The Big Brown Bear

Far away in the Rocky Mountains, a big brown bear lay deep in his winter sleep. Outside the wind howled across the deep snow, but in the cave the big brown bear was dry and warm as he lay on his bed of dead leaves.

Then one day, a little mouse came creeping into the cave. The mouse was cold and wet and when he saw the big brown bear, he thought it was a big brown rug and he crept amongst its curly hair and gave a big sigh of happiness at being warm again.

However, the big brown bear felt the little mouse scratching against his side and woke from his sleep. He gnashed his long yellow teeth and roared:

'Go away and do not disturb me, you miserable little creature!'

So, the mouse ran away.

It was very cold outside the cave and, after a while, the mouse came creeping back and tried to sleep amongst the crackly dead leaves.

Again the big brown bear woke up.

Again he gnashed his long yellow teeth and roared:

'Go away, you miserable little creature!'

Again the little mouse ran away, but not very far.

The Big Brown Bear

The next day a hunter with a big gun came to take shelter in the cave. Through his dreams the big brown bear heard the sound of someone moving.

'That tiresome mouse must be back again,' he thought.

Getting to his feet, the bear charged forward, shouting:

'Be off with you before I kill you.'

How amazed he was when he saw a hunter with a gun standing before him.

The big brown bear was so frightened that he ran out of the cave and has never been seen since.

Then the little mouse crept back amongst the warm leaves and was happy for the rest of the winter.

Which shows that a mouse may get the better of a bear, if it is lucky.

Cinderella

Once upon a time, there lived a happy girl named Ella. However, her happiness was not to last for when her dear mother died, Ella's father married again. The second wife hated Ella and her two daughters were vain and cruel.

Ella was turned out of her pretty

bedroom. She was made to do the housework and wait on her two ugly stepsisters hand and foot.

At the end of each day Ella was always so tired she could do nothing but sit amongst the cinders of the kitchen fire, hoping for a little warmth and rest.

'Sitting amongst the cinders! That is all you are good for!' jeered her ugly stepsisters. 'From now on we shall call you Cinderella.'

Indeed, from that day everyone called the girl Cinderella. She was dressed in rags and smeared with ashes and no one could remember the day when she had been the most important young lady in the house.

5
January

Cinderella

One day, Cinderella's stepmother and ugly stepsisters were atwitter with excitement. A letter had arrived inviting them to a ball at the palace. The prince was looking for a wife and he would choose her from the ladies who danced with him on the great night.

Cinderella looked wistfully at the pretty dresses her sisters had bought to wear at the palace ball.

'Am I invited to dance at the palace too?' she asked.

The ugly stepsisters screamed with laughter.

'You!' they jeered. 'You! Why, you are not fit to be invited anywhere. Go back amongst the cinders where you belong.'

Poor Cinderella crept sadly down the stairs to the kitchen, while her stepmother and stepsisters left the house and rode in a fine coach to dance with the prince at the royal palace.

6
January

Cinderella

Cinderella sat alone amongst the cinders, weeping because she could not go to the ball at the royal palace.

Then, to her surprise, she heard a voice ask:

'Why are you crying, my dear?'

Looking up she saw a beautiful lady dressed in sparkling white and carrying a wand.

'I am crying because I cannot go to the ball,' replied Cinderella, curtsying to the beautiful lady. 'And may I ask who you are?'

'I am your fairy godmother and I have come tonight to grant you a wish,' smiled the lady in reply.

Cinderella's face lit up with joy.

'Oh, please let me go to the ball,' she begged.

The fairy godmother smiled and nodded.

She ordered Cinderella to fetch the biggest pumpkin she could find in the garden. She told her to fetch the six mice from the mousetrap. She sent her to bring the fat rat caught in the rat-trap. She told her to find two green lizards on the warm side of the garden wall.

Then the fairy godmother waved her magic wand. In the twinkling of an eye the pumpkin was changed into a golden coach. The mice were changed into ponies. The rat became a coachman and the two lizards turned into footmen.

Cinderella's rags turned into a lovely ball dress and her worn-out shoes became two glittering, glass slippers.

Cinderella was ready to go to the ball.

7
January

Cinderella

Cinderella was so happy. She could hardly believe that she was going to the ball after all. How pleased she was her fairy godmother had made it possible!

As Cinderella drove away in her golden coach, her fairy godmother called:

'Remember, at midnight my magic spell will lose its power. The coach will turn into a pumpkin and the ponies and coachman and footmen will go back to being mice and a rat and lizards. Your fine dress will turn to rags. Before midnight strikes you must leave the ball and return home.'

'I shall remember. I shall remember,' laughed Cinderella, but she was so happy that she scarcely heard what her fairy godmother was saying.

Cinderella was the most beautiful girl at the ball. The prince fell in love with her at once and would dance with no one else.

Everyone asked who this beautiful stranger could be. No one knew. Not even Cinderella's own stepmother nor her ugly stepsisters recognized her in her fine clothes. The hours flew by. Cinderella was dancing in the prince's arms when she heard midnight begin to strike. Dismayed, she remembered the words of her fairy godmother. Cinderella slipped from the prince's arms and ran across the ballroom. Then as she fled down the steps, her lovely gown turned to rags. Down in the courtyard no golden coach awaited her, only a pumpkin stood there, while some mice and a rat and two lizards scuttled away from the railings.

Cinderella

All that remained of Cinderella's finery were her glass slippers. One fell off her foot as she ran down the steps and one she clutched in her hand as she ran through the streets towards home.

The prince hurried out of the ballroom.

'Have you seen a beautiful princess run past?' he asked the guards.

'No. Only a ragged servant girl,' they replied.

The prince turned back sadly. Then he picked up the glass slipper from the steps. It was all that was left to him of the lovely stranger.

The day after the ball, the ugly sisters could talk of nothing else but the beautiful stranger who had enchanted the prince the night before.

'They say she is a princess from a far land,' they cackled. 'They say the prince is dying for love of her. They say he sits looking at that glass slipper she left behind and will neither eat nor drink. The king and queen are very worried.'

Then the sound of a trumpet rang from the street. A herald from the palace stood holding Cinderella's glass slipper.

'Whomsoever this slipper shall fit, shall be the bride of the prince,' he announced.

Cinderella

At once the ugly sisters called the herald into the house. They were both determined to force their big, bony feet into the slipper, no matter how it hurt.

However, try as they might, they could not make the slipper fit. They were both furious with disappointment. When Cinderella asked if she might try on the slipper, they screamed at her:

'Go away, you ragged lazybones! Why should you marry the prince, if we cannot?'

The herald stepped forward.

'The prince ordered that everyone may try to put on the slipper,' he said.

Cinderella smiled and slid her dainty foot into the glass slipper with no trouble at all. Then she took the matching slipper from her pocket and put it on her other foot. The herald was convinced Cinderella was the one for whom the prince was seeking.

In a flash of light, Cinderella's fairy godmother appeared and once more dressed Cinderella in beautiful clothes.

Cinderella and the prince were married and lived happily ever after. Even the horrid stepmother and ugly stepsisters were happy because Cinderella was kind to them and invited them to all the royal parties.

Kind Kenny

Once upon a time there was a little boy who was very kind. Being kind is nice, but Kenny learned that he had to be sensible as well.

One evening at bedtime, Kenny looked at his cuddly toys.

'Blue Bunny has been good all day,' he thought, 'he should come to bed with me and snuggle down in the warm.'

Kind Kenny picked up Blue Bunny and looked at Woolly Lamb.

'Blue Bunny and Woolly Lamb are such friends, I cannot take one without the other,' he thought.

So he picked up Woolly Lamb.

Then he noticed Pink Piglet sitting by the stairs.

'Pink Piglet was left behind when we went for a walk,' thought Kind Kenny. 'If I leave him behind again, he will be really upset.'

So Kind Kenny picked up Pink Piglet to join Blue Bunny and Woolly Lamb. Then he picked up Spotty Dog because Spotty had worked hard all day being a watch dog and deserved a treat.

Kind Kenny went upstairs and put Blue

Bunny and Woolly Lamb and Pink Piglet and Spotty Dog into his bed. Then he found there was no room for himself.

'Silly Kenny!' smiled Mummy. 'You must be sensible and take one toy to bed at a time. The others must sit on the bedside chair with a blanket round them. I'm sure they will be quite comfortable.'

Kenny agreed, but as he was such a kind boy, he told all the toys a bedtime story before they went to sleep.

Nurse Nancy

Nancy's favourite Christmas present was her nurse's outfit. It was made up of a nurse's striped dress and pinafore, with a smart cap to match.

Then all in the same box were bandages and sticking plaster and ointment, plastic bowls, a thermometer, a toy wristwatch and a notebook and pencil.

Nancy looked smart in the uniform and she learned how to use all the things in the box.

'Nurse Nancy,' the whole family called her and Nancy felt proud.

Then one day Cousin Kate came to visit and brought her doll with her. As they walked up the path to the front door, Cousin Kate tripped over. Kate did not hurt herself, but the doll fell into the mud and scraped her elbow on some gravel.

'My poor dolly!' gasped Cousin Kate. 'She is hurt and dirty. Now she will cry all the while until we are home again.'

At once Nancy ran to put on her nurse's uniform.

'Leave everything to me,' she smiled, 'I know how to make Dolly better.'

12
January

Nurse Nancy

Nurse Nancy washed Dolly clean and put ointment and a bandage on to her scraped elbow. Then she took Dolly's temperature and said:

'Dolly is very shaken up. She needs to lie down and rest.'

Kate and Nurse Nancy put Dolly on a cushion and covered her with a blanket.

A little later they came back to look at her. Nurse Nancy used the toy wristwatch to help her take Dolly's pulse.

'Dolly is quite better now,' said Nurse

Nancy. 'She is fit enough to go home when you are ready.'

Cousin Kate picked Dolly up and cuddled her.

'Thank you,' smiled Cousin Kate. 'It must be wonderful to be a nurse like you, Nancy.'

13
January

Red Riding Hood

Long, long ago when many forests full of wild beasts covered the land, there lived a little girl called Red Riding Hood.

This was not her real name, but everyone called her that because she wore a red hood and cloak which her grandmother had made for her.

Red Riding Hood lived with her mother and father, who was a woodcutter, near the edge of a forest.

Further away, in a clearing in the forest lived the grandmother who had made the hood and cloak.

One day her mother said to Red Riding Hood:

'Your grandmother is ill. You must visit her and take her some food, but do not wander down the green paths into the forest to pick flowers or berries. The forest is full of fierce beasts.'

Red Riding Hood promised to walk along the road and, with the basket of food over her arm, she set out.

The sun was high and the road was hot. How Red Riding Hood longed to step into the green shade of the trees and pick the pretty flowers!

Soon she forgot everything her mother had said and went into the forest.

Almost at once a great wolf came up and spoke to her.

'Good morning,' he said. 'Where are you going to this fine day?'

'Good morning, Mr. Wolf,' replied Red Riding Hood, dropping a curtsy. 'I am going to see my grandmother.'

14
January

Red
Riding Hood

'So you are going to see your grandmother,' smiled the wolf, 'and where does she live?'

'In a pretty cottage not far from here, straight along the road and near a tall beech tree,' replied Red Riding Hood, foolishly telling the wolf how to find her grandmother's home.

'And when you get there, how do you get in?' asked the wolf.

'I tap at the door and Grandmother says, "Lift the latch and come in," and in I walk,' finished Red Riding Hood.

By now the wolf had learned everything he wished to know. Telling Red Riding Hood to be sure to pick a big bunch of flowers, he hurried through the forest to the home of the grandmother.

'I will eat the grandmother first and then gobble up Red Riding Hood when she arrives after picking the flowers,' he thought, feeling well pleased.

The wolf tapped gently at the door of the grandmother's cottage.

'Lift the latch and come in,' called an old voice. The grandmother thought it was Red Riding Hood tapping at the door.

15
January

Red
Riding Hood

The wolf lifted the latch and rushed in through the door and gobbled the grandmother up with one gulp.

Then he put on one of her frilly nightcaps and jumped into the bed and pulled the bedclothes well up under his chin and waited for Red Riding Hood to arrive.

When she had finished picking flowers, Red Riding Hood hurried to her grandmother's cottage and tapped at the door.

'Lift the latch and come in,' called a voice.

Red Riding Hood thought it was the voice of her grandmother, but it was the voice of the wolf.

Red Riding Hood went into the cottage and walked towards the bed.

'Your voice sounds very hoarse, Grandmother,' she said. 'Is your throat sore?'

'Yes, my dear,' replied the wolf. 'Come close and sit on the bed.'

Red Riding Hood stared at the strange face under the frilly nightcap.

'Grandmother, what big eyes you have!' she said.

'All the better to see you with, my dear,' replied the wolf.

'But Grandmother, what big ears you have,' said Red Riding Hood, staring at the pointed ears pushing up under the nightcap.

'All the better to hear you with, my dear,' replied the wolf.

'And Grandmother, what big teeth you have,' gasped Red Riding Hood.

'All the better to eat you with, my dear,' laughed the wolf and leaping out of bed, he sprang at Red Riding Hood.

Poor Red Riding Hood was so surprised that she dropped her basket in fright.

Red Riding Hood

Luckily Red Riding Hood was young and quick. She turned and ran out of the cottage screaming and shouting for help.

Close after her came the wolf, his long, sharp, yellow teeth gleaming in the sun and his tongue hanging out. He had just caught the little red cloak in his paws when Red Riding Hood's own father came running towards the cottage.

He had been felling trees in the forest and he had heard the voice of Red Riding Hood shouting for help.

With one blow of his axe, he struck the wolf dead and then took Red Riding Hood safe in his arms.

'Oh Father,' sobbed Red Riding Hood, 'I fear the wolf has eaten Grandmother.'

'We shall soon see,' replied her father and taking out his knife, he slit the wolf open and out stepped the grandmother alive and well.

The wolf had swallowed her so quickly that his yellow teeth had not even so much as scratched her.

How happily the three hugged and kissed each other! And from that day, Red Riding Hood never wandered in the forest alone again.

17
January

The Snowman

It was wintertime and the snow lay deep on the ground. Grandpa came knocking at the door and asked if Johnny would like to play snowballs.

'Yes, please, Grandpa,' replied Johnny, 'I should love to play in the snow, but could we build a snowman? Building a snowman would be much more fun than playing snowballs.'

'Nonsense!' laughed Grandpa. 'Playing snowballs is exciting. We always played snowballs when I was a boy.'

Outside into the snow went Johnny and Grandpa. They made a pile of large, round,

wet, squelchy snowballs. Then they hid behind a bush.

In a moment Johnny's father came out of the house to clear the snow from the drive. SQUELCH!

Grandpa threw a snowball which landed on the back of Dad's head and ran down inside his collar. Grandpa roared with laughter, but Dad did not seem pleased. He looked at Grandpa and then he frowned at Johnny.

'Can't you think of anything better to do with your grandpa than play snowballs?' said Dad. 'Why don't you take Grandpa for a walk?'

Johnny knew that Dad was cross with Grandpa for throwing the snowball, but did not like to say so.

'Shall we go for a walk?' Johnny said to Grandpa.

'Certainly not,' replied Grandpa. 'Throwing snowballs is fun.'

Johnny thought of his father's angry face and said, 'I don't think it is much fun for the people who get hit by the snowballs.' But Grandpa wasn't listening.

The Snowman

Johnny and Grandpa hid behind the bush once more. In a few minutes Mr. Barnes from next-door came out to collect the mail from his mail box.

WUMP!

Grandpa threw a snowball at Mr. Barnes. It landed in Mr. Barnes' ear and made him jump in the air and shout with surprise.

Mr. Barnes went red in the face and seemed to be very cross, but when he saw it was Grandpa who had thrown the snowball, he swallowed his anger and said:

'Fancy seeing you throwing snowballs at your age, Mr. Lacey. You seem a little old for that sort of thing.'

'Never too old to have fun,' laughed Grandpa, who did not seem to notice that no one liked being hit by snowballs.

'I must stop Grandpa before he gets into real trouble,' thought Johnny. 'Grandpa,' he went on, 'let us build a snowman and throw snowballs at him. That will be real fun.'

Luckily Grandpa agreed. The two of them built a fine snowman and pelted it with snowballs. They both had a great time and no one else was made cross.

'There are times,' Johnny thought to himself, 'when I feel more grown-up than Grandpa. I must make sure he doesn't throw snowballs at people in future.'

How fortunate that Grandpa had Johnny to look after him!

Careful Hans

Once upon a time there was a boy called Careful Hans who always did what he was told without thinking.

One day Hans went to visit his grandmother. He played all day and when it was time to go home his grandmother said:

'You have been a good boy. Take this needle to your mother and put it somewhere safe as you walk home.'

As it happened, Hans walked home behind a cart full of hay. He pushed the needle in amongst the hay, thinking that there was nowhere safer than the farmer's cart.

When he reached home he told his mother what he had done, but although his mother visited the farmer and searched all through the hay she never found the needle.

'You foolish boy, Hans,' she said. 'You should have put the needle in your pocket.'

20
January

Careful Hans

The next day Careful Hans again visited his grandmother. When it was time to go home Grandma said:

'You have been a good boy, Hans. You may have this puppy to take home with you, but remember to carry it somewhere safe.'

Hans remembered what his mother had said about the needle and he pushed the puppy into his pocket. However, the puppy did not like being in the pocket and by the time they reached home, the puppy had chewed a big hole in Hans' jacket.

Hans' mother was not pleased.

'You foolish boy,' she said. 'You should have tied a length of string to the puppy's collar and pulled it along behind you.'

'I will try to do better next time,' promised Hans.

21
January

Careful Hans

The next day Hans again went to visit his grandmother. He played all day and when it was time to go home his grandmother said:

'You have been a good boy. Take this meat home as a present to your mother from me.'

And she gave Hans a fine joint of beef.

Careful Hans remembered what his mother had said about the puppy. He tied a length of string round the meat and dragged it along behind him.

Of course, every dog living along the lane dashed out and took a bite of meat as Hans walked past. By the time he reached home there was very little meat left, and that was unfit to eat.

His mother was cross.

'You foolish boy,' she said. 'You should have wrapped the meat in paper and carried

16

it on your head where no dog could reach.'

'I will try to remember,' promised Hans.

22
January

Careful Hans

The next day Hans again went to visit his grandmother. He played all day and when it was time to go home his grandmother said:

'You have been a good boy. Take this pound of butter home to your mother.'

Hans took the pound of butter and remembering what his mother had said, wrapped it in paper and put it on his head. Then Hans walked along the road home. The sun was hot and the butter melted. It dripped through the paper and ran down his hair and over his jacket.

When his mother saw him she said:

'What a mess! Why are you so greasy?'

When Hans told her about the butter, she said:

'You foolish boy. You will never visit your grandmother again!'

Luckily, as Hans grew older, he learned to be sensible and his mother changed her mind and did allow him to visit his dear grandmother and everyone was happy.

23
January

The Princess and the Pea

Long ago and far away, there lived a prince who wished to marry a princess, but he wanted to be sure he found a real princess.

In those days many young ladies pretended to be princesses in order to make a good marriage.

The prince travelled far and wide and met many so called princesses, but whether or not they were real princesses, he could never decide.

Then one night a terrible storm arose. The lightning flashed and the thunder roared and the rain streamed down. It was very frightening.

In the midst of all the turmoil there was a knock at the castle door. The old king went to answer it.

A princess stood outside the gate, but how terrible she looked from being caught in the rain and stormy weather! Her hat was blown from her head. The rain ran in streams through her hair and down her clothes and filled her shoes to the brim.

'I am a princess,' she declared, 'and I hope you will give me shelter for the night.'

The bedraggled girl did not look like a princess, but the queen invited her in and thought of a scheme to prove whether what the girl claimed was true or not.

24
January

The Princess
and the Pea

'If this girl is a real princess, then my son, the prince, can marry her and that will be an end of all this searching and fuss,' thought the queen.

She went up to a bedroom and took all the bedding off the bed. Then she put a pea on the bedstead and covered it with twenty mattresses. Then she put twenty eiderdowns upon the mattresses and invited the girl to sleep on the very top.

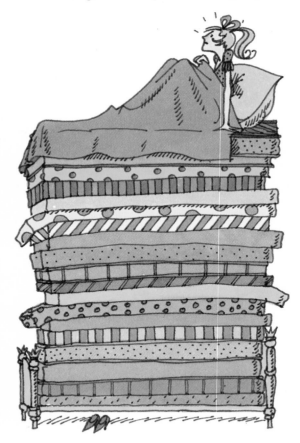

The next day the queen asked the girl how she had slept.

'Oh, miserably!' said the princess, for a princess she was, 'I scarcely closed my eyes. I don't know what was in that bed, but something was under those mattresses!'

Then the queen and the old king and the prince all smiled. They knew they had found a real princess at last, for only a real princess could have been so delicate that she felt a pea through twenty mattresses and twenty eiderdowns.

The prince and princess were married and lived happily ever after and the pea was put in the castle museum.

25
January

A
Special Cake

Not very long ago there lived a little girl who did not like Christmas cake. Her name was Billie Jean and she tried her very best to like the rich, dark, fruity Christmas cake, but she could not.

One day towards the end of January, Billie Jean's mother took her to visit an important friend, who did not have children of her own.

'Remember,' said Mother, 'Mrs. Justso is not used to children about the house. Do not touch anything. Do not run about. Do not talk in a loud voice. Do not interrupt.'

'Do not have any fun,' thought Billie Jean to herself. However she sat still and said nothing and the grown-ups were pleased with her.

Halfway though the visit, Mrs. Justso made some coffee and said:

'Billie Jean is the best behaved child who has ever visited with me. She deserves a special treat. Instead of eating these little cakes, Billie Jean may have my last slice of Christmas cake.'

A Special Cake

With a proud flourish, Mrs. Justso took out a slice of heavy, dark, fruity cake and set it before Billie Jean.

Now Billie Jean did not wish to offend Mrs. Justso, who was a very important person, so she ate the cake and said it was delicious. Billie Jean's mother was proud of her good, kind little girl.

The strange thing was that as Billie Jean ate the cake, she found that she liked it. Mrs. Justso was a good cook. Her Christmas cake was special. Mrs. Justso took such a liking to Billie Jean that she invited her to visit again and learn how to make the special Christmas cake.

Every year after that Billie Jean made the special cake for her own family. She became famous for making delicious cakes and it was all because she had been a well-behaved, polite, little girl when she went visiting with Mrs. Justso.

Three Little Pigs

There was once an old mother pig who had three little pigs. These little pigs grew so fast that the day came when their mother sent them out into the world to fend for themselves.

As the three little pigs were walking along the road, they met a man with a load of straw.

'Please,' said the first little pig, 'will you give me some straw to build a house?'

The man agreed and the first little pig built himself a house of straw.

'Straw is not good enough for us,' said the other two pigs and went on their way.

After a while a big grey wolf came trotting along and saw the chubby little pig living in the house of straw. He knocked on the door and called:

'Open the door and let me in!'

'Not by the hair of my chinny, chin, chin,' replied the first little pig, who knew that wolves liked to eat pigs.

'Then I'll huff and I'll puff and I'll blow your house in,' growled the wolf.

And he huffed and he puffed and he blew the house in. The first little pig had to run for his life.

Three
Little Pigs

The two little pigs walked along the road and soon they met a man carrying a load of sticks.

'Our brother built a house of straw,' said the second little pig. 'But I will build a house of sticks. That will be much stronger.'

He bowed to the man and said:

'Please, will you give me some sticks to build a house?'

The man agreed and the second little pig built a house of sticks while the third little pig went on his way. Sticks were not good enough for him.

After a while the second little pig heard a terrible screaming and squealing and, opening the front door, he saw his brother being chased along the road by a great big wolf.

'Save me! Save me!' shouted the first little pig. He ran into his brother's house of sticks and they slammed the door, not one moment too soon.

'Open the door and let me in,' roared the wolf, in a rage at being cheated of his dinner.

'Not by the hair of our chinny, chin, chins,' replied the two little pigs, laughing and thinking themselves safe in the house of sticks.

'Then I'll huff and I'll puff and I'll blow your house in,' shouted the wolf.

And he huffed and he puffed and he blew the house in. The poor little pigs had to run for their lives. They raced along the road looking desperately for the third little pig and all the while they heard the wolf bounding along behind them.

Three
Little Pigs

While his brothers had been having such frightening adventures with the great big wolf, the third little pig had met a man with a load of bricks.

'That is exactly what I want,' thought the third little pig. He bowed politely and said:

'Please, will you give me enough bricks

to build a house?'

The man agreed.

At once the third little pig set to work and he built a strong house with a big chimney and a thick front door, painted green and with a fine brass knob.

He had not been living there long when he heard a dreadful shouting and screaming and the clatter of trotters and paws on the road.

Looking out, he saw his two brothers being chased by a great big wolf.

'Save us! Save us!' they shouted.

They ran into their brother's house of bricks and he slammed the green front door an instant before the wolf arrived.

'Open the door and let me in,' panted the wolf.

'Not by the hair of our chinny, chin, chins,' replied the pigs, certain they were safe in the house of bricks.

'Then I'll huff and I'll puff and I'll blow your house in,' screamed the wolf.

And he huffed and he puffed and he huffed and he puffed until he had no breath left, but he could not blow the house in.

The three little pigs laughed and laughed.

30
January

Three Little Pigs

The great big wolf was angry that he could not blow down the house of bricks, but he did not give up hope of eating the pigs.

A few days later, he came by and said in a voice of honey:

'Would you pigs like some fat turnips? I can show you a field where you can get as many as you like.'

'Thank you,' replied the third little pig. 'Where is the field and when will you call to take us there?'

'The field is a mile away by a big oak tree,' grinned the wolf. 'I will call for you at seven in the morning.'

The pigs agreed to the plan, but the next morning they went to gather the turnips at six and were safely back home before the wolf knocked at their door.

The wolf was furious, but he did not give up. He waited for a week, then he strolled by the house of bricks and called:

'There is a fair in the village today. If you would like to go, I will call for you at three o'clock this afternoon.'

The pigs agreed, but went to the fair early, thinking they would be back home long before the wolf arrived. However, they spent too long at the fair. As they walked homewards down the hill, carrying a milk churn which they had bought, they saw the wolf walking towards them.

It seemed the wolf had outwitted them.

Three Little Pigs

The three little pigs stood at the top of the hill staring down at the great big wolf. He had not seen them yet, but soon he would and then he would eat them for sure.

The third little pig looked at the milk churn which the pigs had bought at the fair.

'Climb into the milk churn and we will be saved yet,' he ordered.

His brothers did as he said and the third little pig climbed into the churn after them. Before he pulled on the lid, he gave a push and sent the churn hurtling down the hill.

It rolled and bumped and made a loud clattering noise. The wolf thought a large monster was rushing towards him and he ran away and hid for the rest of the day. So, the pigs were able to walk home safely.

The next day the wolf went to visit the house of bricks.

'I am sorry I did not see you yesterday,' he said, 'but a monster chased me away.'

The pigs laughed and jeered at the wolf and told him that the monster had been a milk churn with them inside it.

The wolf was more furious than he had ever been before and could wait no longer to eat the three clever little pigs.

He climbed on to the roof of the house of bricks and started to scramble down the chimney. Luckily the third little pig heard the scratching of the wolf's claws on the roof.

He put a pot of water on the fire and brought it to the boil. When the wolf came down the chimney, he fell into the water. The pigs slammed on the lid and threw the pot and the wolf out of the house.

After that the wolf was so discouraged by his failures he decided never to bother the pigs again. They lived happily ever after and on Sundays went back to visit their old mother.

February

1
February

The Pancake

One day a big fat cook made a big fat pancake. Near the cook waited seven hungry little boys. They all wanted to eat the pancake.

The pancake said:

'I will not be eaten.'

Mr. Pancake gave a hop and a jump and leaped out of the frying pan and rolled away down the road.

'Stop! Stop!' called the cook.

'Stop! Stop!' called the seven hungry little boys.

Mr. Pancake took no notice, but rolled faster and faster. The cook and the seven hungry little boys all ran after the pancake, but they could not catch him.

Presently the pancake met a little man.

'Stop! Stop! I am hungry. I wish to eat you,' said the little man.

'The cook cannot stop me. The boys cannot stop me. You cannot stop me,' replied Mr. Pancake and he rolled on faster and faster.

The little man joined the chase after the pancake, but he could not catch him.

Next the pancake met a chicken.

'Stop! Stop! I am hungry. I wish to eat you,' cackled the hen.

Mr. Pancake replied:

'The cook cannot stop me. The boys cannot stop me. The little man cannot stop me. And you cannot stop me.'

And the pancake rolled along the road faster than ever.

2
February

The Pancake

On the village green, the pancake met a duck.

'Stop! Stop! I am hungry. I wish to eat you,' quacked the duck.

Mr. Pancake did not wish to be eaten. He rolled on his way shouting:

'The cook cannot stop me. The boys

cannot stop me. The little man cannot stop me. The hen cannot stop me. You cannot stop me.'

Quacking loudly, the duck joined the others and ran after the pancake.

After a while the pancake met a pig, who asked him why he was running so fast. The pancake replied that he was running away from being eaten.

'I will run with you,' said the pig.

The pig and the pancake ran on until they came to a river.

'I cannot swim,' said Mr. Pancake.

'Jump on my nose and I will take you across,' said the pig.

The pancake jumped on to the pig's nose and with a jerk of his head, the pig tossed the pancake into his mouth and ate it.

And that was the end of Mr. Pancake.

3
February

Little Bo-Beep

About a hundred years ago there lived a shepherdess called Bo-Peep. Every day Bo-Peep would take her sheep from the safe, fenced field near her father's farm and drive them up on to the hillside.

The grass was green and good to eat on the hillside, but the sheep could not be left there unguarded in case a wolf or a fox or even some naughty boys came to steal them away.

It was Bo-Peep's job to watch the sheep all day and to take them back to the farm at night. Bo-Peep did this task very well, but the day came when things went wrong. The sheep felt naughty and decided they would run away into the village and have fun chewing the flowers in the gardens and stealing the carrots from the shops. Bo-Peep thought she would collect the strands of wool which fell from the sheep's coats and make them into a jacket for her mother.

As soon as Bo-Peep turned her back to collect the wool, the naughty sheep ran away, but they were cunning. They left one sheep behind and told him to bleat the whole time.

'Baaa-baaa! Baaa-baaa! Baaa-baaa! Baaa-baaa!' bleated the one sheep.

Hearing all this bleating, Bo-Peep thought her sheep were safely nearby. All the while the naughty sheep were racing towards the village.

4
February

Little Bo-Peep

The day wore on. Bo-Peep collected a lot of wool and as she worked, she kept hearing:

'Baaa-baaa! Baaa-baaa! Baaa-baaa! Baaa-baaa!' coming from the hill behind her.

At last Bo-Peep had collected enough wool and turned to tell the sheep it was time to go home. How amazed she was to see only one sheep standing still and bleating:

'Baaa-baaa! Baaa-baaa! Baaa-baaa! Baaa-baaa!'

Bo-Peep knew she had been tricked. She was a young lady with a hot temper.

'You run and find those other sheep and tell them to come back to the farm at once or I will be after them with my stick,' she shouted. 'And say if any of their tails have been bitten off by wolves or foxes, or if their wool has been clipped by naughty boys, they will get no more sugar lumps for a week!'

Bo-Peep turned and stamped down the hillside towards the farm. Her father met her and asked why she was not searching for the lost sheep.

'I'm leaving them alone to come home on their own,' replied Bo-Peep, 'and you can be sure that they will bring their tails safely behind them.'

5
February

Little Bo-Peep

Meanwhile everything had not been going well for the naughty sheep.

As they ran down the village street, laughing and bleating and saying how they were going to eat the roses from the garden of Widow Blackweed, the widow herself came out with a broom and chased them away.

When they tried to eat the carrots from Mr. Greengrocer's shop, he set his dog on them.

As the dog chased them, two naughty boys tried to clip off some of the sheep's wool. As the sheep ran away from the boys, a fox yapped at them from the hedgerow.

As they ran away from the fox into the hills, a wolf snapped at their tails.

By the time the one sheep, sent by Bo-Peep, found them, they were all longing to go home, and their tails were safe and unbitten.

So, when anyone says the rhyme:
Little Bo-Peep has lost her sheep
And does not know where to find them.
Leave them alone and they will come home,
Bringing their tails behind them.
you will know what it was all about.

6
February

The Lonely Tiger

Once upon a time there was a big tiger who was always lonely. He would stalk through

the jungle roaring and roaring but he never met anyone.

One day he did see a bird perched high on a tree.

'Doesn't anyone live in this jungle?' roared the tiger. 'I walk about all day but I never see a soul.'

'Of course you never meet anyone,' twittered the bird. 'You frighten everyone with your roaring.'

All the next day the tiger stalked through the jungle whispering in a quiet voice:

'Is anyone there? Is anyone there?'

Still no one waited to talk to him. Again the tiger saw the bird perched high on a tree and asked him why none of the other animals would speak to him.

'I have asked them,' replied the bird, 'and they say it is because you are a tiger and that you will eat them.'

'Oh, but I don't eat *animals*,' laughed the tiger. 'I eat *rice pudding*!'

When the other animals heard the tiger say that, they came out of hiding and the naughty tiger gobbled them up.

And that is why *all* tigers are lonely. You can never believe a word they say, whether they are roaring or whispering.

Sleeping Beauty

Once upon a time there lived a king and queen who were blessed with a lovely baby daughter. Joy bells were rung, bonfires were lighted and a Christening party was arranged.

Thirteen fairies lived in the kingdom, but it happened that the king had only twelve gold plates.

'I cannot afford to buy another gold plate,' said the king. 'We can invite only twelve fairies to the Christening and serve their food on the twelve gold plates we have here.'

'Very well,' replied the queen. 'I will not invite the thirteenth fairy. I do not like her and anyway I believe she is away on holiday.'

On the day of the Christening, the twelve fairies came to the party and gave the baby princess the gifts of beauty and health and happiness and cleverness and so on. When the twelfth fairy was about to bestow her gift, the door burst open with a crash.

The thirteenth fairy stormed into the room, her face twisted with rage.

'So!' she screamed. 'I am not good enough to be invited to the Christening!'

She glared at the baby lying in its cot.

'I will give you a gift,' sneered the thirteenth fairy, 'but it will not be the gift you want. When you reach the age of fifteen years, you will prick your finger with a spindle and fall down dead.'

With a horrible laugh, the thirteenth fairy left the room.

8
February

Sleeping Beauty

The queen burst into tears and the king shook his fist, but there was nothing they could do against the power of a fairy.

Then the twelfth fairy, who had not yet given a gift to the baby, stepped forward.

'I cannot take the curse away completely,' she said, 'but I will alter it. When the princess is fifteen years old, she will prick her finger with a spindle, but instead of dying, she will fall into a sleep which will last a hundred years.'

With that the king and queen had to be content. The years went by. The princess grew into a lovely girl. The king and queen ordered every spindle to be taken from the palace and they came to think that no harm could befall their dear daughter. They had not seen the thirteenth fairy since the day of the Christening and they thought she had gone away and forgotten about them.

The day of the princess's birthday arrived, but no harm befell her. How could it? No spindle was allowed to be brought near the lovely girl. Then, as the princess walked through the garden on the way to her birthday party, she noticed a staircase leading to a tower, which she had never seen before. She walked up the staircase and pushed open the door leading into a room where an old lady was spinning.

9
February

Sleeping Beauty

Of course the old lady was the thirteenth fairy come back to do her evil work.

'Oh, what a strange thing that is!' said the princess, stretching her hand out towards the spindle, because she had never seen one before.

'Would you like to touch it, my dear?' asked the old lady in a cracked voice, and she put the spindle into the princess's hand.

At once the princess pricked her finger and fell down as if dead. The old lady, who was the thirteenth fairy cackled with dreadful laughter and flew away through the window of the tower.

However, the princess was not dead. She had fallen into her deep hundred years' sleep. Not only the princess slept. The king slept on his throne. The queen slept at her embroidery. The cook slept with his hand raised to strike the kitchen boy and the kitchen boy slept with his mouth open ready to cry with the pain of the slap. The courtiers slept before the throne. The horses slept in the stables. The pigeons slept on the roof. The fire flickering in the grate grew still and the roast meat stopped crackling. The wind dropped and not a leaf stirred. Everything in the palace was asleep.

10
February

Sleeping Beauty

At first the local village folk came to stare in amazement, but then a hedge of briar roses sprang up round the palace. Year by year it grew taller and thicker, until it hid the palace from sight. People began to forget what was there. Only a few of the old folk remembered their grandparents saying that behind the thick rose hedge was an enchanted palace where slept a beautiful princess and all her court.

Sometimes a brave young man would try

to break through the hedge of thorny briar roses, but he never succeeded. He would turn away with his clothes ripped to ribbons and his body scratched and bleeding and he would declare that no one would ever get through to the palace.

'Anyway,' folk said, 'if a sleeping princess is behind the rose hedge, she will have grown old and will have died long since. It is useless to bother with the place.'

A hundred years went by and a handsome, brave prince rode along the road at the side of the high briar rose hedge. He had never seen such a dense thicket of thorns before and he asked an old man what lay behind it.

The old man told him the story of the sleeping beauty who lay in the palace behind the thorns. The prince smiled.

'I have had many battles and done many daring deeds,' he said. 'I am the man to break through to the enchanted palace.'

11
February

Sleeping Beauty

The prince dismounted from his horse and walked towards the briar hedge. As his shadow fell across it, it bloomed with soft pink roses. The thorns turned away their spikes. The branches parted. The prince walked through without a scratch and was the first person in a hundred years to see the palace.

Cobwebs and dust covered everything and at first the prince thought he had come to a ruin. Then he saw the horses sleeping in the stables and the doves dozing on the roof. He walked into the palace and saw the king asleep on his throne with the courtiers standing sleeping before him. The prince saw the queen asleep over her embroidery. He looked into the kitchen and saw the cook with his hand raised to strike the kitchen boy and the boy with his mouth open, ready to cry. The flames of the fire stood still in the hearth and the meat glistened with fat as it had a hundred years before.

All these things were amazing to behold, but where was Sleeping Beauty?

12
February

Sleeping Beauty

Turning from the kitchen, the prince wandered across a courtyard, until he saw the staircase which the princess had seen so many years before. Just as the young princess had done, he climbed the stairs and pushed open the door of the room.

On the floor lay the spindle which had pricked the princess's finger and sent her to sleep. Creeping in through the window was a bank of beautiful roses and lying across them was Sleeping Beauty, the young princess, still as lovely as the day she had fallen asleep.

The prince bent over her and kissed her. At once the princess opened her eyes and smiled at him. They fell in love.

In the palace the king awoke. The courtiers stirred and rubbed their eyes. The queen continued with her embroidery, not knowing she had been asleep. The horses neighed in the stables and the doves cooed on the roof. The cook slapped the unfortunate kitchen boy, who cried at last, having opened his mouth to do so one hundred years before. The flames of the fire flickered and the meat crackled.

How amazed everyone was when the prince showed them the hedge of briar roses and told them that they had been asleep for a hundred years.

'No matter,' smiled the king, 'we are awake now and ready to be happy.'

He agreed that the prince should marry the princess and they all lived merrily for many long years.

The Witch's Farm

Once upon a time there was a witch who owned a nice piece of land near a river's edge. As was the habit with witches, she often went away for hundreds of years at a time. One of the times, when she was away, a good man and his wife came and built a farmhouse and made a farm on the land, never dreaming that it belonged to a witch.

Unfortunately for them, after they had lived there for some seven years, the witch returned. She was furious to find someone on her land. She stood outside the farmhouse and shouted at the farmer. She dared not go into the farm because there was a cross over the door.

'You are a wicked man to farm my land,' shouted the witch. 'When you come out, I will take you to be my servant for life.'

The farmer was afraid and would not go outdoors, but his wife said:

'We cannot stay indoors for ever. I know what to do.'

She made some pastry and stuffed it with an iron weight from her scales and plenty of salt. Then she baked the whole thing, wrapped it in a cloth and threw it out to the witch. The witch snatched it up and took a hearty bite. She broke her teeth on the iron and choked on the salt, which is hateful to her kind.

'What is this dreadful thing?' she choked.

'Why, that is supper for all of us,' called the wife. 'If my husband is to be your servant, I will come too and do the cooking.'

'No thank you!' gasped the witch and went away for another hundred years.

Chicken Licken

One day Chicken Licken went to the woods and an acorn fell on her head. She thought that the sky had fallen and decided to go and tell the king.

On the way she met Hen Len and asked her where she was going.

'I am going to the woods for some food,' replied Hen Len.

'Do not do that,' said Chicken Licken. 'I went to the woods and the sky fell upon my poor little head. Now I am going to tell the king.'

So Hen Len turned back to walk with Chicken Licken. On the way they met Cocky Locky. They asked him where he was going.

'I am going to the woods for some food,' said Cocky Locky.

Hen Len said: 'Do not do that, Cocky Locky. I was going to the woods when I met Chicken Licken. Chicken Licken was going to the woods when the sky fell on her poor little head and now we are going to tell the king.'

So Cocky Locky turned back and met Duck Luck. He asked him where he was going and Duck Luck replied that he was going to the woods for some food.

Cocky Locky said: 'Do not do that, Duck Luck. I was going to the woods when I met Hen Len and Chicken Licken. Chicken Licken went to the woods and the sky fell on her poor little head. Now we are going to tell the king.'

15
February

Chicken Licken

So Duck Luck turned back and met Drake Lake and asked him where he was going. Drake Lake replied that he was going to the woods for food.

'Do not do that, Drake Lake,' said Duck Luck. 'I was going to the woods when I met Cocky Locky and Hen Len and Chicken Licken. Chicken Licken went to the woods and the sky fell on her poor little head. Now we are going to tell the king.'

Drake Lake turned back. He met Goose Loose and asked her where she was going. Goose Loose replied that she was going to the woods for food.

'Do not do that, Goose Loose,' said Drake Lake. 'I was going to the woods when I met Duck Luck and Cocky Locky and Hen Len and Chicken Licken. Chicken Licken went to the woods and the sky fell on her poor little head. Now we are going to tell the king.'

So Goose Loose turned back and met Gander Lander. She asked him where he was going and Gander Lander replied he was going to the woods for food.

'Do not do that, Gander Lander,' said Goose Loose. 'I was going to the woods when I met Drake Lake and Duck Luck and Cocky Locky and Hen Len and Chicken Licken. Chicken Licken went to the woods and the sky fell on her poor little head. Now we are going to tell the king.'

16
February

Chicken Licken

So Gander Lander turned back and met Turkey Lurkey. He asked him where he was going and Turkey Lurkey replied he was going to the woods for food.

'Do not do that, Turkey Lurkey,' said Gander Lander. 'I was going to the woods when I met Goose Loose and Drake Lake and Duck Luck and Cocky Locky and Hen Len and Chicken Licken. Chicken Licken went to the woods and the sky fell upon her poor little head.'

Turkey Lurkey decided to turn back too.

Turkey Lurkey walked with Gander Lander, Goose Loose walked with Drake Lake. Duck Luck walked with Cocky Locky. Hen Len walked with Chicken Licken.

As they were going along, they met Fox Lox. They told him that Chicken Licken had been to the woods and that the sky had fallen on her poor little head and now they were going to tell the king.

Fox Lox smiled a terrible smile, showing all his shiny, sharp teeth.

'I know the way to the king,' he said. 'Come with me. I will show you.'

Fox Lox did not take the friends to the king, he took them to his own den where his hungry cubs were waiting. They ate up poor Chicken Licken and Hen Len and Cocky Locky and Duck Luck and Drake Lake and Goose Loose and Gander Lander and Turkey Lurkey.

They never did get to see the king and they never told him that the sky had fallen.

The Cat Bell

Once upon a time all the mice who lived in a house met together to decide what to do about the cat.

After a lot of talking to no purpose one mouse stood up and said:

'A bell should be tied round the cat's neck. Then we should hear it coming and it would not catch any of us any more.'

'Marvellous! Wonderful! Our troubles are over!' said all the other mice.

They gave the mouse who had had the idea a medal and had his portrait painted and cheered him whenever he came from his hole.

Then one very small mouse said:

'I am not clear on just one thing. Who is going to tie the bell round the cat's neck?'

There was a long silence.

Everyone looked at the mouse who had had the idea. He looked up at the ceiling and down at the floor and out of the window, but he said nothing.

The mice looked at each other.

No one offered to tie the bell round the neck of the cat.

'Perhaps it was not such a good idea after all!' said the very little mouse. 'Ideas are only good if you are able to carry them out.'

Then the very little mouse, who was a real little busy body, organized the mice into taking turns in keeping watch for cat. This idea worked well and no more mice were caught. However, keeping watch was hard work and no fun and everyone wished and wished that one day a big, bold mouse would come along, who *could* put a bell on the cat.

18
February

Little Miss Muffet

Not very long ago there was a girl called Matilda Muffet. Little Miss Muffet her family called her, because she was so high and mighty and would never do as she was told.

At breakfast time the other children in the family would sit round the table in the kitchen eating their bread or their porridge, but not little Miss Muffet.

'I want curds and whey! I want curds and whey!' she would shout.

Curds and whey sound rather horrid, but really they are nice, especially with sugar and sultanas stirred into them.

Mrs. Muffet gave the curds and whey to Matilda to keep her from shouting.

Then, instead of sitting with the other children in the kitchen, Matilda ran out into the garden and sat on a tuffet.

'Little Miss Muffet is too good to sit with the rest of us,' said her brothers and sisters.

Living in the garden of the Muffet's house was a big spider.

'Matilda is a nice child really,' he thought, 'but she is growing up spoilt. It is time she was taught a lesson and behaved properly, like the other children.'

The next time Matilda went into the garden to eat her curds and whey, instead of staying indoors with the others, the big

spider came down and frightened her so much she ran back indoors and was good for evermore.

Now when you hear the rhyme:
Little Miss Muffet
Sat on a tuffet,
Eating her curds and whey;
There came a big spider,
And sat down beside her,
And frightened Miss Muffet away.
you will know what it is all about.

19
February

Tom Thumb

Long, long ago, in the days when Merlin the magician lived, a farmworker and his wife were unhappy because they had no children.

They went to Merlin and asked his help.

'We would like a child of any sort,' they said, 'even if he is a little fellow no bigger than a man's thumb.'

Merlin cast his spells and in due course a child was born, a fine boy, handsome and clever, but he never grew bigger than his father's thumb.

Everyone called the little fellow Tom Thumb.

Tom's mother loved him very much. She

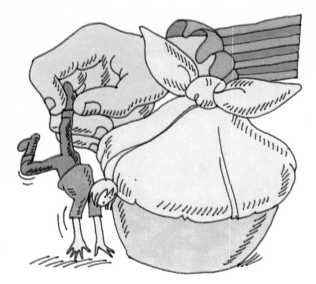

felt it was not safe for such a little boy to go to school, so she kept him at home to help her about the house. Unfortunately staying at home did not stop Tom from having dreadful adventures. One day he fell into the mixing bowl when his mother was making a pudding. She did not notice him and went on beating the mixture until Tom's head ached. It was not until she was tying the pudding into a cloth that Tom's mother noticed his legs kicking and pulled him to safety.

20
February

Tom Thumb

On another day Tom's mother took him to the meadow while she milked the cow. Tom sat on a thistle to enjoy the sunshine, but the cow bit up the thistle with a mouthful of grass.

'Mother! Mother! Help me!' shouted Tom, as he rolled about on top of the cow's fat tongue and tried to keep out of the way of her crunching teeth.

Tom's mother could not think where her son's voice was coming from. She stared round and round and up and down and never dreamed that Tom was in the cow's mouth.

'I see that I must save myself,' thought Tom and he jumped and kicked and pinched and punched at the poor cow's tongue, until the wretched creature opened her mouth and Tom dived between her teeth right into his amazed mother's hands.

'I must keep you out of danger, Tom,' said his mother. 'From now on you must stay indoors.'

One day Tom was sitting by the open window, enjoying the sunshine, when a raven swooped down and carried him off. Over the hills the raven went until it reached a giant's castle. The raven perched on the giant's shoulder and opened its beak and poor Tom fell into the giant's porridge.

The giant was not at all pleased.

'I do not want to eat porridge after some little stranger has been having a bath in it,' roared the giant.

He picked up the bowl of porridge with Tom in it and threw it over the battlements of his castle into the river which ran nearby.

21
February

Tom Thumb

In the river was a fish, which was not as fussy about its food as the giant was.

When the porridge and Tom Thumb came floating down the river the fish opened its mouth and gobbled everything up.

That was the last meal the fish ate. A

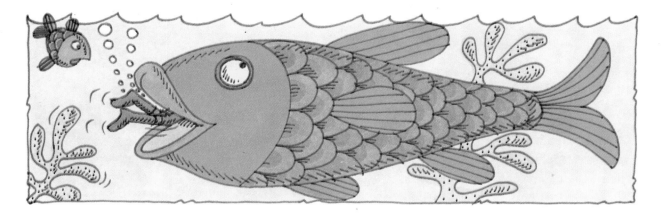

moment later it was caught in a fishing net and taken to market.

'That is a fine fish!' said the royal cook and he bought it for King Arthur's supper. Back at the palace the cook cut the fish open and was amazed to see a pair of kicking legs. Soon Tom Thumb struggled into the daylight.

'You will make a fine present for King Arthur,' said the cook. Giving Tom a wash, he took him before the royal throne and presented him to the king.

The king was pleased with the little fellow who was set before him, and a happy, exciting life began for Tom Thumb.

Tom was given everything his heart could desire. A little house was made for him to live in. He was given fine clothes. He wore the king's signet ring as a belt. He was given a mouse to ride like a horse, with saddle and bridle, and a lance was made for him like the lances used by real knights.

22
February

Tom Thumb

However, after many months, Tom became homesick for his mother and father and felt ashamed he was living a life of such luxury.

Tom Thumb asked King Arthur if he could go home for a holiday and also if he could take some money with him, as his parents were poor.

King Arthur agreed and said Tom could take as much money as he could carry from the royal treasure house. As Tom was so small this was not very generous, but kings are like that, as many people find out.

Determined to do the best he could for his parents, Tom took a silver sixpence from the treasury and carried it on his back all the long way home. This was a great struggle for such a little fellow.

His parents were overjoyed to see their boy whom they had given up for dead. They were also pleased with the silver sixpence which was a lot to poor folk like them.

Tom and his parents were happy for a long while. Then Tom felt he should go back to the royal court and make the best of himself.

It is said that King Arthur welcomed Tom back and that he was a great favourite with the king for many years. Then the little fellow fell ill and the Queen of the Fairies came to take him to live with Merlin and all the other magic people. And that is all that is known of Tom Thumb.

23
February

Five
Little Pigs

Once upon a time a mother lived in a cottage with her five little pigs. Every day the mother had to go out to work at the big house at the end of the lane and the little pigs were supposed to go to school in the village.

Every evening, when the mother came home from work, she would ask the five little pigs:

'Did you go to school today?'

The five little pigs would reply:

'Yes, Mother. We went to school today.'

However, the mother pig found out that the five naughty little pigs hardly ever went to school and she determined to find out what they did do. She spoke to the mouse which lived under the floorboards of the cottage.

'You can scamper about quickly,' she said. 'Tomorrow, run after each of my five children and find out what they do. I will reward you with a fine supper of cheese.'

The mouse agreed. The next day he scampered about, following first one little pig, then the other.

When the mother came home in the evening, she looked at her children and asked:

'Did you go to school today?'

'Yes, Mother. We went to school today,' replied the five little pigs.

24
February

Five
Little Pigs

Then a squeaky voice called from a hole in the skirting board:

'Oh no, they didn't go to school. I followed all five of them and I know they are not telling the truth.'

The mouse came forward and pointed to first one pig, then the other. He said:

'This little pig went to market and this little pig stayed at home. This little pig ate roast beef and this little pig had none. And this little pig cried "Wee, wee, wee, wee," all the way home.'

The five little pigs were furious that the mouse had given away their secrets, but there was no help for it. From then on the little pigs had to go to school every day or the mouse told their mother.

Never again was one little pig able to go to market and one little pig to stay at home, nor could one little pig eat roast beef, while another little pig had none. And never again did one little pig cry 'Wee, wee, wee, wee,' all the way home.

Goldilocks and The Three Bears

Once upon a time there were three bears, a great big Daddy Bear, a medium sized Mummy Bear and a sweet little Baby Bear. They all lived together in a pretty cottage in the forest.

One day Mummy Bear made porridge for breakfast. However, the porridge was too hot and the bears went for a walk while the porridge cooled.

The very same morning, a pretty little girl named Goldilocks was lost in the forest. She wandered for a long while until she came to the cottage belonging to the three bears.

The door was not locked.

'Is anyone at home?' called Goldilocks.

When no one replied, Goldilocks pushed the door open and walked in. She was tired and hungry and wished to rest.

First she sat on the great big chair belonging to great big Daddy Bear. In front of her on the table was Daddy Bear's big bowl of porridge.

'Surely the people who live here will not begrudge me a little porridge,' thought Goldilocks and leaning forward she took a spoonful of porridge from Daddy Bear's big bowl.

'Ugh!' gasped Goldilocks. 'That is too salty.'

She scrambled down from the chair and climbed on to the medium sized chair belonging to medium sized Mummy Bear. Then she leaned forward and took a spoonful of porridge from Mummy Bear's medium sized bowl.

'Ugh!' gasped Goldilocks. 'That is too sweet.'

Goldilocks and The Three Bears

Goldilocks jumped down from the chair belonging to Mummy Bear and instead, sat on the chair belonging to little Baby Bear.

'What a lovely chair!' gasped Goldilocks. 'It is just right for me.'

Then she leaned forward and tasted Baby Bear's porridge in its sweet little plate.

'What delicious porridge!' smiled Goldilocks and ate it all up.

Goldilocks settled back in Baby Bear's chair to rest, but there was a loud crack and the chair broke in two.

'Dear me!' sighed Goldilocks. 'I seem to be too heavy for this chair. Surely the people who live here will not mind if I rest on a bed for a while.'

She climbed up the stairs.

Goldilocks pushed open the door of the bedroom and went in. First she lay on the great big bed belonging to great big Daddy Bear.

'This is too hard,' she grumbled and rolled off on to the floor with a thump.

Then Goldilocks lay on the medium sized bed belonging to medium sized Mummy Bear.

'Dear me, this is far too soft,' muttered Goldilocks, 'I feel quite smothered.'

She slid off Mummy Bear's bed and lay on the sweet little bed belonging to sweet little Baby Bear.

'Oh, how comfortable! This is just right,' yawned Goldilocks and snuggling down, she went fast asleep.

27
February

Goldilocks and The Three Bears

Meanwhile the bears were returning from their walk.

'Our porridge should be cool by now,' said Mummy Bear.

They opened the door of the cottage and walked in.

Great big Daddy Bear glanced round the room and at once noticed that his chair had been moved. He said in a big deep voice:

'Who's been sitting in my chair?'

Then Mummy Bear noticed a dent in the cushion on her chair.

'Who's been sitting in my chair?' she asked in her medium soft voice.

Then Baby Bear noticed that his chair was lying broken on the floor and he squeaked in his little voice:

'Who's been sitting in my chair and broken it in two?'

Great big Daddy Bear stepped close to the table and roared in his big deep voice:

'Who's been eating my porridge?'

And Mummy Bear said:

'Who's been eating my porridge?'

And Baby Bear said in his squeaky voice:

'Someone's been eating my porridge and eaten it all up.'

All this shouting and squeaking wafted up the stairs into the bedroom and disturbed Goldilocks' sleep. She turned restlessly in the sweet little bed belonging to sweet little Baby Bear. The floorboards creaked.

'Someone is upstairs!' said great big Daddy Bear.

28
February

Goldilocks and The Three Bears

Great big Daddy Bear started walking up the stairs on his huge shaggy feet. Medium sized Mummy Bear followed him on her medium sized fluffy feet and sweet little Baby Bear pattered along after them on his pretty little paws.

They pushed open the bedroom door and looked in. First they saw the great big bed belonging to great big Daddy Bear. Its counterpane was ruffled and creased, where Goldilocks had slid about on it.

'Who's been sleeping in my bed?' roared Daddy Bear in a loud angry voice.

They stepped further into the room and looked at the medium sized bed belonging to medium sized Mummy Bear. There was a hollow in the middle.

'Who's been sleeping in my bed?' sobbed Mummy Bear, beginning to feel upset.

Then sweet little Baby Bear pushed forward into the room to see what had happened to his own bed. Lying on it he saw Goldilocks.

At that moment, woken by all the noise, Goldilocks sat bolt upright.

She saw the three bears with their furry skin and Daddy's sharp yellow teeth and Mummy's fairly sharp claws and Baby Bear's indignant little face.

Goldilocks screamed at the top of her voice. She jumped out of the window and did not stop running until she was home.

'What a strange girl!' said the bears.

And Goldilocks never more wandered alone in the forest. She was too scared!

March

1
March

Dick Whittington

About five hundred years ago in a country village in England, there lived an orphan boy named Dick Whittington. He had no relatives left alive and although the kind people of the village gave him what they could, Dick knew he would never be rich.

Dick was a strong lad. He was not content to be poor. He made up his mind to go to London to seek his fortune. Many rich people lived in London and some folk said that the streets were paved with gold.

After many days of walking, Dick, ragged and hungry, reached London. He found no streets paved with gold, just many, many people hurrying about their own business, and rows and rows of houses, more than he had ever seen.

Night fell, and cold and weary, Dick sank down in a doorway, hoping for shelter from the bitter wind.

The cook of the household noticed Dick lying on the doorstep and ordered him away.

'We want no thieves nor beggars here,' she shouted. 'Be off with you.'

Fortunately for Dick the house was owned by a rich merchant named Mr. Fitzwarren, who had a kind heart. He heard the cook shouting and came to look at Dick.

'I know we have to beware of thieves,' said Mr. Fitzwarren, 'but this boy has an honest face. Let us take him in and clean him and feed him. While he works for his keep, he can stay with us.'

2
March

Dick Whittington

Dick had no experience of living in a grand house like that of Mr. Fitzwarren. He was not trained to do anything important, like counting money or tailoring fine town clothes. So he was set to work as a kitchen boy in the charge of the cook who had first found him on the doorstep.

The cook did not like Dick. She gave him all the hardest work to do and was always ready with an unkind word or a blow. Worst of all, she sent Dick to sleep in a bare garret which was infested with rats and mice.

Dick was miserable, but knew he was fortunate to have a roof over his head and food to eat and even a little money, which kind Mr. Fitzwarren gave him from time to time.

One day, when he had an hour off from work, Dick was exploring the streets of London, still half hoping to find the ones which were paved with gold, when he met a girl carrying a fine handsome cat. She was trying to sell it.

'He is a wonderful mouser,' she said, 'but now I am to marry and my future husband has a cat which always fights with mine, so my cat has to go.'

'That cat is what I need to rid me of the rats and mice in my bedroom,' thought Dick.

He bought it at once.

3
March

Dick Whittington

Dick's cat proved to be a fine mouser and soon Dick's life was much more comfortable, with no mice eating his food, nor rats running across his bed at night.

Dick and the cat became fond of each other and the cat slept on Dick's bed. Although the cook was still unkind to Dick, he found a friend and protector in Alice, the daughter of Mr. Fitzwarren. Alice liked Dick and saw that he was given the chance to learn ways to better himself. However,

Dick was still a very poor boy and Alice was a very rich girl.

Then one day, Mr. Fitzwarren, who was a merchant, called all his servants and workers together.

'I am sending a ship full of goods to trade along the Barbary Coast,' he said. 'If any of you have goods you wish to send to be sold, you may send them in my ship and hopefully share in my profit.'

The servants were very excited. This was a fine opportunity. Some sent woollen goods they had made, others knives and metal goods they bought cheap from the blacksmith.

Dick Whittington had nothing to send. He had spent what little money he had on feeding his cat and buying clothes for himself.

'Why don't you send your cat?' said Alice.

4
March

Dick Whittington

At first Dick was upset at the idea of parting from his cat, but the captain of the ship wanted to take him.

'That cat is a fine mouser,' said the captain. 'He will help keep the rats down on my ship. Please let him come with me. I will take good care of him and only sell him if I am offered a fine price.'

So Dick agreed. It seemed that sending the cat was his only chance of becoming rich.

The ship sailed away and many months passed. Ships were often gone for years in those days. Quite often they sank and no one aboard was heard of again.

Alice Fitzwarren, Dick's friend, was sent away to an even grander household to be trained in the ways of fine society. Dick was lonely. Mr. Fitzwarren was busy and took no notice of Dick now Alice was away. The cook, who had always disliked Dick, was more horrid to him than ever.

Suddenly Dick thought it was no use staying in London any longer. The streets were not paved with gold. He would always be a poor boy. He might as well go back to his country village to be amongst people he knew.

Early one morning he packed some food in a cloth and carrying it tied to a stick, he walked north out of London and made his way up Highgate Hill.

5
March

Dick Whittington

Half-way up Highgate Hill, to the north of London, Dick sat down to rest. It was the morning of All Hallows Day and as Dick turned to look back across the great city, he heard the sound of Bow Bells ringing.

All the way from Bow Church on Cheapside the chiming of the bells clanged

through the early morning sunshine. It seemed to Dick that they were calling him to return. Surely he was not mistaken - the bells were speaking to him.

'Turn again, Whittington,' they said. 'Turn again, Whittington. Thrice Lord Mayor of London.'

Young Dick's heart leapt with fresh hope. Forgetting his weariness, he ran back down the hill and along the streets towards the house of his master, Mr. Fitzwarren.

'It is worth staying here and enduring a little hardship if I am to become Lord Mayor of London three times,' smiled Dick.

He reached Mr. Fitzwarren's home and crept back to his bed in the garret before anyone noticed that he had gone.

Meanwhile the captain of Mr. Fitzwarren's ship was enjoying great success along the wild Barbary Coast of Africa.

6
March

Dick Whittington

The captain of the ship was a skilful sailor and a just master. The ship was a happy

Dick Whittington

The dining room at the palace was large and beautiful. The captain and the royal household sat on rugs and cushions on the floor, as was the custom of the country. Dishes of silver and gold were brought and set before the company, but as the lids were lifted from the dishes, there was a great scurrying and scratching and a horde of rats ran from behind the curtains and beneath the floor. They snatched the food from the plates, taking no notice of the servants who tried to drive them away. It was with great difficulty that anyone present managed to eat anything at all.

The captain enquired if the King of the Moors was often plagued in this way.

'Every meal time it is the same,' sighed the King. 'Our lives are a misery. I would give half my wealth to anyone who could rid me of these pests.'

one and all the more happy because Dick Whittington's cat chased and killed every rat or mouse which dared to poke its nose out of its hole.

The cargo was kept safe from their nibbling and the crew's rest was not disturbed by the squeaking of the mice nor the gnawing of the rats – and it was all thanks to Puss.

The ship put in at several harbours and sold most of its cargo at a high price. Finally it docked at the capital of the Moorish kingdom, where the captain hoped to sell the rest of his cargo, buy many goods which he could sell at a high price in London, and then set sail for home.

The captain looked at hard-working Puss.

'I have not sold you to make a fortune for Master Whittington,' smiled the captain. 'However, I will pay him a few pence wages for your work on the voyage.'

Putting on his best suit of clothes, the captain went ashore to bargain with the King of the Moors.

All went well and when business was over the King of the Moors invited the captain to dine with him in the palace. The captain agreed, thinking he would enjoy a fine feast. He was to be disappointed.

At once the captain thought of Dick Whittington's cat.

'I am sure I can help you,' he smiled and he sent a messenger to the ship with orders to bring Puss to the palace. Needless to say, clever Puss rid the dining room of rats in a few minutes. The King and his courtiers enjoyed their first peaceful meal for years.

'Will you sell this cat?' asked the King.

8
March

Dick Whittington

The captain of Mr. Fitzwarren's ship was used to trading and at first he pretended he did not wish to part with Puss.

'I need him to kill the rats and mice on my ship,' said the captain. 'I cannot sell him.'

However the King of the Moors begged and pleaded and held out more and more money, until he was offering a fortune for the cat, which was what the captain had intended all along.

Puss was sold and lived for many, many years in great luxury until every rat was driven away from the land of the Moors. Then he caught a ship back to London and stayed with Dick for the rest of his life.

Meanwhile the captain returned to the house of Mr. Fitzwarren. Everyone was delighted with the success of the voyage and each was given his just share of the profits the captain had brought back. However, Dick Whittington was the richest of all because he was given the fortune the King of the Moors had paid for Puss.

Dick used his new money well. He bought ships and became a successful trader. He married Alice, Mr. Fitzwarren's daughter. He was knighted by the King of England and became Sir Richard Whittington. Three times he became Lord Mayor of London.

And if those who visit London care to go north to Highgate Hill, they will find the stone where Dick Whittington stopped and heard the sound of Bow Bells calling him back. And they will also see a stone statue of Dick's dear cat.

9
March

Old King Cole

Old King Cole,
Was a merry old soul,
And a merry old soul was he.
He called for his pipe,
And he called for his bowl,
And he called for his fiddlers three.

Old King Cole

King Cole lived many, many years ago in the days when the mighty Roman Empire was coming to an end. He did not understand that now the Roman soldiers had to go home to protect Rome and could no longer fight for King Cole.

Everything was very jolly at the court of King Cole. The servants shut the thick doors of the wooden hall in which the king and his court lived and all that could be heard were the sounds of eating and drinking and singing and fiddling.

Many people were not pleased with this.

'Father!' said the king's daughter, Helen. 'The Saxons are coming ashore and stealing our crops and burning the farmhouses and the Danes are sailing up river and destroying our ships. Don't you think you should stop sending for your pipe and your bowl of ale and your fiddlers three and do some fighting instead?'

'Do not be hasty, Helen,' replied King Cole. 'I thought the Roman soldiers were supposed to do the fighting. Why else do I pay my taxes?'

'Father!' said Helen. 'The good old days are over. However many taxes you pay, there will never again be enough Roman soldiers to protect us.'

'I do not wish to hear unpleasant talk like that,' snapped Old King Cole and he went back to his pipe and his bowl of ale and the music of the fiddlers three.

King Cole's daughter, Helen, looked across the burning countryside. Then she looked at the last band of Roman soldiers which was preparing to leave. One of their leaders was a handsome young man named Constantius.

Helen married Constantius and went with him to safety. They had a son called Constantine, who became emperor of what was left of the Roman Empire.

And that is all that is known about Old King Cole.

Rumpelstiltskin

Once upon a time there was a poor miller who had a beautiful daughter. It happened one day the miller went to the palace to sell his flour. Everyone there seemed so rich, the miller felt he had to boast about something, so he said his daughter could spin straw into gold.

Word of this came to the king and he sent for the miller.

'I am interested in anyone who can spin straw into gold,' said the king. 'Bring your daughter to the palace.'

When the unfortunate girl was brought before the king, he took her by the hand and led her to a room filled with straw. He gave her a spinning wheel and some reels for the spun gold and a chair.

'Set to work,' he said. 'If by dawn tomorrow you have not spun all this straw into gold, you will die.'

Then the king went out, locking the door behind him. The miller's daughter sat and wept. She had no idea how to spin straw into gold. Suddenly the door burst open and a strange little man leaped into the room.

'Good evening, Mistress Miller,' he croaked in a cracked little voice. 'Why are you crying?'

The miller's daughter told him she had to spin the straw into gold before dawn or she would die.

'What will you give me if I spin the straw into gold?' asked the strange little man.

'I will give you this necklace,' said the girl, taking some beads from round her neck.

'Very well,' smiled the little man.

He took the beads and worked all night and before dawn the straw was spun into fine, glittering gold and wound on to the reels. With a last laugh, the little man turned round and was gone.

When the king came into the room and saw the gold, he was delighted.

Rumpelstiltskin

The king was delighted, but he was not satisfied. That evening he took the miller's daughter to another room bigger than the last. This room also was full of straw and contained a spinning wheel and reels and a chair.

'Spin all this straw into gold by morning, or you will die,' ordered the king and again left the girl in the locked room. The miller's daughter wept, not knowing what to do.

Suddenly the door flew open and the same little man burst into the room.

'What will you give me to spin this straw into gold?' he asked.

The girl took a ring from her finger.

'I will give you this ring,' she said.

The little man seemed pleased. He took the ring, turned the straw into gold and disappeared. Next morning the king hurried into the room. He was overjoyed to see the gold, but he was still not satisfied.

He took the miller's daughter to an even larger room filled with even more straw and told her she must spin that straw into gold by the next morning or she would die.

'However,' smiled the king, 'if you do spin the straw into gold, I will marry you and you will be Queen.'

13
March

Rumpelstiltskin

Again the miller's daughter sat in a locked room full of straw and again she wept. Suddenly the door burst open and the little man who had visited her before, came running in.

'What will you give me if I spin this straw into gold?' he asked.

'Alas! I have nothing left to give,' sobbed the girl. 'Tomorrow I must die. And yet, if the straw could be spun into gold, the king has said he would marry me.'

'Very well,' smiled the little man. 'I will spin the straw into gold if, after you marry the king, you give me your first born child. I am tired of living alone. I should like a pretty baby to keep me company.'

The girl was not happy with the bargain,

but she thought that if she did not agree, she would be killed. She nodded her head and the little man set to work.

The straw was spun into gold. The king was pleased. He married the miller's daughter and about a year later a pretty baby was born.

As the queen, who had been the miller's daughter, sat rocking the cradle and singing to her baby, the little man came bursting into the room.

'I have come for the baby,' he said.

14
March

Rumpelstiltskin

'When I turned that roomful of straw into gold, you promised to give your first born baby to me,' the little man went on. 'Keep your word.'

The unhappy queen wept.

'Please do not keep me to my promise,' she begged. 'I love my sweet little baby so much. My heart will be broken if you take him.'

The little man felt sorry for her.

'Very well,' he said. 'I will give you a chance to keep your baby. If in three days you can guess my name, then I will not take the baby and you will not see me again.'

With that, he turned on his heels and vanished.

At once the queen sent for pen and paper and made long lists of every name she could think of. She also sent a messenger all over the land to learn every name there was.

'I am sure to guess the little man's name and keep my baby,' she thought.

The next day the little man came back.

'What is my name?' he asked.

'Caspar, Melchior, Balthazar?' guessed the queen, reading the lists of names she had made.

All day long the little man shook his head and finally went away laughing.

The second day he was back again. This time the queen read out all the names her servant had collected on his travels round the country.

Still the little man shook his head.

15
March

Rumpelstiltskin

The queen began to fear for the safety of her baby. Again she sent her servant out to travel the country listening for strange names. When he returned in the evening of the second day he said:

'I have no more lists of names, but as I travelled home I saw a strange thing. As I came round the corner of a wood, I saw a weird little man leaping up and down beside a fire in front of a house. As he jumped about he sang:

Today my wholemeal bread I bake,
Tomorrow, the queen's child I'll take.
She'll never know from whence I came,
Nor that Rumpelstiltskin is my name.'

The queen was filled with joy. At last she knew the name of the strange little man.

On the third day the little man came to see the queen.

'What is my name?' he asked.

At first the queen pretended she did not know.

'Er – Jack? Tom?' she asked.

The little man shook his head.

The queen smiled.

'Is your name, by chance, Rumpelstiltskin?' she laughed.

The little man was furious.

He shook his fist and stamped on the ground so hard that the floor split open and swallowed him up and the little man was never seen again.

16
March

The Boy
Who Cried Wolf

Long ago, when there were not many big towns and most folk lived in the country and were farmers, there was a boy whose task it was to look after a flock of sheep.

All day long the boy stayed alone with the sheep. He was not big enough to fight wolves or lions himself. Everyone knew

Later that day a pack of wolves really attacked the sheep. The boy screamed and waved his arms at the men in the village.

'Wolf!' he shouted. 'Wolf!'

But the men of the village did not help.

'That silly boy is trying to trick us again,' they said. So the sheep were lost.

The lesson of this story is, that folk who tell lies are not believed, even when they tell the truth.

17
March

The Three Billy Goats Gruff

Once upon a time three goats lived in a field. They were called Little Billy Goat Gruff, Big Billy Goat Gruff and Great Big Billy Goat Gruff.

Alongside the field ran a river and over the river was a bridge. On the other side of the bridge was another field with green grass, ripe berries and red apples.

The field where the three billy goats lived was nibbled almost bare from their constant feeding, but the field on the other side of the bridge was untouched and full of food.

However, under the bridge lived a horrid dwarf, who loved eating goats.

that. If a pack of wolves or an old lion came sniffing round the flock, the boy was to shout for help to the men in the village, who would come running to save the sheep.

Now this boy found staying with the sheep very boring. In order to make some excitement on a dull day, he turned towards the village and called:

'Wolf! Wolf! Help! A wolf is attacking the sheep!'

At once the men left what they were doing and ran across the valley. When they arrived panting at the boy's side, he said:

'The wolf turned tail and ran away. He is not here any more.'

The men went back to the village.

A little later on the boy called for help again.

'Wolf! Wolf!' he screamed. 'Help me!'

Again the men came running and again, when they arrived there was no wolf to be seen.

A third time the boy called for help and a third time the men ran over from the village, but this time they guessed what the boy was doing and vowed they would be tricked no more.

Because of this the goats did not dare cross the bridge to the luscious field on the other side.

One day Little Billy Goat Gruff said:

'I will cross the bridge. I will eat the grass and the berries and the apples in the field on the other side.'

'If you do, the dwarf will catch you,' said the other goats.

'I am not afraid,' said Little Billy Goat Gruff and he set off across the bridge.

18
March

The Three Billy Goats Gruff

Little Billy Goat Gruff walked across the bridge and over the place where the horrid dwarf lived.

'Who runs trip-trap, trip-trap, over my bridge?' called the horrid dwarf.

'It is I, Little Billy Goat Gruff,' replied the little goat.

'Then I will eat you,' called the dwarf.

'No. Do not eat me. I am too small,' shouted back Little Billy Goat Gruff. 'Eat Big Billy Goat Gruff when he comes over the bridge. He is plumper than I am.'

'Very well,' agreed the dwarf and he let Little Billy Goat Gruff continue trip-trap, trip-trap over the bridge.

Soon Little Billy Goat Gruff was eating

the green grass and the ripe berries and the red apples. Big Billy Goat Gruff and Great Big Billy Goat Gruff watched him.

'I will cross the bridge, too,' said Big Billy Goat Gruff.

19
March

The Three Billy Goats Gruff

Big Billy Goat Gruff went trip-trap, trip-trap, across the bridge and over the place where the horrid dwarf lived.

'The dwarf did not eat Little Billy Goat Gruff. He will not eat me,' thought Big Billy Goat Gruff.

The dwarf called out:

'Who goes trip-trap, trip-trap, over my bridge?'

'It is I, Big Billy Goat Gruff,' replied the big goat.

'Then I will eat you,' shouted the dwarf.

'No. Do not eat me,' replied Big Billy Goat Gruff. 'Eat Great Big Billy Goat Gruff. He is much plumper than I am.'

'Very well,' agreed the dwarf and he let Big Billy Goat Gruff continue trip-trap, trip-trap over the bridge.

Soon Big Billy Goat Gruff was in the far field eating the green grass and ripe berries and red apples with Little Billy Goat Gruff.

Great Big Billy Goat Gruff watched them.

'I will cross the bridge, too,' he thought.

20
March

The Three
Billy Goats Gruff

Great Big Billy Goat Gruff went trip-trap, trip-trap, across the bridge and over the place where the horrid dwarf lived.

'The dwarf did not eat Little Billy Goat Gruff. He did not eat Big Billy Goat Gruff. He will not eat me,' thought Great Big Billy Goat Gruff.

'Who goes trip-trap, trip-trap, over my bridge?' called the dwarf.

'It is I, Great Big Billy Goat Gruff,' replied Great Big Billy Goat Gruff.

'Then I will eat you,' shouted the dwarf.

'Come up here and try it,' laughed Great Big Billy Goat Gruff.

With one bound the dwarf jumped on to the bridge and stood in the path of Great Big Billy Goat Gruff. The goat was not afraid. He shook his head and stamped his feet. He lowered his horns and ran at the dwarf. He caught him on the points of his horns and tossed him over the side of the bridge and into the water.

'Eat me, would you!' snorted Great Big Billy Goat Gruff. 'Try drinking water instead!'

The dwarf sank deep into the water and was carried away and never seen again.

Great Big Billy Goat Gruff continued trip-trap, trip-trap over the bridge and

joined Big Billy Goat Gruff and Little Billy Goat Gruff in the luscious field. There they all grew fat eating the green grass and ripe berries and red apples.

21
March

Little Boy Blue

Once upon a time there was a farmer's son who had big blue eyes. His mother thought the boy's eyes were beautiful and always dressed her little son in blue to make his eyes look brighter than ever.

Little Boy Blue the child was called.

The boy was too young to do the hard work on the farm, but he liked to think he helped his father, so he was given a horn. Each morning, when it was time for work to commence, the farmer would lift his son to the open window of the farmhouse and the boy, wearing his blue clothes and with his bright blue eyes shining, would blow on the horn. Then everyone would start work and Little Boy Blue felt he was doing an important job.

However, one New Year's Day, when there had been a big party at the farm the evening before, a neighbour came walking by. Though the sun was well risen, he saw that no work was being done.

The sheep had escaped from its pen and was running about in the meadow. The cow had broken out of the cowshed and was eating the corn. And the boy who was supposed to keep an eye on the sheep and

the cow was still asleep by the haystack!

'I can see that Little Boy Blue has not blown his horn to set everyone to work this morning,' thought the neighbour. 'I hope the family is not ill.'

The neighbour hammered on the door of the farmhouse and called:

'Little Boy Blue, come, blow up your horn. The sheep's in the meadow, the cow's in the corn.'

'Where's the boy who looks after the sheep?' asked the farmer, waking up.

'He's under the haystack, fast asleep!' replied the neighbour.

At once, Little Boy Blue and the farmer and his wife and all the farm labourers got up.

'We are not ill,' explained the farmer. 'We had a party last night. We stayed up late and overslept.'

Little Boy Blue quickly dressed in his blue clothes, took up his horn and went to the open window. He blew on his horn and everyone started work and the farm was put to rights again.

22
March

Rapunzel

Long ago and far away, a man and his wife lived next door to a witch. The witch had a beautiful garden in which she grew not only flowers, but herbs and vegetables.

One day, when the man's wife was waiting for a baby to be born, she looked into the witch's garden and longed to eat the rampion which she saw growing there. The wife longed for the rampion so much that she became pale and ill.

At last the man summoned up his courage and crept into the garden of the witch and took some rampion. His wife cooked it and ate it and felt better straightaway.

Every time the wife fell ill, the man stole rampion from the garden of the witch, until at last the witch caught him. She was angry and threatened to turn the man to stone. Nevertheless, when he explained why he took the rampion, the witch relented and said she would let him go, on condition that when the child was born, it would be given to her.

The man and his wife had many other children, so it was agreed that the new baby should go to the witch.

23
March

Rapunzel

The witch took the baby, which was a girl, and named it Rapunzel. She was kind to the child and little Rapunzel grew up happily, although she was never allowed out of the witch's garden.

When Rapunzel came to be twelve years old, the witch fell to thinking.

'This is the age when girls become restless and wish to leave home,' thought the witch. 'Soon Rapunzel will want other companions than me. However, if I let Rapunzel go, who will keep me company and look after me if I become old and sick?'

The witch made up her mind that she would never let Rapunzel go, for although she had been kind to the little girl, the witch was very selfish.

The witch built a tall tower in the woods. There was no entrance to the tower and no staircase. At the top was a single room with a window and a hook at its side.

The witch took Rapunzel and put her to live in the room at the top of the tower. Rapunzel had long, thick hair. When the witch wished to visit Rapunzel, she would stand at the foot of the tower and call:

'Rapunzel! Rapunzel! Let down your hair.'

Then Rapunzel would wind some of her hair round the hook and let the rest fall to the ground and up the witch would climb.

24
March

Rapunzel

Every afternoon, the witch came to visit Rapunzel and would spend several hours chatting with her in the room at the top of the tower.

Rapunzel was fairly happy, because she had never lived with anyone but the witch, nor seen any other human being. She thought this way of life was quite normal.

Several years went by. The witch became rather old and her voice cracked. When she called out:

'Rapunzel! Rapunzel! Let down your hair,' the sound was very quavery and thin.

Then one day a prince was riding through the forest, when he saw the witch standing at the foot of the tall tower, screeching in her croaky voice:

'Rapunzel! Rapunzel! Let down your hair.'

How amazed the prince was when he saw a beautiful young woman lean from the window at the top of the tower and let down her hair for the old witch to climb up.

25
March

Rapunzel

The prince thought this was very strange, but he was busy and it was none of his affair and he rode on his way back to his castle.

However, he could not banish the things he had seen from his mind. Several days later, he rode back to the tower and hid in some bushes and watched.

In the afternoon the witch arrived with a basket of food for Rapunzel and some silks for the embroidery which she did to pass the time.

'Rapunzel! Rapunzel! Let down your hair,' called the witch in her cracked old voice.

Rapunzel looked out of the window, wound her hair round the hook and let it down to the ground. The witch climbed up the hair, stayed with Rapunzel for an hour or two and then went away.

'If that is the way to get into the tower to visit the beautiful young lady, then I will try doing the same,' thought the prince.

He waited until dusk. Then he walked forward and stood under the tower and imitating the croaky old voice of the witch, he called:

'Rapunzel! Rapunzel! Let down your hair.'

Thinking that the witch had forgotten something and come back for a second visit and not being able to see for the evening gloom, Rapunzel let down her hair and the prince climbed up.

26
March

Rapunzel

At first Rapunzel was frightened of the prince, because she had never seen a man before. However, he spoke to her gently and told her about the world outside the tower where there were other young people like herself. Then Rapunzel realized how lonely she was and how selfish the witch was being. When the prince asked her to marry him, she agreed.

'I will gladly go with you,' she said, 'but how shall I get down from this tower?'

Then, after thinking for a moment, she told the prince to visit her every evening and each time bring with him a skein of silk.

'I will twist it into a ladder and when it is long enough, I will climb down it and you can take me away on your horse,' she smiled.

The witch discovered nothing of what was going on, until one day Rapunzel said to her:

'How is it that you are much heavier to pull up than the young prince who will be here before long?'

'You have deceived me, you ungrateful girl,' screeched the witch. Then she cut off Rapunzel's hair and locked her in a house in the loneliest part of the forest.

That evening, when the prince stood under the tower and called:

'Rapunzel! Rapunzel! Let down your hair,' the witch let down Rapunzel's hair. When the prince climbed up and into the room, he found the witch waiting for him.

'Your ladylove has gone and you will never see her again,' screamed the witch, pushing the poor prince back through the window, so that he fell with a crash to the ground.

The prince struck his head and now wandered between the trees, hardly knowing what he was doing. Fortunately the woodland fairies guided his feet to the

house where Rapunzel was imprisoned. The sound of her voice calling for help brought him back to his senses. He released his beloved sweetheart and they went back to his castle, where the witch could not find them, and lived happily ever after.

27
March

The Lion and the Mouse

One day a mouse happened to run into the mouth of a sleeping lion. The lion woke up and was about to eat the mouse, when the little fellow said:

'Let me go and I will be forever grateful.'

The lion smiled and let the mouse go, saying:

'You have found me in a good mood, so I will set you free, but I do not care whether you are grateful or not. A mighty lion like me will never need help from a small mouse like you.'

Sometime later the lion was caught by hunters and bound by ropes to a tree. The mouse heard his roars and creeping close, gnawed through the ropes and set the lion free.

'You laughed at me and said I was too small to help you,' squeaked the mouse, 'but now you see you were wrong.'

This story shows there come sudden changes of fortune when the most powerful will need help from the weakest.

28
March

The Legend of Johnny Appleseed

Once, in the East of America lived a little man named Johnny, who had a fine orchard. Every year the trees were loaded with apples. Johnny surely knew the right way to grow apple trees.

Then one year, Johnny saw a long line of wagons creaking past his gate.

'Where are you folks going?' asked Johnny.

The people replied that they were going to start new lives out West where there was plenty of land and the soil was rich and the rivers were full of fish.

'Ah, but are there any apple trees out in this wonderful land to the West?' asked Johnny.

'I reckon not,' replied a lady in a blue sunbonnet, 'and I shall miss them. There is nothing my boys like better than some of mother's homebaked apple pie.'

Johnny watched the wagon train roll away into the sunset.

'It seems a mighty shame that those fine folks aren't going to eat apples any more,' he thought. Then he sat down for a sleep under one of his trees.

As he slept, he dreamed that an angel came down from an apple tree and told him that he ought to go out West and take a sack of apple seeds with him.

'I can't go out West,' replied Johnny. 'The West is for big tough men and I'm a little fellow.'

'Nonsense!' replied the angel. 'The folks out West need apple dumplings and baked apples and apple sauce and apple cider and it will never be true America without apple pie. You must go.'

'I reckon I will then,' smiled Johnny.

The next week he set off West with a sack of appleseeds over his shoulder.

The Legend of Johnny Appleseed

Johnny did not bother much about clothes or luggage. He took a tin cooking pot, which he often wore on his head to save the bother of carrying it, and he took the clothes he stood up in and that was all – apart from the precious appleseeds.

Johnny lived off the land and slept wherever he happened to be when night fell. If he was lucky, he found a lonely cabin where the good folks would take him in for the night and feed him; and always before leaving, Johnny planted some appleseed.

Johnny would find a good spot with water for the young seedlings. He would put the appleseeds into the ground and pat it firm. He would build a little fence around the seeds to protect the young trees as they grew. Then Johnny would go on his way.

As the years went by, folks could stand on a hill and look across the land and from the trail of apple trees, they could see where Johnny had been visiting.

Johnny was happier than he had ever been in his life. No animal ever harmed him, because the animals knew they had nothing to fear from the little man who planted appleseeds.

The farmfolk always welcomed Johnny, hoping he would leave a present of apple trees behind. And whenever Johnny went back to see how his trees were growing, the farmers' wives welcomed him and gave him a big slice of apple pie.

Without Johnny Appleseed there would have been no apple pie.

For over forty years Johnny Appleseed wandered across the West. Then, one year, he was seen no more. Folks said the angel had fetched Johnny to plant appleseeds in heaven. Perhaps that was true.

The Goose that laid Golden Eggs

Once upon a time there was a fortunate man who owned a goose which laid golden eggs. On the first day of every month the goose laid the precious egg. The man would sell it and live well on the money he gained.

Then one day a friend said to him:

'Why do you wait to get one egg a month? If you killed the goose and took all the eggs at once, you would be the richest man in the world and have everything your heart desired.'

'What a wonderful idea,' gasped the man. 'Why didn't I think of that myself?'

He killed the goose and looked inside it for all the golden eggs.

However, the goose was as other geese. There was no store of golden eggs. And now the goose was dead, the man had lost his one golden egg a month.

The lesson of this story is, if you are fortunate, be satisfied. Do not be too greedy.

31
March

Humpty Dumpty

Once upon a time there was an egg named Humpty Dumpty.

Humpty Dumpty liked to sit on the high brick wall which ran round his house and call out to his neighbours as they went by.

'I see you are wearing a new coat, Mrs. Martin,' he would say. 'The colour does not suit you. You should have chosen brown.'

Or he might call into the next garden:

'Those roses look very small, Mr. Jones. You did not prune them properly in the spring.'

As you may imagine, none of the neighbours liked Humpty Dumpty. They liked him even less when they learned he was spying on them and telling tales to the king.

Sometimes the neighbours got so cross they shook their fists at Humpty Dumpty and swore at him. But he just laughed at them and rolled from side to side.

When, one day, Humpty Dumpty fell off the wall, none of the neighbours went to his help. At last the king found out, but although he sent all his horses and all his men, they could not put Humpty Dumpty together again.

The neighbours sang:
'Humpty Dumpty sat on a wall,
Humpty Dumpty had a great fall.
All the king's horses and all the king's men,
Couldn't put Humpty together again.'

The lesson of this story is that a frail egg should be careful where it sits and what it says!

April

1
April

The Emperor's New Clothes

Many years ago there lived an Emperor who was very fond of clothes. He took no interest in his army, nor in going to the theatre, nor in farming his wide lands. He thought of nothing and talked of nothing but clothes from morning till night. He had a suit for every hour of the day.

One year two swindlers came to town. They said that they were weavers and that they knew how to weave fabric more beautiful than had ever been seen before. Moreover, they claimed that their fabric had the quality of becoming invisible to anyone who was not fit for the office he held or who was stupid.

'I must have clothes made from this fabric,' thought the Emperor. 'Not only shall I look grand in the beautiful material, but I shall be able to tell which of my officials is unfit to hold his job or is stupid.'

The Emperor paid the swindlers a lot of money in advance, so that they might start their work. The two men ordered the finest silk and pure gold thread, all of which they hid away. Then they worked far into the night on empty looms.

2
April

The Emperor's New Clothes

After a few days the Emperor sent his wise and faithful chief minister to see how the two men were progressing with their weaving.

The good man went into the room where the two swindlers were working at empty looms.

'Heaven help me!' thought the chief minister. 'I can see no material. This means I must be unfit for my job or I am stupid.'

The two swindlers beckoned the chief minister to come closer.

'Does not the gold thread in the material glitter in the sunshine?' they said. 'Is not the pattern most original?'

'Oh, yes, yes. Indeed! Indeed!' gasped

the poor old man, who did not wish to lose his job. He listened carefully while the two swindlers described the material to him and explained why they were using certain colours and certain patterns. Then the chief minister went back to the Emperor and told him every detail about the material and said how charming and lovely it was.

Immediately the weavers demanded more money and more gold thread, all of which they hid while they went on pretending to weave at empty looms.

3
April

The Emperor's New Clothes

The Emperor sent several of his court officials to see how the wonderful new material was coming along. They all saw nothing, for there was nothing to see. However they went back to the Emperor and reported that the material was beautiful because they did not wish to lose their jobs.

At last the Emperor decided to look at the material himself. With several of his courtiers, including those who had already been sent to look at the material, the Emperor walked into the room where the two swindlers were hard at work over their empty looms.

Wishing to prove how clearly they could see the material, the courtiers hurried forward and remarked how elegant the patterns were and how beautiful the gold thread glittered in the sun.

The Emperor was horrified that he could see nothing.

'No one must guess that I cannot see the material,' he thought, 'or they will say I am stupid and not fit to be Emperor.'

'This material is magnificent,' he nodded. 'You may make it up into clothes for me to wear in the Easter procession.'

The swindlers smiled and asked for more money and continued to pretend to work.

4
April

The Emperor's New Clothes

The swindlers burned candles late into the night pretending to take material from the looms and cut it with scissors. Then they

sewed it with needles with no thread in them and at last said the clothes were ready. They took the clothes to the Emperor in his dressing room.

'Please take off your old clothes, Your Highness,' they smiled, 'and we will dress you in your new clothes.'

Not daring to say he could see no new clothes, the Emperor took his old clothes off and let himself be dressed in nothing!

'Our wonderful clothes are as light as cobwebs,' said the men. 'You will not feel their weight at all.'

'Indeed I cannot,' agreed the Emperor, quite correctly, for he had nothing on.

Not wishing anyone to think them stupid or unfit for their jobs, all the servants and courtiers exclaimed how fine the Emperor looked in his new clothes and how they were the best he had ever worn.

The Emperor held his head high and stepped out of his palace to walk in a parade through the streets of his realm.

5
April

The Emperor's New Clothes

The citizens of the country leaned from their windows and stood in the streets, eager to see the Emperor's wonderful new clothes.

'How beautiful! The clothes fit to perfection,' they said.

None could see the clothes because, of course, the clothes were not there. Everyone believed that the clothes were invisible only to those who were stupid or unfit for their jobs. No one dared to say they could not see the clothes.

Then a little child looked down from a window and called out in a clear voice:

'But he has got nothing on! The Emperor has no clothes!'

'My innocent child can see the Emperor has no clothes,' said the father of the boy. 'It is true. The Emperor has no clothes!'

Soon the entire crowd was laughing and shouting at the foolish Emperor.

The Emperor squirmed, for he knew what they shouted was true, but he would not admit that he had been cheated. He walked more proudly than ever and his courtiers went on pretending they could see the invisible suit of clothes.

6
April

The Sun and the Wind

Once the Sun and the Wind fell to arguing which of them was the stronger. They could not agree and decided to test their strength upon a passing traveller walking along the road.

'Whichever of us can make that traveller take his cloak off first shall be reckoned the stronger,' said the Wind, and the Sun agreed.

The Wind blustered around the unfortunate man as he trudged along the road. He roared and whistled and pulled at the cloak. He threw rain and hail and snow down on the man. The man merely pulled his cloak tighter about him and strode firmly on his way.

Next day the Sun tried his strength. He stood high in the sky and shone warmly down on the traveller's back. Soon the man ceased his walking and flinging off his cloak lay at the side of the road to rest in the comfort of the Sun's rays.

So the Sun won the contest and proved that more is to be gained by being warm and gentle than by being harsh and rough.

7
April

Paul Bunyan and Babe

Lumberjacks are big strong men, but there was never one bigger and stronger than Paul Bunyan.

Even when he was a baby, Paul was so strong his folks hardly knew what to do with him. When he cried the trees fell over for miles around and when he kicked and stamped his baby feet, why, the neighbours grew tired of putting their roofs back on!

Paul's folks thought they would put him where he could do no harm. They built him a cradle as big as a battleship and put him to rock in the harbour. When Paul woke up, he started to roll to and fro and made a tidal wave which flooded the country for miles around and his ma and pa had to take him home again.

When Paul grew up he became a lumberjack and ran a fine camp, where the food was the best in the country.

Everyone who went to the camp talked about the strange pet Paul had. It was a blue ox, the biggest blue ox in the world. Paul called it Babe.

Paul found Babe when it was a baby, lost and half frozen in the snow. He took it to camp and kept it warm and fed it eighteen gallons of milk a day and soon the young ox was right as rain and they were friends for life.

Babe grew to be so huge that folks mistook it for a mountain. When Babe was lying down near camp, Paul would say to strangers:

'There's Mount Bluebabe.'

Then Babe would get up and walk away and the strangers would near die with fright.

Even Paul was surprised at how quickly Babe grew. One night Paul put Babe to sleep in a barn. Next morning Paul looked out and was surprised to find the barn gone.

He went to look for Babe and found him eating hay in a field and growing apace. On Babe's back was a small building.

It was the barn. Babe had outgrown it in one night!

Babe was really useful to Paul.

Once there was a wiggly road near the lumber camp. Paul harnessed Babe to one end of the road and set him to pull.

It was a real hard job, but after a few tugs, Babe had pulled the road as straight as a ruler.

Yes, Babe was a fine pet for a big fellow like Paul Bunyan.

8
April

Paul Bunyan and Johnny Inkslinger

Paul Bunyan was the biggest, strongest logger who ever felled a tree. With him in his lumber camp he had some fine friends. One of them was Johnny Inkslinger. In those days folk wrote with pen and ink, which was how Johnny got his name.

Johnny kept the account books for Paul Bunyan and they sure took some keeping. Paul cut down so many trees, so swiftly, and sold them so quickly, it took volumes of books to keep account of the comings and goings.

Johnny Inkslinger sat at his desk writing so fast he had to have a fountain pen with a long hose fastened to a barrel of ink, so that he had enough ink to write with.

Ten barrels of ink a day Johnny Inkslinger would use and that seemed too much, so he stopped crossing the t's and dotting the i's and he saved six barrels of ink in a week.

Paul thought Johnny was the best bookkeeper in the world and he was right.

9
April

Paul Bunyan and the Cornstalk

Paul Bunyan was not only good at logging. He was a mighty fine gardener too. He grew onions as big as wagon wheels and potatoes as large as pillows.

One thing he was never keen on growing and that was corn. He tried it once and swore never again.

It happened this way. Paul was standing in his garden about to eat a grain of corn, when he thought - why not plant it instead - so he did and then went off logging, giving no more thought to the corn.

Suddenly the blacksmith came calling him and telling him he should get back to his garden. Back Paul went and found the cornstalk growing as thick as a tree trunk and with its head in the clouds.

The blacksmith was the best climber in the camp, so Paul sent him shinning up the tree to see where it went. Pretty soon the blacksmith shouted back:

'I can't reach the top. It's growing too fast!'

'Come down then,' Paul shouted back.

Pretty soon the blacksmith's voice shouted down:

'I can't do that either. It's growing up faster than I can climb down.'

'I've got a problem here,' thought Paul Bunyan and he was right.

10
April

Paul Bunyan and the Cornstalk

Paul Bunyan looked up the monstrous cornstalk which was growing in his garden.

'Don't worry,' he called to his friend, the blacksmith, who was up the cornstalk. 'We'll soon get you down.'

Paul sent for a dozen of the best axemen in the logging camp. While he was waiting for them to arrive, he loaded his musket with apple pies and shot them into the air.

'The blacksmith must have something to eat while he is waiting,' thought Paul, 'or he will starve.'

The axemen arrived and hacked at the cornstalk faster than rain falling on a tin roof, but the stalk was growing so quickly, the axes never hit the same place twice.

'Don't worry,' Paul called out to the blacksmith and his voice shook the snow from the mountains a hundred miles away. 'I'll get you down.'

Paul ran to the railroad and pulled up four hundred yards of track. He took it back to the garden and tied it tight round the tree.

'Now let that stalk grow,' he said, 'the fatter the stalk grows, the more the track will cut into it, until it fells itself.'

That is what happened. The cornstalk came tumbling down and the blacksmith with it. He hung on till he was five feet from the ground, then he stepped off as light as a feather.

'I'll never grow corn again. We'll have carrots instead,' said Paul. And they did. Carrots as long as broomhandles!

11
April

The Fox and the Grapes

One day a fox saw some grapes hanging high on a vine. The grapes were ripe and sweet and juicy. The fox wished to eat them very much.

The fox tried every way to reach the grapes. He jumped up and snapped at them. He tried to climb the wooden stalk of the vine. He walked along a wall and tried to reach across to the grapes.

Everything was useless.

The fox could not reach the grapes. Tired and scratched with his efforts, the fox

cast one last glance at the fat, sweet grapes.

'I'm sure they are sour anyway,' he snarled and, believing what he said, he went on his way.

Which only shows that some folk can make themselves believe anything if they want to.

12
April

The Gingerbread Boy

Once a little old woman and a little old man lived in a little old house. They had no little children to share the house with, so the little old woman said:

'I will make a boy out of gingerbread. I will use sugar frosting for his coat, sugar candy for his eyes and mouth, a fat currant for his nose and nuts for his toes.'

She made the gingerbread boy and put him into the oven to bake. Presently she heard a little voice calling:

'Let me out! Let me out!'

She opened the oven door and out hopped the gingerbread boy. He ran through the open kitchen door and down the street.

The little old woman and little old man both called to him to stop, but he would not. He ran on, calling:

'Run, run, as fast as you can. You can't catch me, I'm the gingerbread man.'

And they could not catch him. He ran on and on until he met a cow.

'Stop,' said the cow, 'you look good to eat.'

But the boy ran faster and shouted:

'I have run away from a little old woman and a little old man. I can run away from you, I can. Run, run, as fast as you can. You can't catch me, I'm the gingerbread man.'

13
April

The Gingerbread Boy

Next, the gingerbread boy met a horse.

'Stop! You look good to eat,' neighed the horse.

The little gingerbread boy merely ran the faster, and called over his shoulder:

'I have run away from a little old woman

and a little old man and a cow. I can run away from you, I can. Run, run, as fast as you can. You can't catch me, I'm the gingerbread man.'

The horse tried to catch the boy, but he could not, and the boy began to have a big opinion of himself.

'No one can catch me,' he laughed.

Then he met a sly old fox.

'Wait,' said the fox. 'I want to talk to you.'

'You can't catch me with that trick,' said the gingerbread boy and he started to run. The fox ran at his side.

'I don't want to catch you,' he said. 'I want to help you. I will help you cross this river to get away from the little old woman and the little old man and the cow and the horse who are chasing you.'

The gingerbread boy caught hold of the fox's tail and they started across the river. Presently the fox said:

'You are too heavy for my tail. Jump on my back.'

So the little gingerbread boy jumped on to the fox's back. Then the fox said:

'Dear little gingerbread boy, my back is sinking. Jump on to my head.'

So the little gingerbread boy jumped on to the fox's head.

Soon the fox's feet touched the bank on the other side of the river. He tossed the gingerbread boy into the air. He opened his mouth and SNAP went his teeth.

'Dear me,' said the little gingerbread boy, 'I am a quarter gone.'

Then he said: 'Why, I am half gone.'

Then he cried: 'I am three-quarters gone.'

And after that the little gingerbread boy said nothing at all.

14
April

I had a Little Pony

Once there was a girl who owned a pony and she was very fond of it. The pony was a dapple grey colour and the girl kept him clean and well fed and rode him well.

One day a fine lady came to stay nearby for a holiday. She asked if she could hire the pony to go riding.

The girl agreed because she thought the money would be useful for paying for the pony's food. However, when the lady returned the pony, it was in a dreadful state. It had been whipped and ridden

through mud and water. The girl wished she had never let the lady ride the pony and she made up a poem about it. Here it is.

'I had a little pony,
His name was Dapple-grey.
I lent him to a lady,
To ride a mile away.
She whipped him, she lashed him,
She rode him through the mire;
I would not lend my pony now,
For all the lady's hire.'

15
April

Snow White and Rose Red

Long ago and far away, there lived two sisters named Snow White and Rose Red. They were good girls and helped their widowed mother with the housework and in the dark evenings they would sit before the fire spinning, while their mother read to them.

One evening the three of them were sitting comfortably together, when there came a tap at the door.

'Make haste and open the door, Rose Red,' said her mother. 'Perhaps there is some traveller outside who needs shelter.'

Rose Red drew back the bolt and opened the door. However, instead of a traveller, a bear poked his nose in through the doorway. Rose Red screamed with fear. Snow White hid behind the bed, but the bear said:

'Do not be afraid. I will do you no harm. I am half frozen and wish only to come in and warm myself.'

'Poor bear!' said the mother. 'Come in and lie down by the fire, but take care not to burn your coat. Snow White and Rose Red, do not be afraid. The bear will not hurt you.'

All through that winter the bear spent the nights in the cottage and in the daytime he roamed through the forest. The two girls came to treat him as a friend and had no fear of the huge creature.

16
April

Snow White and Rose Red

As spring returned, the bear said to Snow White:

'Now I shall leave and not return for the whole of the summer.'

'Where are you going, dear bear?' asked Show White.

The bear replied:

'I must go into the forest and guard my treasure from the evil dwarfs. In winter, when the ground is frozen, the dwarfs have to stay in their holes and cannot break out.

Now the sun is warming the earth, the dwarfs will scramble free and steal all they can.'

Snow White was sorry the bear would be away for so long. She opened the cottage door so slowly, that as the bear hurried through he tore his fur on the latch and through the tear Snow White thought she saw the glitter of gold, but she could not be sure.

After the bear had gone, the family carried on as before. One day the girls were out gathering sticks for the fire, when they saw a dwarf with an old wrinkled face and a snow white beard a yard long. The beard was caught in a slit in a fallen tree and the dwarf was struggling vainly to free himself.

17
April

Snow White and Rose Red

The dwarf caught sight of the sisters.

'Don't stand there staring!' he shouted. 'Do something to help me.'

'How did your beard get stuck like that?' asked Rose Red.

The dwarf danced with rage.

'You silly goose,' he shouted, his red eyes burning, 'don't waste time asking silly questions. Do something to free my beard.'

Although she felt the rude little man did not deserve help, Snow White took out a pair of scissors from her pocket and cut off the end of the beard.

As soon as he was at liberty, the dwarf snatched up a sack of gold which had been lying between the roots of the tree.

'You stupid girl!' he shouted at Snow White, as he hurried away. 'Could you think of no other way of freeing me than by cutting off part of my lovely beard? Bad luck to you!'

The two girls went home hoping they would never see the dwarf again, but they were not to be so fortunate.

18
April

Snow White and Rose Red

Twice more Snow White and Rose Red helped the dwarf when he was trapped.

They saved him from a fish which was trying to pull him into a pond and they dragged him from the clutches of a bird which was carrying him off in its talons. Each time the dwarf had a sack of treasure, but he gave no reward to the kind girls.

Then again, by chance, the girls came upon the dwarf, when he was not in trouble, but was counting his treasure. The dwarf was furious. Being a thief himself, he thought everyone else was the same and he thought Snow White and Rose Red would try to steal his treasure from him.

He was about to attack them, when a huge bear ran up and felled the dwarf with a blow. The girls had turned to run home, when they heard the familiar voice of the bear who had shared their cottage through the winter. They turned and smiled and, as they watched, the fur coat of the bear fell away and a handsome young man dressed in gold stood before them.

'I am the son of a king,' he said, 'and this dwarf stole my treasure and put a spell on me. Now I have found him and he is dead, the spell is broken and I may return to my father.'

Snow White married the prince and Rose Red married his brother. They were rich, for the prince now had the treasure and, together with the girls' mother, they all lived happily ever after.

19
April

The Dog in the Manger

Once there was a cow who had a fine manger from which she ate happily.

On the same farm lived a dog, who had a good kennel and plenty of meat to eat.

However, the dog enjoyed sleeping in the cow's manger and barked at the cow which made her too afraid to eat.

The dog did not eat the food in the manger, and did not need to sleep there.

The moral of this story is that to stop someone from having something that you do not need yourself, is selfish.

20
April

The
Leak in the Dyke

Holland is a very flat, low-lying country. Much of it is below the level of the sea. Huge dykes hold back the cruel sea and everyone in Holland knows that if the water floods through the dykes, homes will be destroyed and people drowned.

One day a boy called Peter was walking home when he saw a trickle of water across his path. Looking closer, he saw that the water was coming from a small hole in the dyke. On the other side of the dyke the sea roared and pounded and Peter could see that a storm was blowing up.

Peter knew that if the hole was not blocked at once it would grow bigger, the dyke would collapse and many people would be in danger. The brave boy pushed his arm into the hole and stopped the water from coming through.

Then he called for help, but none came. The light faded, the air grew chilly. Peter became cold and hungry, but still he kept his arm thrust into the hole in the dyke.

At last Peter's mother and some friends came to find him. They took the frozen boy home, while the men mended the hole.

Everyone knew that if it had not been for Peter, they would have lost their homes, if not their lives. All the people in Holland praised the courage of the brave boy.

21
April

The Frog Prince

In the olden days there was a king who had nine daughters. The youngest was as beautiful as the sun and the king gave her a valuable golden ball as a toy.

The girl liked to go to a well in the woods and play at tossing the golden ball into the air and catching it. One day the ball slipped through her fingers and rolled into the well and sank deep into its dark waters.

The king's youngest daughter cried, for she loved the golden ball. A frog heard her weeping and came and asked what she would give if the ball could be retrieved from the pond.

'I will give anything you like,' said the princess to the frog, 'my best dress, my pearl necklace, my crown, anything.'

'Those things are of no use to me,' replied the frog, 'but if you would love me and have me for your companion and let me sit by you at table and eat from your plate and sleep in your bed, then I will fetch the golden ball for you.'

'Oh, yes! I will promise all that,' agreed the princess, thinking to herself, 'What nonsense! As if a frog could ever come into the palace and behave like that!'

At once the frog sank down out of sight into the water and then came to the surface with the golden ball in its mouth. It tossed the ball in front of the princess, who snatched it up and ran towards the palace.

'Wait for me,' called the frog, but the princess did not wait. She had no intention of keeping her promise to the frog.

22
April

The Frog Prince

The next day the king's youngest daughter was sitting at table with the king and all his court when there was a pitter-patter on the marble stairs and a knocking at the door. A voice cried:

'King's youngest daughter, let me in!'

The youngest daughter got up and ran to the door to see who could be there. When she opened the door, she saw the frog sitting outside. She slammed the door shut and went back to her place at table.

The king noticed that the princess had gone pale, and asked her what was wrong.

'There is a green, slimy frog outside,' she replied. 'Yesterday he rescued my golden ball for me and in return I promised that he could be my companion, but I did not dream that he would ever come to the palace and expect to sit with me at table and eat from my plate. It is ridiculous! Frogs do not do things like that.'

The king looked stern.

'A promise is a promise,' he said. 'You may not like the frog, but you must bring it in and let it be your companion.'

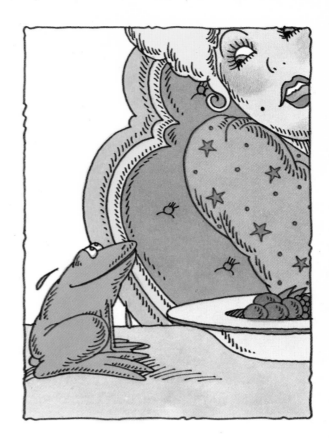

23
April

The Frog Prince

'That which you have promised, you must now perform,' added the king, and the princess was obliged to open the door and let the frog in. It hopped at her heels until she reached her chair. Then it croaked:

'Lift me to sit by you.'

The princess pretended not to hear, but the king ordered her to do as the frog asked. No sooner was the frog on the chair than it wanted to be on the table. It said:

'Push your golden plate close to me, that I may share your food.'

The princess did so, but everyone could see she loathed having the slimy frog near her. The frog ate well, but the princess scarcely nibbled a mouthful.

'I have had enough food now,' said the frog at last. 'Pick me up and carry me to your room and make ready your silken bed, so that I may sleep.'

With the king watching her, the princess again obeyed the frog, but as soon as they were in her bedroom, she dropped him in a corner and climbed into her silken bed alone.

24
April

The Frog Prince

However, the frog was not content to stay in the cold corner.

'I am tired and wish to sleep in a comfortable bed,' it said. 'Lift me up or I will tell your father.'

The princess looked at the frog's bulging eyes and green wet skin. She picked it up in her fingers and all of a sudden, she felt sorry for the ugly creature. Bending down, she kissed the frog tenderly.

At once the frog turned into a tall, young prince and he and the princess fell in love. Soon they were married. A carriage pulled by eight white horses came to the palace gates and behind the carriage stood Henry, the prince's faithful servant.

'How pleased I am to see you released from the spell of the witch who cursed you so long ago,' he said to his master.

Henry drove the newly married prince and princess back to the prince's kingdom where they lived happily ever after.

25
April

The Tubby Teddy Bear

Once there was a teddy bear, who lived quite happily in the toy cupboard, until a new toy lion came to stay. The lion was a little deaf and when the white toy rabbit introduced him to Teddy Bear, the lion thought the white rabbit said Tubby Bear.

'Nice to meet you, Tubby,' smiled the lion. 'Your name certainly suits you. You do look as if you have been eating too many doughnuts lately.'

Teddy Bear was annoyed.

'My name is Teddy Bear, not Tubby Bear,' he growled, 'and I have not been eating too many doughnuts. We teddy bears are supposed to be plump.'

Unfortunately the lion was not only deaf, he was also forgetful. He was an old lion, and had once belonged to someone's grandfather.

Every time visitors came to the house, the lion would say to them:

'I want you to meet my good friend, Tubby Bear. He is very nice, but he does eat too many doughnuts.'

Teddy Bear would be very annoyed and say:

'My name is TEDDY Bear, not TUBBY Bear and I do NOT eat too many doughnuts.'

'Of course! Of course!' the lion would smile. Then he would whisper to the visitors. 'Tubby is very sensitive about being plump, you know.'

The little girl who owned all the toys noticed what was happening. She made a t-shirt for Teddy with the name TEDDY written across the front.

After that there were no more mistakes. Everyone, including the lion, knew that the bear's name was Teddy.

However, for a while, the lion went round muttering:

'Whatever happened to that Tubby Bear fellow? I used to like him.'

26
April

The Clever Puppy

Once upon a time there was a clever little puppy. He knew everything that went on in the home where he lived.

When it was time for the children to go to school, he ran out and sat in the car ready to drive off.

When it was time for the children to walk home from school, the puppy would be at the window watching for them.

At meal times, he was waiting at the side of his food bowl with a happy look on his face.

The strange thing was that the puppy knew when it was Saturday or Sunday and when it was the school holidays. At those times he never went out to the car in the mornings and he never waited by the window in the afternoons.

'How does he know all these things?'

people would say, looking at the clever puppy. 'He must be the cleverest puppy in the world.'

One night the little girl who lived in the house dreamed that the puppy could speak and she asked him how he knew which was Saturday and which was Sunday, which were school holidays and so on.

'How do you know?' the puppy replied.

The little girl thought.

'Well, I guess on Saturdays and Sundays and at holiday time, our mother does not get up early and she does not shout at us to get up and she lets us wear comfy old clothes. That's how I know it is the weekend or holiday time.'

'Then that's how I know too,' smiled the puppy. 'And in the afternoon, when you children are due home from school, your

mother gets a snack ready and keeps looking at the clock. That's how I know it's time to watch for you from the window. And I know when it's meal times because you keep asking when dinner will be ready.'

The next morning the little girl went downstairs and looked at the puppy.

'I see you aren't all that clever after all,' she said, 'but don't worry. I won't give away your secrets. I'll let everyone go on thinking you are the cleverest puppy in the world.'

27
April

The Milk Pail

In the olden days, when many people kept cows of their own, a country girl, who had just milked her cow was walking home carrying the pail of milk on her head.

'The money for which I shall sell this milk will buy me three hundred eggs,' she thought. 'Even allowing for bad eggs, I

should get two hundred and fifty chicks. I will fatten them up and take them to market at Christmas, when poultry fetches high prices. With the money from the chickens I will buy material for a gown. I will buy green. Green matches my eyes. When I wear my new green gown, all the boys will want to dance with me, but I will be fussy and only choose the most handsome.'

With that, the girl tossed her head proudly, as she meant to toss it at the boys. The pail of milk spilled to the ground and all was lost.

The lesson of that story is – don't count your chickens before they are hatched.

28
April

The Polar Bear

Once, way up in the north of Canada, a young brown bear met a polar bear for the first time.

'Goodness!' gasped the brown bear. 'You poor thing! You must have had a terrible fright to turn white like that!'

'I did not!' the polar bear replied frostily. 'Polar bears are not frightened of anything. My fur is white so that no one can see me against the snow.'

'How very clever!' replied the brown bear. 'But why don't you want anyone to see you? Are you running away from someone?'

'I am not running away from anyone,' growled the polar bear. 'I am running towards them so that I may catch them and eat them.'

'Oh, well, in that case I think I will be going,' said the brown bear.

The brown bear hurried south and warned the other brown bears about the polar bear.

'If the weather is ever snowy and a bear you cannot see runs towards you, hide

quickly, or he will eat you,' he said.

The other bears laughed.

'How can we hide from a bear we cannot see?' they giggled.

But the young brown bear was giving good advice and those who take it will never be eaten by a polar bear.

29
April

Little Jack Horner

Little Jack Horner sat in a corner, eating his Christmas pie. He put in his thumb and

pulled out a plum and said:

'What a good boy am I!'

'No, you certainly are not,' said his big sister, who was sitting up at table and eating her pie properly.

She walked to the corner and took the pie away from Jack Horner and put it on the table. Then she made Jack wash his hands, tie a bib round his neck, sit up at the table on a chair and eat his pie with a spoon.

When he had finished, the little fellow had to help clear the table and wash up.

'It's lucky you have a big sister to teach you the correct way to behave,' the big sister said to Little Jack Horner.

The lesson of that story is, if you wish to be naughty, do so when your big sister is not looking.

30
April

Why the Bear's
Tail is Short

As all folks who have ever looked at a bear will know, nowadays bears have short tails. This has not always been so. Long ago bears had long, bushy tails, but because of a trick by Mr. Fox, they lost them.

It happened like this.

One cold winter's day a fox saw a man taking home a load of fish. The fox jumped up into the wagon and while the man was not looking, the fox threw several of the fish over the back of the wagon on to the road.

Soon the man was out of sight and the fox started to eat the fish. However, along came Mr. Bear.

'Good morning,' said Mr. Bear. 'Those are fine fish. I like eating fish. Will you share them with me?'

The fox did not wish to share the fish with anyone, but as Mr. Bear was so big, the fox was afraid to refuse him.

'Of course I will share the fish with you,' smiled the fox, 'but there are far finer fish in that pond over yonder and all you need do to catch them is to hang your tail into the water.'

'Really!' replied Mr. Bear. 'I have never heard of catching fish that way before.'

Nevertheless he ambled over to the pond and hung his tail in the water. It was icy cold.

After a while the bear called out:

'Mr. Fox, I cannot feel any fish biting my tail. Perhaps I should come and eat your fish after all.'

'No, Mr. Bear. You stay there a little longer and you will get some wonderful fish,' replied the fox.

On and on sat the bear, for hour after hour, until even he realized that the fox had finished eating the fish and had gone away. It had all been a trick. With a roar of rage the bear leaped to his feet, but his bushy tail was frozen hard into the ice on the pond. The bear could not get free until his tail broke off short.

That is why these days bears have short tails, and very smart they look too, as surely everyone will agree.

May

1
May

Jack and the Beanstalk

Many years ago, a widow lived in a cottage with her only son. The widow spoiled the boy and he grew lazy and good-for-nothing. He did not tend the garden, nor watch the sheep. Soon they had nothing left to sell, but a cow.

On market day the widow told Jack to take the cow to town and sell it for a good price, then buy food with the money.

Feeling annoyed that he had to stir himself from bed, Jack drove the cow along the road. He had not gone far when he met a man with some beans in a bag.

'Will you exchange that cow for these beans?' asked the man.

Jack agreed at once, glad to be saved the bother of walking all the way to town. Of course his mother was furious when Jack returned home with nothing but a bag of dry beans. She threw the beans out of the window and sent Jack to bed.

The next morning Jack woke up to find his room strangely dark. The sun was not blazing in through the windows as it usually did. Jack scrambled out of bed and looked outside. A beanstalk had grown thick and tall during the night. Now it reached so high into the sky, it disappeared amongst the clouds.

'Mother! Mother!' called Jack. 'I am going to climb up the beanstalk.'

'If you do, you do it without breakfast.' snapped his mother, who was still angry.

So Jack set off up the beanstalk with an empty stomach.

2
May

Jack and the Beanstalk

After hours of climbing Jack reached the top of the beanstalk and stepped on to a strange land. It was flat and like a desert, with scarcely a bush to be seen. Suddenly Jack saw a young woman dressed in white

and holding a magic wand. She told him that she was a fairy and that she had made him buy the beans and climb the beanstalk.

'You must go to the home of an ogre,' she said. 'Many years ago, before you were born, the ogre stole your father's wealth. It is your task to get it back.'

With that the fairy disappeared and Jack was left to trudge across the unfriendly countryside.

After several miles, Jack came to some trees surrounding a farm and a garden. A large house stood in the garden and, knocking at the door, Jack asked for food and shelter for the night.

The tall woman who answered the door stared at Jack in amazement.

'Do you not know that this is the house of an ogre?' she asked. 'No one comes here to ask for shelter. You are either very brave or very foolish.'

'I am most certainly very hungry,' sighed Jack, 'please give me food and a bed.'

3
May

Jack and the Beanstalk

The ogre's wife, who was a kind-hearted woman, took Jack into the huge kitchen and sat him in front of the fire and gave him

bread and cheese to eat and milk to drink. However, Jack had scarcely finished his meal, when the house shook with the sound of mighty footsteps. The gate slammed back on its hinges like a tree falling. The door of the house was unlatched and crashed open like the sound of thunder. A big, red-faced, hairy ogre strode into the kitchen and sniffed.

'Fee-fi-fo-fum, I smell the blood of an Englishman!
Be he alive, or be he dead,
I'll grind his bones to make my bread.'

'Oh nonsense!' replied his wife. 'There is no one here but we two. You must be smelling that meat pie I am cooking for your supper. Now sit down and eat.'

While they were talking, Jack, shaking with fear, hid in the oven at the side of the fireplace. Leaving the door open a crack, he watched while the awful ogre ate the meat pie, two sheep, six loaves of bread and a barrel of apples. Then the ogre ordered his wife to fetch his hen.

'Lay!' he shouted at the hen and the hen laid an egg of solid gold.

4
May

Jack and the Beanstalk

Waiting until the ogre fell asleep and the ogre's wife went to bed, Jack crept from his hiding place and picked up the hen. It squawked and clucked, but as the ogre was snoring as loud as cannon fire, no one heard the hen and Jack could escape. He ran to the beanstalk and climbed down to earth. With his mother they now lived well on the money they got from selling the golden eggs at market.

The weeks went by and although Jack was rich, he was bored.

One day, in spite of his mother's pleading, he climbed the beanstalk and again knocked at the door of the ogre's house.

This time Jack was well dressed and well fed and the ogre's wife did not recognize him as the hungry boy she had seen before.

However, she did say:

'It is no use asking for shelter here. Last time I took pity on a young fellow, he stole a fine hen.'

Just then the ground shuddered and the voice of the ogre could be heard shouting:

'Fee-fi-fo-fum, I smell the blood of an Englishman!
Be he alive, or be he dead,
I'll grind his bones to make my bread.'

The wife hid Jack in a cupboard in the kitchen and told him to be quiet or the ogre would find him and eat him.

5
May

Jack and the Beanstalk

After eating an enormous supper, the ogre ordered his wife to bring out his bags of gold and silver. She obeyed, and peeping from his hiding place, Jack saw the ogre count his treasure and put it neatly into its sacks. Then the huge, hairy fellow fell asleep sprawled across the supper table.

Silently Jack crept forward, picked up the sacks of gold and silver and escaped down the beanstalk to his own home.

That was enough excitement for Jack for a while, but after several months he climbed up into the clouds for a third time.

He went to the ogre's house and tried to persuade the ogre's wife to let him in.

'No, I will not,' she said. 'I let two other young fellows into the house and they were thieves. You cannot come in. Besides, if my husband sees you, he will eat you.'

However, Jack, who had by this time grown into a handsome young man, begged and pleaded saying that the wind was so cold and there was no other shelter for miles. At last the woman let Jack in and hid him in the washtub and said he could sleep there for the night.

That evening after supper, the ogre shouted for his harp. The wife fetched the prettiest little harp Jack had ever seen. It was magical, as well as pretty. When it was set on the table, it played itself with no one needing to touch the strings.

'My mother would like that,' thought Jack, peeping from his hiding place.

6
May

Jack and the Beanstalk

As soon as the ogre was asleep, Jack crept forward and picked up the harp, expecting to escape as easily as he had done twice before.

However, when he opened the door, the harp called to the ogre:

'Master! Master! Wake up! I am being stolen!'

The ogre leaped to his feet and saw Jack

with the harp in his hand. He roared with rage and lunged forward. Luckily for Jack, the ogre had eaten such a huge supper, he could not run quickly. Jack raced towards the top of the beanstalk on his swift, young legs and the ogre swayed after him.

Trembling with fear, Jack scrambled and half fell down the beanstalk. Back on the ground he thrust the harp into his mother's startled hands and rushed into the woodshed to fetch his axe.

When he got back to the beanstalk, it was shaking and swaying with the weight of the ogre as he came climbing down. In the distance the voice of the ogre roared.

Jack's mother turned white with fear.

'What have you done, my son?' she gasped.

Then Jack worked harder than he had ever worked in his life. He chopped and chopped at the beanstalk, until at last it broke and fell. The ogre crashed to the ground with such force, his body went right

into the earth and he was never seen again.

Then Jack told his mother all about his adventures at the top of the beanstalk and explained where their sudden wealth had come from.

'Thank goodness the beanstalk is destroyed,' she said, 'and that you will never go to such a dangerous land again.'

7
May

The Fox in the Well

One day an unlucky fox fell into a well. He cried out for help and a passing wolf heard him and looked into the well to see what was wrong.

'Ah, my good friend,' called the fox. 'Lend me your hand and pull me out.'

'You poor creature!' said the wolf. 'How did this happen? What were you doing that you did not see the well? I must speak to someone about putting up a proper fence. How cold you must be! I know how upset you must feel at being down there in the dark. I was once shut in a cupboard and it was terrible. I know exactly what you are going through. How the water must be spoiling your fur. I was once caught in a

dreadful rain storm and my fur was not right for a week afterwards.'

The fox interrupted the wolf.

'Your sympathy is very fine, but this is not the time for it,' he said. 'First pull me out of the well. Then I shall feel in the mood for listening to you.'

The lesson of that story is, when you find someone in trouble, deeds are better than words.

8
May

Mary and Her Little Lamb

Lots of children have puppies which follow them to school. The puppies run into the playground and chase the little children. They bark at the teachers and dodge into the schoolrooms and knock over chairs.

There is always a lot of fuss, and parents have to be phoned to come to school in their cars and take the puppies away.

Imagine how much more fuss there

would be if a lamb followed a little girl to school. Lambs aren't as well behaved as puppies. They have hard little hooves and sharp teeth.

A lamb followed a girl named Mary to school one day and ate the roses from the garden outside the headmaster's window. It ran into the cloakroom and nibbled at the children's coats. There was a terrible to do and someone wrote this poem about it:

'Mary had a little lamb,
Its fleece was white as snow;
And everywhere that Mary went,
The lamb was sure to go.
It followed her to school one day,
Which was against the rule.
How the children laughed and played,
To see the lamb at school.'

9
May

King Midas and the Golden Touch

Long ago, in Greece, there lived a king named Midas. In those days, gods lived in Greece, too, at the top of a mountain called Olympus.

It so happened that King Midas was able to do a favour for the god Dionysus, and in return Dionysus said he would grant King Midas a wish.

Midas was a greedy man and although he was already wealthy, he asked that everything he touched might turn to gold.

'I will fill my store houses with gold and be the richest king in the world,' he said.

The next morning, when Midas woke up, he touched his bed with the tips of his fingers. At once the sheets turned to spun golden thread.

The king was delighted.

He was not so pleased when he pushed his feet into his slippers and found they became stiff and uncomfortable to wear, as

the leather hardened into gold.

'Never mind,' he thought, kicking off the slippers. 'Managing without slippers is not a high price to pay for being the richest king who ever lived.' He walked out on to the terrace and the stones turned to gold slabs beneath his bare feet. He touched the roses and the pink petals turned golden in the sunshine.

'That is rather a pity,' he sighed. 'I like pink roses. Never mind. I will eat breakfast now and then start thinking of how I shall spend my new wealth.'

10
May

King Midas and the Golden Touch

The king clapped his hands and ordered the servants to put food on the table. As he sat in his chair and pulled it forward to eat, he noticed that the grain of the wood turned yellow as the chair was transformed to gold.

Then the king's pleasure turned to horror. He raised a cup of milk to his lips, but not only did the cup turn to gold, the

82

milk hardened into metal and could not be drunk. Bread turned to gold under the king's fingers. Desperately he touched eggs and apples. They too turned into the now terrifying yellow metal.

The king began to regret his greed. It would seem that he was doomed to starve and thirst to death.

At that moment his dear daughter ran into the room. King Midas jumped up to greet her and to tell her about his troubles.

As he rested his hands on her shoulders and kissed her hair, the girl turned into a golden statue.

King Midas was heartbroken and hurried to Mount Olympus to speak to Dionysus.

'Take away the gift of the golden touch,' begged the weeping king.

Fortunately Dionysus was in a good mood.

'Bathe in the waters of the River Pactolus in Lydia,' he said, 'and the golden touch will be taken from you. Take the water and sprinkle it on your daughter and she will come back to life.'

Eagerly King Midas did as he was told and was overjoyed to become a normal human person again and have his daughter restored to him.

People do say that if you go to the River Pactolus you will find gold lying along its bed where the gift of gold washed from the fingers of King Midas.

11
May

King Midas and the Ass's Ears

Poor King Midas does not seem to have been a lucky man. First he was given the Golden Touch, which went so wrong and had to be taken away. Then Midas made an enemy of the god Apollo.

Midas went to a musical competition in which Apollo was taking part. The judges gave Apollo first prize, but foolish Midas went round saying that he did not think Apollo was the best and that he did not deserve any sort of prize.

'I think Apollo should have come last,' Midas was jeering in a loud voice, when he noticed a funny feeling in his ears.

He rushed to a mirror and saw to his horror that two large ass's ears were growing in place of his human ears.

'Anyone who thinks I am not good enough to win first prize is an ass and should have ass's ears,' said the voice of Apollo. And that was that.

Midas pulled a hat over his head and hid the terrible truth from everyone. However, he could not keep the secret from his barber, who cut the king's hair once a month.

The barber promised not to tell anyone about King Midas's ass's ears. However, promises are difficult to keep. The barber began to feel he would explode if he did not tell his interesting secret to someone.

He went to the fields outside town and dug a hole. Then he whispered into it:

'King Midas has ass's ears.'

He covered the hole with earth and went home feeling a weight lifted from his mind.

However, there were grass seeds in the hole. The seeds grew and the grass stalks blew gently in the breeze, whispering to each other:

'King Midas has ass's ears. King Midas has ass's ears.'

Soon everyone knew the king's secret and laughed at him as he walked about always wearing his hat.

Poor King Midas! What an unlucky man!

12
May

Old Mother Goose

Nowadays, folks think nothing of flying. They fly away on their holidays and they fly to visit their relatives.

Of course they fly in aeroplanes, but in the days before aeroplanes were invented, some folks still managed to travel through the air.

One of those people was Mother Goose. She was a plump lady, who kept a goose farm. Dozens and dozens of geese she had on the farm and some of the young ones were naughty, as young folks will always be.

Instead of staying shut up in the farm at night, where they were safe, the wild youngsters would creep out and go to parties and dance in the moonlight.

'The foxes will get those youngsters for sure,' Mother Goose would say and calling the biggest gander on the farm, she would climb up on his back and fly over the fields and hedges calling to the young geese to go home or there would be no breakfast.

What a busy time that lady had! Her work was never done. People used to say a rhyme about her:

'Old Mother Goose, when she wanted to wander,
Would fly through the air on a very fine gander.'

Now, if you ever see a plump lady flying through the air on a big goosey-gander, you will know that it is Mother Goose.

13
May

The Moon in the Millpond

A story about Brer Rabbit
An old man called Uncle Remus used to tell stories about naughty Brer Rabbit to a

little boy. This is one of the stories he told.

There were times, in the old days, when all the animals were friendly together, with never a cross word between them. When one of these times had been going along for several months, Brer Rabbit began to feel restless. He lay in the sun and he swatted at the gnats and kicked up the sand.

'Brer Terrapin,' he said, when he met the terrapin that evening, 'I feel like some fun.'

'Then you have come to the right person,' replied the terrapin. 'I feel like some fun too.'

'Well, then,' said Brer Rabbit, 'we will arrange to meet Brer Fox and Brer Wolf and Brer Bear at the millpond tomorrow night. I will do the talking and all you need do is agree with everything I say.'

And with that Brer Rabbit scampered home, but Brer Terrapin started for the mill pond because he was a slow walker and he wanted to make sure of getting there in good time.

The Moon in the Millpond

'We'll get to the pond after dark and we'll do some mighty fine fishing,' Brer Rabbit said to the other animals and they all said what a good idea it was and they could not think why they had not thought of it.

Then Brer Rabbit called on his friends, Miss Meadows and Miss Motts to come and watch the fun, and come nightfall, there they all were at the millpond.

Brer Bear brought a hook and line. Brer Wolf brought a hook and line. Brer Fox brought a dip net and not to be outdone Brer Terrapin brought the bait. Miss Meadows and Miss Motts did not bring anything. They just stood near the edge of the pond and squealed every time Brer Terrapin shook the box of bait at them.

Brer Wolf said he would fish for horny-heads. Brer Bear said he would fish for mud-cats. Brer Fox said he would fish for perch and give them to the ladies, but Brer Rabbit winked at Brer Terrapin and said he was fishing for suckers.

15
May

The Moon in the Millpond

Everyone got ready to fish and Brer Rabbit stepped up to the edge of the pond, as if he intended to cast his hook into the water. Then he stopped, as if he had seen something strange. The others all looked at him as he scratched his head and stared down into the water.

The girls began to feel uneasy and Miss Meadows upped and shouted out:

'Lawsakes, Brer Rabbit. What on earth is the matter?'

Brer Rabbit went on scratching his head and looking into the water and Miss Motts lifted up her skirts and said she hoped there were no snakes about, because she could not abide snakes.

Brer Rabbit went on scratching his head. Then by and by he took a deep breath and said:

'Ladies and gentlemen, we might as well make tracks away from this place, because there will be no fishing tonight.'

Then Brer Terrapin remembered that he was supposed to agree with everything Brer Rabbit said, so he scrambled to the edge of the pond and looked in and said:

'To be sure! To be sure! No fishing tonight!'

Then Brer Rabbit said:

'Ladies, do not be scared. I will take care of you, come what may, but I have to tell you that the moon has fallen into the millpond and if you do not believe me you can look for yourselves.'

16
May

The Moon in the Millpond

Brer Bear, Brer Wolf, Brer Fox, Miss Meadows and Miss Motts all looked down and saw the moon a-swinging and a-swaying at the bottom of the pond. At least, they thought they did. Really it was only the moon's reflection, but they were too scared to realize that.

'There'll be no fishing unless we can think of a way of getting that moon out of the millpond,' said Brer Rabbit.

Then Brer Terrapin, he spoke up and said he had an uncle who had a big dredge net and he reckoned he would lend it to Brer Rabbit, if he asked real polite. So Brer Rabbit, he went off to fetch the dredge net while Brer Terrapin told the others how he had heard that anyone who pulled the moon out of the millpond always found a pot of silver in the net with it.

When Brer Rabbit returned, Brer Bear and Brer Wolf and Brer Fox said to him:

'As you have been so kind as to fetch the dredge net, we will do the fishing for the moon.'

Well, Brer Rabbit took off his jacket and made as if he really wanted to fish that

moon out of the water. The others insisted that they would not dream of letting a fine fellow like Brer Rabbit get his feet wet, so he handed the net over to them and they stepped into the pond.

17
May

The Moon in the Millpond

Brer Bear and Brer Wolf and Brer Fox pushed the dredge net before them and took a sweep across the water. They found no moon, nor did they find the pot of silver Brer Terrapin had said would be with it and they were very puzzled.

They stepped further into the pond and took another sweep. Water got into Brer Bear's ears and he stumbled about shaking his head. Water got into Brer Wolf's eyes and he tripped forward as he rubbed them. Water got into Brer Fox's nose and he slipped over as he sneezed.

All three of them fell into the deep part of the pond and went under the water and came up smothered in mud and pond weed. By the time they scrambled up the bank, Miss Meadows and Miss Motts were a-giggling and a-snickering and asking them where was the moon and where was the pot of silver.

And Brer Rabbit was a-pointing up into the sky and saying, there was the moon, so it couldn't have fallen into the pond and he must have been mistaken all along.

Brer Bear and Brer Wolf and Brer Fox slunk home feeling mighty foolish and that naughty Brer Rabbit and Brer Terrapin went off laughing with the girls.

The Naughty Teddy Bear

Once upon a time there was a rather naughty teddy bear. He would never wear a bib when he was eating.

The other teddy bears always wore bibs and if they did happen to spill a little food, it landed on the bib and did no harm. If they did happen to dip their paws into the jelly to take an extra mouthful when no one was looking, and their paws became sticky, then they wiped their paws on their bibs and no one was the wiser.

This particular teddy bear would never wear a bib.

'Bibs look silly,' he would say. 'They are for babies. I am too old to wear a bib.'

The result was that when he dropped little bits of food, as everyone does at some time or another, they stained the front of his furry chest. When he dipped his paw into the jelly, as all naughty bears do at some time or another, he wiped his sticky paw down his furry side.

'You know what is going to happen to you,' said a wise old bear, 'you will be washed in the washing machine and pegged on the line by your ears to dry.'

No-bib Teddy, for that was what the others called him, went pale.

'No one does things like that nowadays,' he said. 'No one would do that to me.'

'You get messy enough and they will,' said the wise old teddy bear. 'Believe me.'

No-bib looked at the children who owned him.

'They are far too kind to put me in the washing machine and peg me on the line by my ears to dry,' he thought and he went on being messy.

He looked at the mother of the children who owned him and he said:

'She is far too kind to put me in the washing machine and peg me on the line by my ears to dry.' And he went on being messy.

Then one week the family went on holiday and a friend came to stay in the house while they were gone.

'What a messy teddy bear,' she said, picking up No-bib Teddy. 'I will make him clean for when the children come home.'

She put No-bib Teddy into the washing machine and pegged him on the line by his ears to dry. Poor Teddy!

Ever after that he always wore a bib and was a very good little bear.

19
May

The Dog
and His Reflection

Once a dog was crossing a bridge with a fine bone in his mouth. As he trotted along, he happened to glance down into the water and saw his reflection.

He thought that another dog was looking up at him from the stream. Being greedy, the dog thought it would have the bone in the other dog's mouth, as well as his own.

He opened his mouth to bark at the other dog, to frighten him into handing over the bone. At once his own bone fell into the stream and was washed away.

He looked down at his reflection.

'How strange! That other dog lost his food at the same time that I did,' he thought and went on his way.

The lesson of that story is that you should be content with what you have.

20
May

Georgie Porgie

Once upon a time, there was a little boy named Master George Porgie and there was nothing wrong with that.

He was very fond of eating puddings and pies, and there was nothing much wrong with that.

However, when it was time to go to school, George would stay at home eating puddings and pies. There was something wrong with that. It was naughty!

When he had finished eating all the puddings and pies in the house and with jam and treacle still sticking round his mouth, George would creep to school and hide in the playground. There was something wrong with that. It was naughty and messy.

When the girls came out to play, George would jump out at them and give them sticky, jammy, treacly kisses. The girls hated it and started to cry and George roared with laughter. There was something

wrong with that. It was unkind.

When the boys came out to play, they saw what a naughty boy George was being and chased him away.

After that the teacher had a word with George's father and George had to behave himself, like the other children.

However, no one ever forgot how naughty George Porgie used to be and the children used to chant this rhyme about him:

'*Georgie Porgie, pudding and pie,*
Kissed the girls and made them cry;
When the boys came out to play,
Georgie Porgie ran away.'

21
May

The Green Children

Hundreds of years ago a strange thing happened at a village called St. Mary's of the Wolf Pits.

The country folk found a boy and his sister wandering near the mouth of one of the pits. The children had limbs like normal people, but the colour of their skin and hair was green.

No one could understand the speech of the green children and not knowing what to do with them, the good folk who found them, took the weeping children to the home of Sir Richard de Calne.

There the children were offered bread and honey and milk, but although they were obviously hungry, the children would not eat.

At last some green beans, still on their stalks, were brought to the table. The children seized them eagerly and tore open the stalks, as if they expected to find the beans there. When they saw the stalks were empty, they cried bitterly.

The ladies of the household opened the pods and showed the beans to the children. They ate eagerly and for a long while would eat nothing but beans.

As no one could be found who knew anything about them, the children stayed on in the home of Sir Richard. They learned to like many different types of food and gradually lost their green colour.

22
May

The Green Children

Unfortunately, after a while, the boy fell sick and died. The girl was unhappy, but she kept in good health and gradually learned to speak English and was then able to tell her story.

She said that she came from a country where all the people were green. The sun did not shine there, but a soft, green glow filtered down as if through dense forest leaves, and a great river ran through the land.

One day, when the girl and her brother were tending their green sheep, they came upon the entrance to a cavern. They went in and were enticed forward by the sound of lovely music. On and on through the

twisting, turning cavern they went, until suddenly they stumbled out into blinding sunshine.

They had never seen such glaring light before and they staggered forward with their eyes shut and not knowing where they were going. As last they fell down, sick with the light and the heat of the sun. When they awoke they were found by the good country folk.

23
May

The Green Children

As soon as Sir Richard heard the girl's story, he ordered her to be taken back to the wolf pits, where she had been found.

The girl and the servants of Sir Richard searched for hours, but they could not find the cavern through which the girl said she

had come with her brother.

The girl grew up and a husband was found for her. She lived for many years on Sir Richard's estate.

Many times she slipped away and tried to find the entrance to the cavern and the way back to her own people, but she never did find it.

24
May

The Lark
and Her Young Ones

Once a mother lark built her nest in a cornfield. As the baby larks grew up, so the corn ripened. Every day the mother lark looked to see if the reapers were coming, for when the corn was cut, she would have to take her babies to safety.

Every morning, before the mother lark set out in search of food, she said to her babies:

'Listen to all you hear and tell me about it when I come home.'

One day the farmer came to the field and looked at the corn and said:

'It is full ripe and ready to be reaped. I

must call in my neighbours to help me with the harvest.'

When the mother lark returned to the nest, the frightened babies told her what had been said and cheeped that they should leave the nest at once.

'I don't think so,' replied the mother. 'If the farmer is depending on his neighbours, it will be a while yet before the field is harvested.'

Sure enough, the next day no reapers came, but the farmer came by and said:

'The sun is hot and the corn is full ripe. I can wait no longer. I must send for my relatives and ask them to help me.'

That evening, in greater fear than before, the baby larks told their mother what had been said. They begged her to take them away from the nest before the knives of the reapers sliced it in two.

'There is no need for haste,' smiled the mother lark. 'The farmer's relatives will be busy getting in their own harvest first.'

Sure enough, the next day no reapers came, but the farmer looked at the corn and said:

'The grain is falling to the ground for want of cutting. Tomorrow I must harvest it myself.'

That evening the baby larks reported to their mother the words the farmer had said.

'Then it is time to leave,' said the mother. 'When a man depends on others to do his work, nothing will happen. When he does it himself, it is done.'

And the little family flew to safety well in time.

Hickory, Dickory, Dock!

Mice like eating very strange things. Once there was a mouse which liked eating the grease which was spread on the works of a grandfather clock.

The mouse nibbled a hole in the wooden case of the clock and crept in and licked at the grease and thought it was delicious.

All this was not good for the clock. Without the proper amount of grease spread on them, the wheels of the clock would not go round properly.

First the clock was slow, then it ran fast. The people who owned it could not think what was wrong.

'We are not winding it enough,' they said.

'We are winding it too much,' they said.

They never dreamed the trouble was being caused by a little mouse.

Then one day, the mouse crept into the clock at the moment the clock was due to strike 'one'. The mouse had never before been in the clock when it was striking. The sound was terrible. The mouse's head rang. It scurried down from the clock and had a headache for a week.

How the other mice laughed! They were clever mice and knew better than to venture into a chiming clock. They made up this rhyme about the mouse with the headache:

'Hickory, dickory, dock!
The mouse ran up the clock.
The clock struck one,
The mouse ran down.
Hickory, dickory, dock!'

The little mouse never went into the clock again. It raided the larder and the barn, like ordinary mice.

And the people who owned the clock never knew why first it went wrong and then it went right, but we know.

26
May

Will-o'-the-Wisp

Here is another story told by Uncle Remus.

A little while after he had played the prank about the moon in the millpond on Brer Bear and the others, Brer Rabbit took to thinking that he would call on Brer Bear.

Considering how mad Brer Bear was still feeling, this was a mighty strange thing to do. Then again, when you consider that Brer Rabbit decided to call when Brer Bear was out, it made a little more sense.

Brer Rabbit, he sat himself by the side of the road and waited for the bear family to go by. Pretty soon they came out of the house, old Brer Bear himself, Mrs. Bear and the two cubs, Kubs and Klibs.

Brer Rabbit waited until they had gone a-shuffling and a-scrambling along the road. Then he said to himself:

'Well, I think I'll go a-calling on Brer Bear now.'

Into the house he went. Soon he was ransacking the place, poking in here and peeping in there and while he was scraping about under some shelves a bucket of honey fell all over him.

27
May

Will-o'-the-Wisp

The honey covered Brer Rabbit from head to heels. He had to sit there and let it run away from his eyes before he could see his hand before his face.

'Well, what am I going to do now?' thought Brer Rabbit. 'If I go out, the flies and bees will swarm all over me. If I stay here, goodness gracious knows what Brer Bear will do to me!'

Then he had an idea. He ran quickly to the woods and rolled in the dead leaves, hoping the honey would wipe off on the leaves. Instead of that the dead leaves stuck to the honey. The more he thrashed about, the more Brer Rabbit became covered with leaves. Soon he looked a very strange sight, as he wriggled and jumped and squirmed and the dead leaves quivered and rattled and shook.

At last Brer Rabbit realized that there was no help, but to hurry home as fast as he could. Down the road he ran, a-squirming and a-squiggling with the itchiness of the honey and the crackling leaves, when whom should he meet, but Sister Cow.

She took one look at the terrifying figure a-wriggling and a-dancing towards her and she took off, like the dogs were after her.

Brer Rabbit walked straight down the centre of the road towards Brer Bear, taking good care to jump and prance and shake till the dead leaves rattled like the wind at midnight in a dead oak tree.

He truly looked a frightful sight, like no creature anyone had ever seen before. Brer Bear stopped dead in his tracks, and Mrs. Bear shook like a leaf.

Old Brer Bear, he stood and looked, but Mrs. Bear couldn't stand a minute of it. She flung down her parasol and bolted up a tree. For a while it looked as if Brer Bear might stand his ground. Then Brer Rabbit stepped forward and wailed like the wind round a snowy mountain and Brer Bear, he took off so fast, he knocked down a whole strip of fence as he went.

As for the cubs, Kubs and Klibs, they clutched their hats in their hands and they went rushing away through the bushes faster than a herd of bolting horses.

28
May

Will-o'-the-Wisp

The next person Brer Rabbit met was a farm girl carrying a basket of turnips. At the sight of Brer Rabbit, she jumped a foot into the air, spilled her turnips all over the road and squealed and yelled, the likes of which had never been heard before.

All this made Brer Rabbit feel mighty biggity.

'I think this might be a good time to pass by Brer Fox's house,' he smiled, but while he was turning that over in his mind, Brer Bear and his family came sauntering along.

Brer Rabbit felt more biggity than ever and went on swaggering down the middle of the road.

Will-o'-the-Wisp

That very same afternoon, Brer Wolf and Brer Fox were strolling down the road plotting how they could catch Brer Rabbit. Little did they know that Brer Rabbit was walking towards them. In fact they had their heads together so close, they did not look up until Brer Rabbit was upon them.

When they did catch sight of Brer Rabbit covered in shivering, shaking, rattling leaves, they didn't crowd him. They gave him all the room he wanted.

For a moment, Brer Wolf tried to show off, because he wanted to look big in front of Brer Fox. He asked Brer Rabbit who he was.

Brer Rabbit, he jumped up and down in the middle of the road and shouted:

'I'm Will-o'-the-Wisp. I'm Will-o'-the-Wisp. And you are the one I'm after!'

Then Brer Rabbit jumped up and down some more and made like he was going to chase Brer Wolf and Brer Fox. The way those two lit out of there was a caution to behold. They didn't stop running until they were in their homes with pillows over their heads.

Quite a while later, after Brer Rabbit had been home and washed off all the honey and the leaves and taken things easy for a day or two, he came up with Brer Wolf and Brer Fox.

Standing well out of reach, he shouted:

'I'm Will-o'-the-Wisp. I'm Will-o'-the-Wisp. And you are the one I'm after.'

Then Brer Wolf and Brer Fox realized how Brer Rabbit had fooled them and they slunk home feeling mighty silly.

Everyone, including Miss Meadows, came to hear the story and next time Brer Fox went calling on Miss Meadows, she asked him if he wasn't frightened that Will-o'-the-Wisp might come knocking at the door. Then she giggled and sniggered and Brer Fox was mighty mad.

Car Bear Teddy

In the land where teddy bears are made, there once lived a bear who loved riding in cars. All the bears were waiting for Father Christmas to give them as presents at Christmas time and as they sat brushing their fur and tying the ribbons round their necks, they chatted about what sort of teddy bears they were going to be.

They agreed that all teddy bears were Cuddly Bears. Then some said they wanted to be Sit-in-the-window-watching-for-the-children-to-come-home Bears. Some said they wanted to be Go-out-in-the-pushchair Bears. Some said they wanted to be Sit-on-the-bed-and-cuddle-up-at-night Bears.

But one bear wanted to be a Car Bear.

'I want to ride around in cars all day long,' he said. 'I love cars.'

'You won't get your wish,' said the other teddy bears. 'Teddy bears are given to children and although children ride in cars sometimes, they do not ride about in them all the while.'

However, this bear had made up his mind. He had a special word with Father Christmas and then made himself very useful cleaning out the reindeers' stable and polishing the sleigh and getting into Father Christmas's good books.

31
May

Car Bear Teddy

On Christmas Eve, Father Christmas smiled at the teddy who liked cars and said:

'I have found just the home for you. I think you will be very happy there.'

When the bear woke up on Christmas morning, he found himself in a parcel addressed 'To Tom from Grandma'.

To the bear's surprise Tom was not a little boy, he was a young man, who had passed his driving test the day before Christmas.

As Tom opened the parcel with the teddy bear in it, grandma said:

'I gave you the teddy bear you had when you were a little boy, but he is rather worn out. This new bear is a lucky mascot for you to keep with you when you are driving. He can sit on the back seat and see that no harm comes to you.'

Then the bear noticed that he was dressed in a smart jumper with a car knitted on the front. Tom was very pleased with him and put him in the car at once.

For ever after that the bear sat in whichever car Tom drove and he was known as Car Bear Teddy and Tom never came to any harm.

June

1
June

The Sorcerer's Apprentice

Long ago and far away a boy went to the market place looking for work. To his surprise he heard a man saying he wanted an apprentice who could neither read nor write.

This was unusual, as most masters wanted a boy who had as many skills as possible. Now this boy could both read and write, but he needed work badly, so he pretended that he could not.

'What does it matter?' he thought. 'If I do not need reading or writing for my work, how can it be of any consequence that I have these skills, but do not use them?'

The boy was healthy and strong looking and the man took him on as his apprentice. They walked to the man's house, which was in a lonely spot outside town. As soon as they entered the workshop, the boy realized that his new master was a sorcerer. A copper cauldron hung over a huge fireplace. A shelf was lined with books. A mortar and pestle stood on a bench. Bottles and scales and powders and sieves and funnels were everywhere.

'I should like to learn something about sorcery,' thought the boy.

2
June

The Sorcerer's Apprentice

The sorcerer's apprentice worked hard for many months, sweeping the floor, grinding up herbs and berries, washing bottles and jars, and all the while never letting his master know that he could read and write.

Then one night the boy found the courage to creep out of bed while his master was sleeping, and read the heavy books of magic which stood on the high shelf. The books were difficult to understand, but the boy studied diligently, night after night, until at last he was able to understand some of the potions his master was mixing and the spells he was casting.

The boy was upset to find that the man was a wicked sorcerer and that his potions and spells were meant to do harm. However, he stayed on, still learning as much as he could.

About this time the sorcerer started to go away on journeys, sometimes for a day at a time. This gave the apprentice the chance to try out some spells. He was not always successful, such as the time he tried to turn the cat into a kitten and it became a tiger; luckily for only a few seconds. And when he told the broom to sweep the floor, it swept him out of the house with the dust! However, with every experiment, he learned more skill.

3

June

The Sorcerer's Apprentice

Then one dreadful day, when the sorcerer's apprentice thought he was alone and was trying to turn a small bread roll into a large meat pie, because he was feeling hungry, the sorcerer returned early and unexpected from a journey.

He pushed open the door and swept into the room and glared around him.

'I thought so!' he roared. 'I thought you had been meddling with my powders and potions. I will teach you to deceive me!'

He lunged forward to grab the apprentice. However the boy, praying that he was remembering the spells correctly, changed himself into a bird and flew into the trees.

Not to be outdone, the sorcerer transformed himself into an eagle and flew after the bird. Shaking with fear and mumbling spells as fast as he could, the boy changed himself into a fish and - splash - flopped into the pond. In an instant the sorcerer had become a huge pike and again was after the boy. At once the boy changed himself into a cat and stood at the edge of the pond, pawing at the pike. By this time the sorcerer was becoming flustered and changed himself into a grain of wheat and hid between the paving stones to get away from the cat. With a chuckle, the clever boy became a chicken and with one gulp pecked up the grain of wheat and swallowed it and that was the end of the sorcerer.

From then on no more wicked potions were made in that workshop. The boy

became the sorcerer and made spells only
for some good purpose.

4
June

The Wise Tailor

In the olden days, when most clothes were
made by a tailor working in a little shop, a
sailor brought home a length of cloth he
had brought from abroad.

He took it in to Mr. Snip, the tailor, and
said:

'I want this cloth cut to make me a fine
coat with large cuffs and deep pleats at the
back and plenty of cross-over at the front.'

The tailor looked at the cloth.

'I have to cut the coat according to the
cloth and I cannot make such a coat from
this amount of cloth,' he said.

The sailor was disappointed, but decided
to make the best of things.

'Very well,' he said. 'I will have a slim
fitting coat with no pleats, no cuffs and no
cross-over at the front.'

The tailor looked at the rather fat sailor
and the length of cloth and said:

'I have to cut the coat according to the
cloth and I cannot make even a slim fitting
coat for you out of this cloth.'

The sailor was disappointed, but decided
to make the best of things. He gave up
eating cakes and biscuits and buns and pies.
He became slim and much more
handsome.

He went back to Mr. Snip, the tailor, and
asked:

'Now can you make me a coat from that
cloth?'

'Yes,' replied the tailor and he did make
the coat, and the slim sailor looked so fine
in it that the prettiest girl in town agreed to
marry him.

The lesson of that story is that you can
only make a grand coat if you have a lot of
cloth.

However, if you do happen to buy too
little of the cloth, it is always possible, like
the sailor, to make the best of things.

5
June

The Cat
and the Birds

Once a group of birds lived together in an
aviary.

A cat heard that they had fallen sick. He
dressed himself as a doctor in a smart hat
and coat and, holding a doctor's bag in his
paw, he went a-knocking at the birds' door.

'Who is there?' called the birds.

'The doctor,' replied the cat, 'come to
make you better.'

The birds peeped out and saw the cat's
furry paws sticking from the sleeves of the
coat and his tail swishing to and fro behind
him.

They were wise little birds and they had
no intention of letting a cat into the aviary.

'We shall do better without a doctor like you,' they said. 'Go away.'

The cat went away and the birds recovered from their sickness.

The lesson of that story is that even if a villain disguises himself as a good man, he will not deceive those who are careful.

6
June

The Seaside Teddy

Not long ago, there was a little boy who had a grandmother who lived at the seaside. One sunny summer, the grandmother invited the boy to stay with her for a holiday.

Unfortunately, in all the excitement of packing and travelling, the boy's own teddy bear was left behind at home.

When bedtime came, the boy was upset to be in a strange bed and without Teddy.

'Never mind,' smiled Grandma. 'Tomorrow we will go out and buy a teddy bear for you to have while you are staying with me. We will knit him a navy blue jumper like the sailors wear and we will call him Seaside Teddy.'

Seaside Teddy was a real pal to the little boy all through the holiday. He even helped the boy write a picture postcard to the teddy who had been left at home.

'You must not take Seaside Teddy home in case your own teddy is jealous,' said Grandma. 'Leave him here with me and he can be your pal whenever you come visiting.'

The boy thought this a good idea and it meant that when the time came for him to go home, Grandma would have Seaside Teddy to keep her company.

So ever after that, the boy had a Seaside Teddy and a Home Teddy.

Wasn't that nice!

7
June

To Market
To Market

Out in the country there lived a jolly farmer, who was getting rather old. His son had taken over most of the farm work, but the jolly old farmer liked to think he could be useful sometimes.

For instance, whenever it was time to buy a new pig, he would say:

'Let me go to the market to buy the new pig. I have a way with pigs.'

His son would agree, but as the jolly farmer grew older, his son said:

'You can never walk all the way to market and back, father, it is too far for your poor old legs.'

'Me and my poor old legs can manage,' the jolly old farmer would say.

One market day, the son was so anxious about his jolly old father and his poor old legs, that he walked to meet him and the new pig.

To his amazement he saw his father riding home on the back of the pig.

'I walked to market, but I rode home. I told you I have a way with pigs,' he cried!

The jolly old farmer went on buying the new pigs and riding them home for many more years and his son made up a rhyme about it:

'To market, to market, to buy a fat pig,
Home again, home again, jiggety-jig.
To market, to market, to buy a fat hog,
Home again, home again, Juggety-jog.'

8
June

The Elves
and the Shoemaker

There was once a shoemaker, who through no fault of his own had become poor. As he finished work, one evening, he had enough leather left for only one pair of shoes. He cut the leather out, left it on his work bench, said his prayers and went to bed.

The next morning he went to the work bench to start making the shoes, but to his amazement, he saw that the shoes were finished. He picked them up and examined them. Not a stitch was out of place. They were the best made shoes he had ever seen.

At that moment a customer came into the shop and being much pleased with the shoes, he paid a higher price for them than normal.

With the money, the shoemaker bought enough leather for two pairs of shoes. He cut them out, left them on the work bench, said his prayers and went to bed for the night. The next morning the shoes were finished, just as the others had been.

The shoemaker found such fine shoes easy to sell and then he bought leather for four more pairs. He cut them out and the next morning found the shoes completed again.

This went on night after night and the shoemaker became a rich man.

At last he said to his wife:

'Shall we sit up tonight to see who it is who lends us such a helping hand?'

The wife agreed. They left a lighted candle in the workroom and hid under some clothes which were lying in the corner.

9
June

The Elves
and the Shoemaker

At midnight two ragged little men came into the room and sat at the work bench. They picked up the leather and with their tiny fingers, they stitched and hammered so fast, the shoemaker could scarcely believe his eyes. They did not stop until the work was completed and then they ran away.

The next day the wife said to the shoemaker:

'Those little men have made us rich. We should do something in return. They were dressed in rags. I will make them little shirts and coats and waistcoats. I will even knit them tiny stockings and you can make

them each a pair of little shoes.

The shoemaker agreed. The night after the clothes were completed, they were laid out on the work bench. The shoemaker's wife lit a candle and she and her husband hid in the corner of the room.

At midnight the little men came skipping out, but instead of the cut out leather, they found the tiny clothes. They were delighted and put the clothes on with obvious pleasure.

Then they sang a song:

'Now we're boys so fine and neat,
Why cobble more for others' feet?'

They hopped and danced about and jumped over the chairs and ran out of the door.

After that, they never returned, but the shoemaker remained fortunate all his life.

10
June

Johnny
at the Fair

Once upon a time a brother and sister named Johnny and Mary lived on a farm about five miles from the nearest village.

Once a month a fair was held in the village at which the farm folk sold their produce and other traders came to sell pretty things like hair ribbons and pins and brooches.

Johnny and Mary looked forward to going to the fair, but one month Mary had a bad cold and had to stay at home. At the end of the day she sat at the window of the farmhouse waiting eagerly for Johnny to come from the fair. However, he was late in returning and as she sat at the window, Mary sang:

'Oh dear, what can the matter be?
Oh dear, what can the matter be?
Oh dear, what can the matter be?
Johnny's so long at the fair.

He promised to buy me a bunch of blue ribbons,
He promised to buy me a bunch of blue ribbons,
He promised to buy me a bunch of blue ribbons,
To tie up my bonnie brown hair.'

Then, at last, to her joy, Mary saw her brother walking along the road, but he was not alone. Walking with him was Mary's sweetheart, Billy, returned from the sea.

Billy and Johnny had met at the fair and they stopped not only to buy a bunch of blue ribbons to tie up Mary's bonnie brown hair, but also a wedding dress so that she and Billy could get married.

That was why Johnny was late from the fair. Mary was so happy to see her sweetheart again that she gladly forgave Johnny for making her wait so long. She put on her wedding dress and tied her bouncy brown hair with the blue ribbons. Then she and Billy were married and lived happily ever after.

One Swallow Does Not Make a Summer

Swallows were always the sign of summer. When the flocks of swallows were seen swooping overhead, folk knew that the long, warm days had come at last.

Once upon a time, after a hard winter and a cold spring, a young woman saw a single swallow flying over her garden.

The sun was shining and the young woman laughed:

'There is a swallow. Summer is here at last. I can throw off those winter woollies which make me look shapeless and fat. I need not bother to collect wood for the fire. I will wear a pretty cotton dress. How lovely!'

However, when the rash young woman went out, a cold wind was blowing. A shower of rain soaked her to the skin. She hurried home to get warm and dry, but there was no fire.

She scowled out of the window to where the single swallow sat miserably huddled up in the shelter of the stable.

'You stupid bird!' she shouted. 'I thought swallows were supposed to be a sign of summer!'

'I came ahead of all the others,' sighed the swallow. 'I wanted to claim the best

place for my nest. The others said I was flying here too soon. How I wish I had listened to them!'

The girl dragged on a coat, went out to gather some wood and hastily lit a fire, which kept her and the swallow warm until the better weather arrived.

The lesson of that story is: one swallow does not make a summer.

12
June

The Golden Goose

There was once a young woodchopper named Simpleton. Each day this boy would go into the forest with a bottle of water and a loaf of bread and work at chopping down trees.

One day a little old man came up to him and asked him for a drink of water and a bite of bread. Simpleton shared his food with the stranger and when he had finished, the little old man said:

'As you have such a good heart and have shared your food with me, I will grant you good luck. There stands an old tree. Cut it down and take what you find amongst the roots.'

So saying, he disappeared.

When Simpleton cut down the old tree he found a goose with feathers of pure gold sitting amongst the roots. Simpleton picked it up and went to stay at an inn.

The innkeeper had three daughters. When the eldest saw the golden feathers on the goose she wanted one for herself. While Simpleton was eating his dinner, the girl reached out her hand to pluck a golden feather. At once her hand stuck fast to the bird and she could not pull it away.

13
June

The Golden Goose

Soon afterwards, the second sister came along, also wishing to take a golden feather. She had no sooner rested her hand on her sister's arm, than she was stuck fast too.

Finally the third sister arrived.

'Keep away! Keep away!' screamed the other girls.

However, the third girl thought:

'If they are taking golden feathers, why shouldn't I?'

Soon she was stuck as fast as her sisters

and so they had to stay all night.

Next morning, taking no notice of the girls, Simpleton picked up the golden goose and went on his way. As he was walking across the fields, they met the parson. He stared at the girls in dismay.

'For shame, you bold girls!' he said. 'You should not run after a boy like that.'

He caught hold of the youngest girl's arm to pull her away and became stuck himself. He had to run along with the others behind Simpleton.

Soon afterwards the sexton caught sight of the parson running along behind Simpleton and the three girls. He was amazed.

'What are you doing there, Your Reverence?' he asked. 'Do not forget you are due at a Christening.'

He dragged at the parson's sleeve and then he was caught with the others.

14
June

The Golden Goose

The little group of five was stumbling and tripping reluctantly along the road, when the sexton saw two peasants whom he knew. At once he begged them to free him and the parson. Alas, as soon as the peasants tried to help, they became stuck as well. Then there were seven people running behind Simpleton and the goose.

By and by they reached a town where a king had a daughter who would not smile.

'If anyone can make my daughter smile,' said the king, 'he can marry her.'

It happened that the king's daughter was standing on the palace balcony as Simpleton ran by holding the golden goose and tugging the three girls, the parson, the sexton and the two peasants, struggling and tripping after him.

They really were a funny sight!

The princess burst out laughing and the townsfolk said to Simpleton.

'Go and speak to the king at once. You are entitled to marry his daughter.'

The king glared at Simpleton and did not like what he saw.

'You cannot marry the princess until you have found a man who can drink a barrel of wine, eat a mountain of bread and invent a carriage which can float on water and run on the road,' he said, thinking that all such things were impossible.

Then he turned Simpleton and the others out of the palace and said to his daughter:

'I am not letting you marry a poor simple woodchopper! But have no fear. He will never be able to fulfil the three tasks I set him. I am quite, quite sure this is the last we shall ever see of him.'

15
June

The Golden Goose

Immediately the princess started to look miserable again, because she had wanted to marry Simpleton.

Meanwhile Simpleton went back to the forest and found the little old man, who had given him the golden goose.

'I am thirsty enough to drink a barrel of wine and hungry enough to eat a mountain of bread and I have made this carriage which runs on land as well as water and now I do not want it,' said the little old man.

'Then come with me,' said Simpleton.

He took the little grey man to see the king.

'Thank goodness you are back,' gasped the king, who was tired of looking at his daughter's miserable face.

'Don't worry about the barrel of wine or the mountain of bread or that carriage. Marry my daughter and take her away, please.'

So Simpleton and the princess were married and lived happily ever after. The little grey man released the girls and the parson and the sexton and the two peasants from the goose. The goose went to live with Simpleton, who became rich from its golden feathers.

Even the king was happy because the rest of his children liked smiling and the palace rang with laughter from then on.

16
June

Blue Teddy and Pink Teddy

Blue Teddy Bear had lived with the family for several years. His fur was worn a little thin and his bow was rather bedraggled, but everyone knew that he was the best bear in all the world.

Then a new baby came to join the family and after a year or two, this baby was given a pink teddy bear of his own.

Pink Teddy Bear was young and his fur was thick and glossy. The bow at his neck was crisp and smart.

'I can't understand all this talk I hear about your being the best teddy bear in all the world,' he said. 'It is quite clear that I am better than you. I am new and nice and you are old and worn. I must be the best teddy bear in all the world.'

BONK! Blue Teddy hit Pink Teddy on the nose.

'No Johnny-come-lately is talking to me like that,' he growled.

WUMP! Pink Teddy hit Blue Teddy on the ear.

'No worn-out-old-has-been is getting the better of me,' he snarled.

Even teddy bears can be fierce when they are angry.

17
June

Blue Teddy
and Pink Teddy

Dolly looked up from her teaset.

'If you are going to fight, I will put on my red cross outfit and be a nurse,' she said eagerly. 'I love being a nurse. I will give you doses of salt water for medicine and tie bandages round your grazed knees. You will graze your knees, won't you?'

At once the bears stopped fighting. The last thing they wanted was for Dolly to be a nurse. She was always so bossy.

'I would rather be friends than drink Nurse Dolly's salt water medicine,' said Blue Teddy.

'I would rather be friends than wear one of those uncomfortable bandages she ties on,' said Pink Teddy.

'Let's shake paws then,' Blue Teddy suggested. 'After all, we teddy bears have to stick together.'

They thought for a minute and then came to a splendid agreement. They would take it in turns at being the best bear in the whole world. Pink Teddy would be best bear one day and Blue Teddy would be best bear the next.

After that they were good friends and there was no more fighting.

Bossy Dolly was quite disappointed.

18
June

Mercury
and the Woodman

Once, long ago, a woodman was felling a tree near the bank of a river, when the axe slipped from his hand and fell into the water. The woodman knelt by the river bemoaning his ill fortune.

The god Mercury heard him and diving into the river brought up a golden axe.

'Is this yours?' he asked the woodman.

'No. No,' the man replied.

Again Mercury dived into the river and this time lifted up a silver axe.

'Is this your axe?' he asked.

'No,' replied the man. 'That is not mine.'

For the third time Mercury dived into the river and this time brought up the woodman's own axe.

'That is mine, thank you,' said the man joyfully.

Mercury was so impressed with his honesty, that he gave the woodman all three axes.

The woodman related his good fortune to his friends. The next day one of them went to the same part of the river and contrived to drop his old axe into the water.

Mercury appeared as before and diving into the river, brought up a golden axe.

'Is this your axe?' he asked the man.

'Oh yes, yes, it is,' replied the man, not able to restrain his greed.

Mercury was so disgusted at the man's dishonesty that he gave him neither the golden axe, nor dived to fetch the one the man had dropped in the river.

The lesson of that story is that honesty is the best policy.

19
June

The Ugly Duckling

A little while ago, in the springtime, a mother duck was puzzled by one of the eggs in her nest. It was larger than the other eggs and took longer to hatch.

An old duck came to look at it.

'Mark my words. That is a turkey's egg,' she said. 'I hatched a turkey's egg once. An ugly thing the little creature was. It could not swim and it pecked my other babes. Take my advice and leave that egg alone.'

'Oh, I will sit on it a little while longer,' smiled the kind mother duck and she sat on the large egg until it cracked open and out hopped an ugly-looking creature.

This newcomer was nothing like the pretty yellow ducklings already swimming on the pond.

'Perhaps he is a turkey,' sighed the mother duck. 'I should not have bothered with him.'

However, the Ugly Duckling jumped into the water and swam well, better than the other ducklings.

'He is certainly not a turkey,' smiled the mother duck. 'He must be my own. I will look after him.'

Like any mother, mother duck loved all her babies, one as much as the other.

20
June

The Ugly Duckling

The proud mother duck took her babies to the farmyard to introduce them to the other creatures.

'Those little yellow fellows are a credit to you,' said the big gander. 'They may visit here with pleasure, but that ugly thing is certainly not wanted. Turn him out.'

The mother duck pleaded for her ugly baby, but it was no use. The other farmyard creatures pecked and chased the Ugly Duckling, until he fled over the farmyard fence.

Night was falling and the Ugly Duckling

wandered up on to the wide moor, where the wild ducks lived. There he spent a cold and miserable night and at dawn the wild ducks opened their eyes and looked at him.

'What sort of bird are you?' they asked.

'I am a duck,' replied the Ugly Duckling.

The wild ducks roared with laughter.

'Then you are the ugliest duck we have ever seen,' they quacked. 'However, you can fly with us, if you keep yourself to yourself.'

The Ugly Duckling was grateful for even this little kindness and stayed for a few days until two wild geese flew by. They were quite young and the Ugly Duckling liked them because they were nearer to his own size and age.

21
June

The Ugly Duckling

'Fly with us,' invited the wild geese and the duckling did.

However as they went over the marshes, there was a sharp - CRACK! CRACK!

Both wild geese tumbled to the ground and looking down, the duckling saw men with guns and dogs. He was afraid.

The Ugly Duckling crept through the marsh and managed to escape from the hunters and their dogs. At last he came to a poor cottage. Pushing through a gap in the door, he found an old woman living with her cat and a hen. They were all rather bad-tempered. The old woman had no time for the duckling because he did not lay eggs. The cat looked down on him because he could not arch his back, nor purr as she could. The hen became very impatient with the Ugly Duckling because he could not cluck as she did and would keep talking about how nice it was to go swimming.

'Swimming! What a ridiculous idea,' clucked the hen. 'What sensible person ever wanted to go swimming? Take my advice and put all that nonsense out of your head and settle down to scratch round the yard as I do.'

But the Ugly Duckling was most unhappy to stay in the yard. He tried scratching round the place and he tried to put all thought of water and swimming out of his mind.

22
June

The Ugly Duckling

However, as he grew older, the Ugly Duckling longed to dive and splash in a river and at last he said goodbye to the hen and went down into the valley. He slipped into the river and floated over the water like a graceful sailing ship.

Coming from under some willow trees, the Ugly Duckling saw the most beautiful birds he had ever beheld. They were white and large and graceful.

'How I should love to swim with those birds,' thought the Ugly Duckling. 'I must join them, even though they will peck me and hate me as other creatures do.'

He paddled across and joined the white birds, who were swans. To his surprise they welcomed him and were friends. He was amazed that for once he was not driven away. Then he caught sight of his own reflection in the water. He was white and graceful like the other lovely birds.

At first the Ugly Duckling could not believe he was gazing at himself. He stretched his neck and opened his wings.

He was a swan!

The Ugly Duckling had shed his dowdy feathers and had grown into an elegant and beautiful bird, and lived happily for the rest of his days.

23
June

Polly Put
the Kettle On

Milly and Molly were going to visit their cousins Polly and Sukey.

'We do like a nice hot cup of tea,' they said. 'Do not put the kettle on until you see us walking up the garden path. Then the tea will be fresh when we arrive.'

On the day Milly and Molly were due to visit, Sukey kept watch from the window. At a quarter to four she saw Milly and Molly coming through the garden gate.

'Polly, put the kettle on. Polly, put the kettle on,' she called.

Then, down by the garden gate, Milly and Molly saw the postman walking in the lane, and they went out for a chat.

'Sukey, take the kettle off,' called Polly, who could see no one in the garden. 'They've all gone away.'

Sukey lifted the kettle from the heat and said. 'I'm sure I saw Milly and Molly coming through the garden gate.'

She looked through the window once more and by this time Milly and Molly had finished talking to the postman and were walking up the garden path.

'Polly, Polly, put the kettle on,' called Sukey.

While Polly was putting the kettle on for the second time, Milly and Molly noticed Sukey's tortoise trying to run away through a gap in the fence, and they bent down to pick it up.

It was a very friendly tortoise and it did not hide in its shell. Milly and Molly decided to play with it for a minute or two.

24
June

Polly Put
the Kettle On

Polly could not understand where Milly and Molly had got to. It all seemed very strange.

Polly opened the kitchen door and looked up the garden. She could not see Milly and Molly because they were bending low over the tortoise.

'Sukey, take the kettle off again,' she said. 'They've all gone away.'

Sukey took the kettle off, but felt impatient at all the muddle. She ran out into the garden and met Milly and Molly walking up the path with the tortoise.

'Why do you keep appearing and disappearing?' she asked.

'We didn't know that we did,' replied Milly and Molly.

They went indoors. Polly put the kettle on and made tea, and over a nice hot cup, Milly and Molly explained what they had been doing. The girls made up a rhyme about the whole muddle. This is it:

'Polly, put the kettle on,
Polly, put the kettle on,
Polly, put the kettle on,
We'll all have tea.

Sukey, take it off again,
Sukey, take it off again,
Sukey, take it off again,
They've all gone away.'

25
June

The Crow
and the Pitcher

It had been a long, hot summer. The ponds and rivers were all dried up. At last a thirsty crow found a pitcher with some water at the bottom. However, try as she might the crow could not reach the water. The pitcher was too tall and narrow.

It seemed that the crow was about to die of thirst within sight of water. But the crow was not going to give up just like that. She knew her very life depended on her getting to the water.

Then the crow thought of a clever plan. She dropped pebbles into the pitcher. With each pebble, the level of the water rose until it reached the brim and the crow was able to drink.

The lesson of this story is that necessity is the mother of invention.

26
June

Calling the Tune

Once, the animals held a dance in the old barn. A piper was playing merry music and most creatures were enjoying themselves.

However, a little lamb felt he would like to dance to the tune of Danny Boy. As he danced past the piper, he called out:

'Please play Danny Boy next.'

In a moment a pig danced past the piper and called out:

'Play Yankee Doodle Dandy next, please.'

To the lamb's surprise, the piper played Yankee Doodle Dandy for his next tune.

'That isn't fair,' thought the lamb. 'I asked first.'

It was the same all through the evening, no matter how politely any one else asked for a tune to be played, the piper always played the tunes asked for by the pig.

At last the lamb asked the piper why he always did as the pig requested

'The pig is paying me,' replied the piper.

The lesson of this story is that he who pays the piper calls the tune.

27
June

Androcles
and the Lion

Hundreds and hundreds of years ago, when the Romans had a huge empire and were strong and powerful, there lived a boy named Androcles.

Androcles was the son of poor forest folk and when his parents died, he was left to fend for himself in the wild. He took to living in a cave, but one dreadful day a lion came walking in and Androcles shook with fear.

However, the lion did not attack him, but lay down and licked at its paw as if it were in pain. Androcles crept forward and saw that the paw was red and swollen. Daring to take the paw in his hand, Androcles found that a thorn had become deeply embedded and was poisoning the lion's foot.

With many soothing words to the great beast, Androcles pulled out the thorn, bathed the paw and bandaged it.

For several days he looked after the lion and they became friends. The lion hunted by night and slept in the cave by day. Androcles went about his business by day and slept in the cave at night. This arrangement went on for several years and the two became familiar companions.

28
June

Androcles and the Lion

One day the Roman army came marching through the forest. Androcles was taken captive and sold as a slave in Rome. He did not like being a slave and was disobedient.

As a punishment, he was sent to a place called the Coliseum where crowds came to watch slaves and prisoners being made to fight wild beasts.

Androcles was pushed out into the huge arena and the watching crowd of Romans hissed at him.

'This will teach you to be disobedient,' they yelled. 'See how you like fighting a lion.'

A door swung open and a lion came running across the sand towards Androcles. At first it seemed as if it would leap upon him, then it paused and sniffed. The lion circled Androcles, staring at him. Then it

rubbed against his legs and licked his hand.

It was Androcles' old friend from the forest. He had been captured and brought to Rome too.

The crowd were amazed when they saw the lion making friends with Androcles. It even trotted at his heel as he walked round the arena. Such a thing had never happened before.

By order of the emperor, Androcles and the lion were freed and given a home to live in outside Rome.

So at least one story of ancient Rome had a happy ending.

29
June

Beware of Mermaids

Long ago a young fisherman called Jack Tar lived by the seashore. He often heard the old men talking about mermaids, but Jack did not believe what they said.

'Mermaids sit on the rocks combing their long hair,' said the old men. 'They sing with beautiful voices and they try to lure sailor lads to drown on the rocks. If you should see a mermaid, block your ears and turn away your eyes and row as fast as you can in the opposite direction.'

Jack would only laugh.

Then, early one morning, pirates attacked the village where young Jack Tar lived. They stole money and food and dragged Jack with them back to their longboat on the shore.

'You look a strong lad,' they said to Jack. 'You must sail with us and serve our captain.'

They started to row out towards their big sailing ship, riding the waves near the shore.

Poor Jack was in despair, when suddenly the sound of beautiful singing floated across the water. Everyone in the boat turned to

see who was making the lovely sound. Sitting on the rocks combing their hair were some mermaids.

At once Jack Tar remembered the words of the old men. He blocked his ears and turned away his eyes. The pirates had never been given such good advice. One by one they threw themselves into the water and swam towards the rocks and were never heard of again. When Jack realized he was alone in the boat, he seized two oars and rowed for the shore where his mother and father greeted him with tears of joy.

From that day on Jack Tar believed in mermaids, but although they had saved him from the pirates, he was still afraid of them and their songs.

30
June

The Fairy Baby

Long ago a country man and his wife lived in a lonely cottage. One night they were visited by two of the Little People or Fairy Folk, as they are often called.

The Little People had a baby with them.

'If you will look after this baby for us, we will pay you well,' they said.

The country man and his wife agreed.

The baby was left with them and also a jar of ointment.

'Rub the ointment on to the eyes of the baby every day,' said the fairy man, 'but never put it on your own eyes.'

Every day that the country man and his wife cared for the fairy baby, they found a piece of gold on their doorstep and they were well content.

Then one day the man could not resist putting the ointment on to his own eyes as well as on the eyes of the fairy baby. He felt no ill effect, but when he went to market, he saw the fairy man and at once spoke to him.

The fairy man was furious.

'You have rubbed your eyes with the ointment,' he shouted, 'otherwise you would not be able to see me.'

He blew on the eyes of the country man, who at once fell down in a deep sleep.

When he awoke, he hurried home. The

baby was gone. The ointment was gone and no more gold coins ever appeared on the doorstep.

Forever more the country man regretted the day he had disobeyed the orders of the Little People. From that day on, there were no pieces of gold left on their doorsteps.

July

1
July

Rip Van Winkle

Many years ago there lived a good-for-nothing fellow named Rip Van Winkle. He always had plenty of time for chatting with the village children, or hunting with his dog, but when it came to work, somehow Rip Van Winkle was too busy.

As can be well understood, this made his wife angry. When the house needed painting, Rip Van Winkle was nowhere to be seen. When the yard needed sweeping, Rip Van Winkle was nowhere to be seen. When the vegetables needed digging, Rip Van Winkle was nowhere to be seen.

But, when meals were to be eaten, or games were to be played, or someone called for a chat, why, there was Rip Van Winkle, bright and ready and smiling.

One day, when Mrs. Van Winkle had been grumbling and when the wood needed chopping, Rip Van Winkle decided this was a good time to go for a walk. He whistled for his dog, picked up his gun and tramped through the trees and up the mountainside.

Suddenly he heard someone calling to him:

'Rip! Rip! Come and help me,' called a thin old voice and looking down the mountain, Rip Van Winkle saw a little old man with a long beard.

2
July

Rip Van Winkle

The little old man was carrying a keg upon his back.

'Carry this for me,' he begged Rip and although Rip Van Winkle was lazy, he was also kind-hearted, so he picked up the keg and followed the strange little man.

They walked high into the mountains to

a part where Rip Van Winkle had never been before. Suddenly a small valley opened before them. The floor of the valley was flat and grassy and standing in it were twenty more little men like the man walking with Rip.

The men were dressed alike in tall red caps, coats with large brass buttons, short trousers and shoes with large silver buckles.

The men were playing ninepins with great wooden balls and as the balls struck the pins, a sound like thunder rumbled across the mountains.

Rip began to feel rather frightened, but he put the keg on the ground and when he was told, he filled some mugs from it and handed the drinks round to all the little men.

Being Rip Van Winkle, he soon found

the courage to try the drink himself. At once he felt very tired and he lay by an oak tree to sleep with his gun and his dog at his side.

3
July

Rip Van Winkle

When he awoke, Rip Van Winkle saw the sun was up and the birds were singing.

'I must have slept here all night,' thought Rip, rubbing his eyes. 'Mrs. Van Winkle will grumble at me when I get home.'

He reached for the gun he had left at his side. It was not there, only a rusty old firelock lay on the grass.

'What a mean trick,' he thought, 'to take away my nice new gun and leave that rotten old thing.'

He stood up and whistled for his dog. The dog did not come and Rip felt amazingly stiff in the joints.

'These outdoor beds are hard,' he thought. 'They make you feel old.'

Rip Van Winkle took up the rusty gun, and walked to the village where he lived.

He met some children and was puzzled because he did not know them.

'I thought I knew every child in the village,' he muttered, 'and what strange clothes they are wearing!'

4
July
Rip Van Winkle

The strange children Rip met kept looking at his chin and then stroking their own chins. Rip put his hand to his chin and found a long straggly beard there.

'How could this grow in a night?' he thought. 'It must be because of that drink the strange little men gave to me.'

He walked into the centre of the village. It had changed. It was bigger. There were different names over the doors. Strangers stared at him from the windows.

He hurried to his own house. It was in ruins and the garden had run wild. He walked through the empty, crumbling rooms calling for his wife and children. No one answered.

By this time a crowd of the strangers,

who seemed to have taken the village over, were following at Rip's heels. At last a man stopped him and asked why he was walking through the streets with a gun in his hand.

'I mean no harm,' said the desperate Rip. 'I live in this village. Where are my old friends? Nick Vedder or Brom Dutcher will tell you who I am.'

'Nick has been dead these twenty years,' called one of the onlookers, 'and Brom Dutcher was killed in the war.'

'Does nobody here remember Rip Van Winkle?' Rip asked.

A young woman with a baby in her arms stepped forward.

'My father was Rip Van Winkle,' she said. 'He went away some twenty years ago and has never been heard of since. His dog came home without him, but no trace of Rip was ever found.'

Rip took the young woman by the arm.

'I am your father,' he said. 'I was young, but now I am old. Don't you remember me?'

Then the woman did recognize her father and he told everyone the story of the high valley and the strange little men.

Ever after that when folk heard thunder in the mountains, they said it was the little men playing ninepins.

5
July

The Farmer
and his Servants

Not long ago, there was a farmer who employed two servants. He kept them hard at work, making them rise every morning as soon as the cock crowed.

The servants hated getting up so early, especially in winter. One day they took the cock from the farmyard and sold it to a passing tinker.

'Now we shall be able to lie abed in the mornings,' they smiled. 'The cock will not wake the farmer with his crowing and he will not wake us.'

Unfortunately, although their plan worked for one morning, every morning after that, the farmer woke earlier than ever. He was so fearful of losing working time, he scarcely slept at night and being restless himself, did not see why others should sleep.

After the cock left, the poor servants worked even longer hours than before, but they only had themselves to blame.

The lesson of this story is that it is often better to leave well alone.

6
July

The Grand
Old Duke of York

The grand old Duke of York was a soldier. That is what dukes were for in the olden days. It was their job to gather an army together and train it and then to fight for their country.

The grand old Duke of York had ten thousand well-trained men, all dressed in smart uniforms and with bright shiny swords.

However, the grand old Duke of York and his men had been lucky. For years there had been no wars and they had not had to do any fighting.

Then one day a messenger rushed into the room where the grand old Duke of York was eating breakfast and said what sounded like:

'The enemy is coming!'

The Duke of York was becoming a little old and deaf, but he knew how to do his duty. He called all his soldiers into battle order and marched them to the top of the hill.

He looked around the countryside, but he could see no enemy army approaching.

'I wonder what I should do now?' muttered the grand old Duke of York who had never been in a war before. 'I know. I'll march the men down the hill again.'

7
July

The Grand
Old Duke of York

'Oh, I don't know, though,' said the Duke, changing his mind again. 'Perhaps it would be better to be at the top of the hill where we can see everything.'

He marched his men to the top of the hill once more.

Then the messenger, who had rushed into the breakfast room said:

'I hate to criticize you, Your Grace, but why are you doing all this, just because King Henry is coming? I am sure he would have been satisfied if you had prepared a hot meal. There was no need to turn out the whole army!'

Then the grand old Duke realized that the messenger had not said, 'The enemy is coming' but 'King Henry is coming!'

Oh, how foolish he felt then!

With rather a red face, the grand old Duke of York marched his men down the hill and prepared a hot meal for King Henry.

Folk made up a rhyme about the Duke's mistake, which went like this:

'Oh, the grand old Duke of York,
He had ten thousand men,
He marched them up to the top of the hill,
And he marched them down again.
And when they were up, they were up,
And when they were down, they were down,
And when they were only half-way up,
They were neither up nor down.'

8
July

The Pedlar of Swaffham

Long ago there was a pedlar named John, who lived in a village called Swaffham in the county of Norfolk in England.

Night after night the pedlar had the same dream. In the dream a voice told him that if he went to London and stood on London Bridge, he would hear a wonderful piece of news.

John the pedlar took no notice. In those days there was no way to get to London, but to walk and it was a long way.

However, the dream was so persistent, it almost made the wretched man ill and he

packed some food and set out on the long walk south.

For days he walked, sleeping under hedges at night and at last he arrived in London, tired and cold. He easily found his way to the famous London Bridge, which in those days had houses and shops upon it.

He stood at one end and waited, but no one spoke to him. No one even noticed him. Night fell. Poor John slept as well as he could in a shop doorway.

Next day John stood at the other end of London Bridge, hoping that someone would give him the wonderful news about which he had dreamed. Still no one spoke to him. For days John loitered about on London Bridge until all his food and his little bit of money was gone.

'I had better go home,' he thought, 'my dream must have been nonsense.'

9
July

The Pedlar of Swaffham

As he was about to leave, a shopkeeper strolled across to speak to him.

'I've noticed you standing about on the bridge for days,' said the man. 'You don't beg. You don't sell anything. You do not speak to anyone. Satisfy my curiosity and tell me why you are here.'

'Well,' said the pedlar. 'I am from a long way away in the country and in a dream a voice told me that if I came to London Bridge, I should be told a wonderful message. So I have come and that is why I am standing here.'

The shopkeeper burst out laughing.

'What a fool you must be to come all this way and hang about in the cold because of a dream,' he chuckled. 'Only a country bumpkin would do a ridiculous thing like that. If we all took notice of our dreams, we should be dashing across the country like scalded rabbits. Why, do you know, only last night I dreamed that a voice told me to go to a village called Swaffham. I've never even heard of the place. The voice said that if I went to this Swaffham place and dug under an oak tree in the garden of some pedlar fellow, I should find a mighty treasure. What rubbish! I'm not going to be such a fool as to go traipsing round looking for the house of a pedlar in Swaffham, I can tell you.'

With that the shopkeeper went back to his shop.

John hurried home to Swaffham and dug under the oak tree in his garden and found a chest of gold coins. He gave money to repair the village church and kept the rest of the treasure for himself. And he lived a happy man.

10
July

The Wise Farm Boy

Once upon a time a farm boy was ploughing a field. In the middle of the field he found a circle where the grass and earth were beaten flat, as if many tiny feet had been dancing there.

Now, the farm boy was a good boy who often visited his old grandmother. Many times she had told him of how she had seen fairies dancing in a fairy ring.

'If this is a place where the fairies like to dance, then I must not plough it,' thought the boy.

He marked a circle round the ring and did not disturb it with his plough.

At midday the boy was hungry and took out the small piece of bread and cheese, which was all his mother could give him.

Suddenly, to his amazement, he saw a table in the centre of the fairy ring. The table was spread with roast meat and pies and fruit and wine. The boy ate as if at a banquet. When he had finished, the table disappeared. He never knew where the food came from, but from that day onwards, he was always lucky.

His grandmother said the fairy folk were thanking him.

11
July

Puss in Boots

Long ago there was a miller who had three sons. When he died, he left all he had to be divided amongst the three of them.

The eldest son took the mill. The second son took the donkey and all that was left for the youngest son was the cat.

The boy looked at the cat ruefully.

'I shall not become rich by owning a cat,' he sighed.

'Indeed! And why not?' replied the cat. 'Dear master, buy me a leather sack and a pair of fine boots and I shall surprise you.'

The boy spent the last of his money on doing as the cat wished. Looking splendid in some wonderful top boots and with the leather sack over her shoulder, Puss set out.

First she went into the garden and picked some lettuce, which she put into the

sack. Then she placed the open sack at the entrance to a rabbit hole and sat and waited in the sunshine.

Presently a fat rabbit came out of the hole and crept into the sack to nibble the lettuce. The cat leaped forward, pulled tight the strings of the sack and the rabbit was caught.

With the sack over her shoulder, Puss marched up to the gates of the palace and demanded to see the king.

Impressed by her fine boots, the guard let Puss through and she was announced to His Majesty.

Bowing low, Puss presented the rabbit to the king and said:

'This is a present from my master, the Marquis of Carabas.'

The king accepted the present with pleasure and Puss went home to the mill to her young master.

12
July

Puss in Boots

Next day, Puss put some grain into her leather sack and went out into the fields. She left the sack lying on the ground with its mouth open and lay at its side with her feet in the air, pretending to be dead.

After a while two plump partridges came down and ventured into the sack to peck at the corn. In a moment, Puss leapt up and tied the neck of the sack. The partridges were caught.

Walking proudly in her fine boots, Puss went to the palace. This time the guards knew her and she was waved through to see the king in a moment.

Puss bowed low and presented the partridges to the king.

'These are a present from the estate of my master, the Marquis of Carabas,' she said.

'How very kind,' smiled the king. 'Thank your master for me.'

Puss bowed and backed away from the king. However, before she left the palace, she listened to the gossip and learned that the next day the king intended to drive by the river with his daughter, the princess.

13
July

Puss in Boots

Puss scampered home to her master and told him all about her visits to the palace and how the king was going riding by the river the next day.

'Now, dear master,' said Puss, 'do exactly as I say and your fortune will be made.'

The boy agreed and Puss told him to go to the river the next day, leave his clothes on the bank and go swimming.

'Most important of all,' she purred, 'if

anyone should ask your name, say that you are the Marquis of Carabas.'

It all seemed very strange to the boy, but he had nothing else to do, so the next day he went swimming in the river and left Puss to guard his clothes.

Puss hid the clothes and watched for the king and the princess and their attendants to come driving by. As the golden coach rolled past the place where the boy was bathing, Puss ran out shouting:

'Help! Help! The Marquis of Carabas is drowning.'

The king recognized Puss and ordered his carriage to stop and sent his servants to rescue the drowning Marquis. The boy, who was not drowning at all, allowed himself to be pulled from the river.

'Oh, how fortunate that you were passing by at this moment,' said Puss to the king. 'Thieves have stolen my master's clothes. He will die of the cold.'

At once the kindly king sent his servants to fetch a fine suit from his own wardrobe. Soon the miller's son was dressed in a silken suit embroidered with golden thread.

Puss in Boots

He really looked like a Marquis.

'We should be pleased if Your Majesty would dine with us at our estate,' said Puss.

The king was curious to see the fine lands of the Marquis of Carabas, of whom Puss had told him so much and he accepted the invitation eagerly. He invited the miller's son to ride in his carriage and they proceeded along the road.

At once Puss raced ahead and taking a short cut, came out well in front of the others at some fine broad farmlands. Some simple peasants were cutting the corn.

'Listen to me,' said Puss in a grand and threatening manner, 'when the king rides by and asks to whom these fields belong, you are to say that they belong to the Marquis of Carabas. If you do not say that, I shall have you chopped into mincemeat.'

The peasants were frightened and did as Puss said.

Meanwhile Puss ran ahead still further to

where some more peasants were making hay in a lovely wide meadow.

She shook her paw at them and bared her teeth.

'Look here, you fellows,' she said. 'The king will be passing here soon. You tell him that these meadows belong to the Marquis of Carabas, or it will be the worse for you.'

'Worse in what way?' asked one of the peasants, who was not as timid as the others.

'Worse in that if you say anything else the king will have your head chopped off,' replied naughty Puss.

'Yes, that is worse,' agreed the peasant and he and the others did as Puss said.

Puss left the peasants and ran on until she came to a fine house where a terrible ogre lived.

15
July

Puss in Boots

The ogre was big and hairy and so horrible that no one would live with him for love or money. When Puss knocked at the door, the ogre had to open it himself.

'Good afternoon, Your Mightiness,' said Puss. 'I have heard so much about the clever things you can do, that I have called to see for myself. Is it true that you can turn yourself into a wild beast?'

Now, the ogre was vain and loved showing off.

'Of course I can,' he shouted. 'Step inside for a moment and I will show you.'

Puss stepped into the house. The ogre shut his eyes and took a deep breath and in a moment he had turned into a great roaring lion, who chased Puss up the curtains.

How the ogre laughed when he saw Puss clinging to the curtains by her claws! He turned himself back to his normal shape and asked Puss how she had liked the lion.

'Not much,' replied Puss. 'Of course it must be easy for a huge ogre to change himself into a large creature like a lion, but to change yourself into a mouse! Now that would really be clever. I don't suppose you can do that. It would make you the cleverest ogre in the world.'

16
July

Puss in Boots

The vain ogre laughed.

'I can change into a mouse as easily as winking,' he said. 'Nothing is too difficult for me.'

In a moment he had changed himself into a tiny mouse. With one pounce, Puss killed it and that was the end of the ogre.

Meanwhile, the king and the princess and the miller's son had been driving along and asking to whom all the fine fields belonged. The king was very impressed when he heard they all belonged to the Marquis of Carabas. So was the miller's son, who was pretending to be the marquis.

Finally, they came to the ogre's house. Puss stood bowing in the doorway.

'Welcome to my master's home,' she said. And as the ogre was dead, the house was free for the miller's son to occupy.

Puss ushered everyone into the dining room where a huge dinner had been prepared for the ogre. The king was so impressed, he gave the miller's son, or the Marquis of Carabas, as he was known from then on, permission to marry his daughter and they lived happily ever after.

Of course Puss lived in the grand house too. She never did any work, but strolled around in her fine boots being admired by everyone.

17
July

The Darkest Hour

Some travellers were journeying in the mountains of a far country. Suddenly a huge hungry mountain lion ran out and attacked them. The terrified travellers ran in all directions. Two climbed up a tree and clung to the high branches. Two others ran into a shepherd's deserted mountain hut and slammed shut the thin wooden door. The youngest of them raced down the trail towards the village far away in the valley.

He glanced over his shoulder as he ran and saw the lion leaping up at the travellers in the tree. When he had stumbled further, he glanced back once more and saw the lion pounding with its huge paw at the door of the shepherd's hut.

'I must fetch help,' panted the young fellow, for he knew he could never fight the lion without weapons. 'The villagers will surely help me.'

He ran to the village as fast as he could and the good men who lived there agreed to return with him and rescue his friends. However, night was falling and the men said it was useless to go up into the mountains in the dark.

'If the lion does not kill us, we shall fall over a cliff and perish on the rocks below,' they said.

18
July

The Darkest Hour

Meanwhile, the travellers in the tree and in the hut were in fear for their lives. The lion prowled and growled, waiting for one of the men to fall from the tree through tiredness or the cold. It slammed and chewed and pounded at the door of the hut, until long cracks appeared and the hinges sagged. It seemed to the men inside that at any moment the lion would break in and eat them.

The sun set, but the moon rose. There was still light enough for the travellers to see each other and give each other comfort. Then the moon set and clouds hid the stars. During the hour before dawn there was no light at all. The travellers lost hope, thinking that the night would never end.

They prepared themselves for death, expecting the lion to break in at any moment.

Then, suddenly, the bright warm sun rose above the shoulder of the mountain. Their friend and the village men came shouting up from the valley, waving sticks, banging drums and with dogs barking round their heels.

The lion took fright and ran away. The travellers were saved.

As so often happens, the darkest hour had been just before the dawn which brought rescue.

19
July

Baa, Baa, Black Sheep

Most sheep are white, but some sheep are black and once there was a black sheep who lived with Farmer Giles at Buttercup Farm.

This black sheep was strong and healthy and grew thick, glossy wool on his back. Everyone wanted wool from the black sheep to knit up into smart black clothes.

'Black clothes are so much better to wear for visiting town,' the ladies would say to each other.

The black sheep had a wonderful time. He was always being invited here and asked to dinner there. Platesful of carrots and apples the ladies would give him and all so that they could snip some thick black wool from his coat.

Farmer Giles, who owned the black sheep, became cross. When he came to clip the black sheep in the springtime, hoping for enough wool for a new suit for himself or for a coat for his little grandson, who lived down the lane, or for a dress for Dame

Giles, his wife, he was disappointed. There were only a few small patches of wool left on the black sheep's back.

This made Farmer Giles very cross indeed. After all, the black sheep belonged to him. He wagged his finger at him.

Baa, Baa, Black Sheep

'This is not good enough,' Farmer Giles said to the black sheep. 'You live on my farm. You eat my food most of the time. Just because you get a free meal from the ladies now and then, that is no reason to let them take wool which should be mine.'

'You are quite right,' agreed the black sheep, 'but you know how naughty we black sheep are. I will try to do better in future.'

And the black sheep really did try. He did not let the ladies snip any of the thick black wool from his coat . 'I'd rather do without the carrots and apples,' he said.

For the whole of the next winter, the black sheep was good. He let no one clip wool from his back. When springtime came and Farmer Giles came to shear the wool from the black sheep, this is what he said:

'Baa, baa, black sheep
Have you any wool?
Yes, sir, yes, sir,
Three bags full.
One for my master,
One for my dame
And one for the little boy
Who lives down the lane.'

Farmer Giles was pleased and gave the black sheep extra carrots for his dinner.

The Tinder Box

Long ago and far away, a soldier came marching home from the wars - left-right, left-right.

An ugly witch stood at the side of the road.

'Good evening, soldier,' she said. 'You are a fine looking fellow. Do as I say and you can have as much money as you please.'

'Thank you kindly, witch,' replied the soldier, 'but what do I have to do to earn that money?'

The witch pointed to a big tree at the side of the road and said:

'At the top of that tree is a hole. Let yourself down, right under the tree. I have a rope you can tie round your waist and I will haul you up again, when you call. Beneath the tree is a wide passage, lit by a hundred blazing lamps. In the passage are three doors, which you can open, for the keys are in the locks. Go into the first room and you will see a box in the middle of the floor. Sitting on the box is a dog with eyes as big as saucers. However, there is no need to be afraid. I will give you my blue-checked

apron. If you lift the dog and sit him on the apron, he will not hurt you. Open the box, which is full of copper coins and take as much money as you wish. However, if you prefer silver, go into the next room.'

22
July

The Tinder Box

'In the next room, sitting on another box, you will find a dog with eyes as big as millstones. Do not be afraid. Lift him on to my blue-checked apron and he will not hurt you. Fill your pockets with silver from the box. However, if you prefer gold, go into the next room. Sitting on a box in the next room, you will find a huge dog with eyes as big as round towers. He is a fierce dog indeed, but if you sit him on my blue-checked apron he will not hurt you. You may take as much gold as you wish.'

'That sounds good,' replied the soldier, 'but what about you, old witch? You must want something for yourself.'

'I don't want any money,' said the witch, 'but while you are down there, you might as well bring up the old tinder box my grandmother left there some years ago.'

The soldier smiled and said:

'Very well. Tie the rope round my waist. Give me your blue-checked apron and I will go down the hole and fetch the tinder box for you.'

The soldier slid down the rope to the passage beneath the tree. It was lit by a hundred lamps, as the witch had said. The soldier unlocked the first door and walked into a room where a frightening dog with eyes as big as saucers sat on a box. Quickly lifting the dog on to the blue-checked apron, the soldier opened the box and took out as many copper coins as he could put into his pockets.

23
July

The Tinder Box

Then he went into the next room where sat the dog with eyes as big as millstones.

'Good doggie,' said the soldier, lifting the dog to sit on top of the blue-checked apron. He opened the second box and found it full of silver coins, just as the witch had said. Turning the copper coins from his pockets, the soldier replaced them with silver.

Then, picking up the blue-checked apron, he unlocked the door of the third room and went in. Sitting on a box in the middle of the room was a truly fearsome dog with eyes as big as round towers.

'Good evening,' said the soldier, saluting politely, for he had never before seen such a dog. He waited for a moment, wondering if he had the courage to touch such a frightful looking creature. Then, thinking of the gold, he lifted the dog from the box and sat him on the blue-checked apron. The dog did nothing, so the soldier opened the box, threw away the silver coins, then filled his pockets, his knapsack, his boots and even his cap so full of gold he could scarcely walk.

He put the dog back on the box, picked up the blue-checked apron, locked the door and went back to the foot of the tree.

'Haul me up,' he called to the witch.

'Have you got the tinder box?' the witch shouted back.

'No. I've forgotten it,' said the soldier. He walked back, picked up a shabby tinder box and returned to the tree. The witch hauled him up into the fresh air and he stood on the road, a rich man.

24
July

The Tinder Box

The witch took no interest in the gold bulging from the soldier's every pocket.

'Give me the tinder box,' she said, stretching out an eager hand.

The soldier was puzzled.

'Tell me why you want the tinder box and not a share of the gold,' he said. 'You are behaving in a most peculiar way.'

The witch screamed and stamped with rage and said: 'I will not tell you why I want the tinder box. It is none of your business. Give me the tinder box!'

With that the soldier drew his sword and at once the witch took to her heels and ran

away. The soldier tucked the tinder box into his pocket and ran off in the opposite direction. He never saw the witch again. Then the soldier made his way to the nearest town. He went straight to the best hotel, booked into the finest rooms, ordered a banquet to eat and sent for the town's most skilled tailors to make him some suits. The soldier was rich and he felt that only the best was good enough for him.

Many so-called friends flocked round the soldier to help him spend his money. There were trips to the theatre, picnics in the woods, parties in the hotel and laughter and gossip from morning till night. They hardly left themselves time to sleep.

25
July

The Tinder Box

At the parties, the soldier was interested to hear of the princess who had been seen by no one outside the palace. Folks said she lived in a copper tower and was guarded day and night, because it had been foretold that she would marry a common soldier and the king did not care for that idea.

'I should like to see her,' thought the soldier, 'but I don't suppose I ever shall.'

Then he went back to spending his money.

Needless to say the day came when the soldier had spent all his gold and had only a few pence left. He had to move from his fine rooms to a cold attic. He had to sell all his rich new clothes and go back to wearing his soldier's uniform. None of his new friends bothered to visit him any more.

The soldier sat in a dark room without even the price of a candle in his pocket. Then he remembered the tinder box and the scrap of candle he had seen inside it. He opened the box, took out the candle and struck light with the flint. At once the dog with eyes as big as saucers, whom he had last seen in the cavern under the tree, stood before him and said:

'What does my lord command?'

'Good heavens! This is a fine tinder box if it can give me whatever I want,' gasped the soldier. 'No wonder that witch wanted it.' He looked at the dog. 'Bring me money,' he ordered.

26
July

The Tinder Box

The dog ran away and came back in a few minutes with a bag full of copper coins.

The soldier was delighted. He found that if he struck the flint twice, the dog with eyes as big as millstones came and brought him a bag of silver coins, and if he struck the flint three times, the fearsome dog with eyes as big as round towers came and brought him a bag of gold.

Now that he was rich once more, the soldier moved back into the finest rooms in the hotel. All his friends came flocking round and said what a wonderful fellow he was and where had he been hiding himself lately.

Then the soldier fell to thinking about the princess in the copper tower.

'I should like to see her,' he said.

The soldier took the flint from the tinder box and struck it once. WHOOOSH! The dog with eyes as big as saucers ran into the room.

'I know it is the middle of the night,' said the soldier, 'but I should like to see the princess who is kept locked in the copper tower.'

In an instant the dog rushed from the room. In a few minutes he was back with the sleeping princess on his back, who was quite unaware of what was happening. She was so beautiful, the soldier could not resist kissing her. Then the dog took her back to the copper tower.

All this time the princess never woke up, not even when she was kissed.

The Tinder Box

The next morning at breakfast, the princess said to the king and queen:

'I had the strangest dream last night. I dreamed a dog carried me on his back to visit a soldier who kissed me.'

The king and queen were not pleased. That night, they set a serving woman to watch the princess as she slept. Again the soldier sent the dog with eyes as big as saucers to fetch the princess. The dog rushed into the princess's bedroom and carried her off on his back. Fortunately the serving woman was both faithful and brave. She dragged on her boots and followed the dog through the streets. She watched him take the princess into a large house.

'Now I know where the soldier lives,' she thought and marked the door with a large cross. Then she followed the dog and the princess back to the copper tower.

However, on his return to his master's house, the dog noticed the cross on the door. He took some chalk and made crosses on every door in town.

The next day the king and queen went with the servant to find the soldier and ask what he meant by sending the dog with eyes as big as saucers to steal the princess.

They were furious when they found a cross on every door.

The Tinder Box

That night the queen thought of a new plan. She tied a bag of grain to the princess's back and cut a slit in the bag. As the dog ran through the streets with the princess, he did not notice that a trail of grain was falling to the ground and leading from the palace to the soldier's home.

The next day the king's men tracked down the soldier. He was thrown into prison and condemned to death. The poor soldier was in despair. He had left the tinder box behind in his bedroom and he could not summon the magic dogs to help him. Then he felt in his pocket and found a penny. He called to an urchin lingering near the prison and said he would give him the penny, if he would fetch the tinder box. The urchin agreed.

With the tinder box in his pocket, the soldier felt safe. He waited until the day of

his execution, when the king and the entire court were gathered to watch. Then he asked if he might smoke a pipe as a last request. The king agreed. Taking out the tinder box, the soldier struck the flint once, then twice, then three times. The dog with eyes as big as saucers appeared. The dog with eyes as millstones appeared. The terrible dog with eyes as big as round towers appeared. The soldiers ran away. The king shook with fear.

'I will do anything you say, anything,' he squealed.

'Then let me marry your daughter,' said the soldier. The king agreed. The marriage feast was arranged and all three dogs sat at the table and stared around them with their mighty eyes, while everyone cheered the soldier and his princess bride.

29
July

I love Little Pussy

Not long ago, a little boy was given a pussycat as a pet. He had never had a real live pet before and he did not know how to treat her. He made the little pussycat very cross, because he played with her as if she were a toy, pulling at her tail and tossing

her out of the room when he was bored with her.

'You must not treat a live animal like that,' said his grandmother, and she taught the boy this little rhyme, so that he would know the correct way to treat a kitten:

I love little pussy, her coat is so warm,
And if I don't hurt her, she'll do me no harm.
So I'll not pull her tail, nor drive her away,
But pussy and I very gently will play.
She shall sit by my side and I'll give her some food.
And pussy will love me because I am good.'

30
July

The Wolf in Sheep's Clothing

Once a wolf, who considered himself to be very clever, thought of a way to prey on a flock of sheep without being noticed by the shepherd.

He dressed himself in a sheepskin and mingled with the sheep, bleating 'Baaa, baa,' and behaving meekly as a sheep should.

The plan worked well and the wolf was penned in with the sheep for the night. Baring his teeth, the wolf was about to start slaying the sheep, when the shepherd returned to the pens looking for a sheep to kill for dinner.

'That looks a fine big animal,' he thought, seizing the wolf in the sheep's clothing. Immediately he realized he had hold of a wolf and threw him into the depths of the freezing river.

The lesson of this story is to beware of a wolf in sheep's clothing, but also to be beware of trying to be too clever.

31
July

The Dog
and the Crow

Once a crow was sitting in a tree with a piece of cheese in her beak. A dog saw her and decided that he would like the cheese for himself.

He sat under the tree and looked up at the crow and said:

'What a beautiful bird! How fine her feathers are! How strongly her claws grip the branch of the tree! How brightly her beak gleams in the sun!'

The crow was very flattered by all these remarks and listened carefully, hoping to hear more.

'If that lovely bird's voice is as beautiful as the rest of her, she must be the most wonderful bird in the world,' went on the dog.

Wishing to prove that she was the most wonderful bird in the world, the crow opened her beak and uttered a harsh screech, which was the best she could do.

The cheese fell from her mouth and the dog snatched it up and ate it.

'Madam,' he called up to the crow. 'You may or may not be beautiful, for beauty is in the eye of the beholder, but you are not very clever.'

The lesson of that story is, if people flatter you, try to think of the reason why.

August

1
August

The Magic Horse

Long ago, in Persia, the emperor was holding a great feast in his palace. A Hindu bowed before him and showed to the whole court an artificial horse, saddled and bridled and so cleverly made it appeared almost real.

'This is the most marvellous thing ever brought before Your Highness,' said the Hindu. 'I can mount this horse and be transported to the most distant places in just a few moments and I will sell this wonderful invention to Your Highness if you so wish.'

The emperor was greatly interested and asked the Hindu to prove the horse could do as he said. He pointed to a mountain about three miles away. A certain unusual tree grew on its slopes.

'Fly to that mountain and bring me back a leaf from the tree which grows there,' said the emperor. 'Then I will believe you.'

The Hindu mounted the horse, turned a peg in its neck and at once flew high into the air towards the mountain. Soon he was so tiny no one could see him. In a quarter of an hour he returned, circled over the palace and then landed gently, with the leaf of the tree in his hand.

2
August

The Magic Horse

Everyone exclaimed with wonder at such a feat. The emperor asked the price of the horse. He was furious when the Hindu said he would only part with it if he could marry

The Magic Horse

Meanwhile Prince Firoze had risen into the air, without realizing his danger. It was not until he tired of the view and thought of descending that he understood his helplessness. He turned the peg in the horse's neck to and fro, but that did not help. Desperately he felt all round the horse's neck and back, but found nothing. Then by chance his hand fell on a peg in the horse's ear. He turned it and to his relief saw that he was returning to earth.

By this time, night had fallen. The prince did not know where he was and he could not see where he was going. He let the reins lie loose on the horse's neck and hoped for the best. Presently the horse alighted gently and the prince scrambled from its back faint with hunger and thirst.

Prince Firoze looked about him and saw that he was on the terrace of a magnificent palace. All was dark and silent as the prince groped his way forward, hoping to find someone who would give him food.

Finding a half open door, he stepped inside. To his horror, he found he was in a

the emperor's daughter.

'What insolence,' he shouted. 'My daughter could never marry a common fellow like you!'

The Hindu turned and said he would take the horse and offer it to another king. However, the emperor's son, Prince Firoze, could not bear to think that the horse should be lost to them. He jumped on to its back and turning the peg in the horse's neck, as he had seen the Hindu do, he soared into the air. Away he went until he became a tiny speck and finally vanished into the clouds.

Prince Firoze did not return.

The emperor was grief stricken and blamed the Hindu for his son's misfortune.

'It is not my fault if your son stole my horse without bothering to learn how to ride it,' protested the man.

Nevertheless, he was thrown into prison and guarded day and night.

The emperor told the Hindu that if Prince Firoze did not return safely within three months, he would be killed. Then everyone waited and waited, but the prince did not come back.

room filled with men holding drawn swords. Fortunately they were asleep, but the prince realized he must be in the apartments of a very important person.

4
August

The Magic Horse

Once more Prince Firoze crept forward, stepping over the sleeping men. Being a prince himself, he hoped to appeal for help to whoever was lying in the inner room. He crept through a curtained archway into a richly furnished chamber. Sleeping on a raised bed in the middle of the room was a beautiful princess. Prince Firoze tiptoed to her side and touched her arm. She woke in alarm at seeing a stranger at her bedside. She opened her mouth to call the swordsmen to slay the prince, but he begged her to be silent and then told her his strange story.

The princess was amazed when she heard he came from Persia.

'This is Bengal,' she said, 'hundreds of miles from your father's palace. However,

do not despair. Go back to the terrace and I will send my handmaidens out to receive you. They will bring you food and show you to a room for the night. In the morning we will talk of what can be done to help you.'

Prince Firoze was a handsome young man and the princess, who was the daughter of the Rajah of Bengal, fell in love with him. The prince returned her affection and stayed for many weeks living in the palace.

5
August

The Magic Horse

Prince Firoze knew he must return to Persia to his own kingdom for the sake of his father. He asked the princess if she would marry him, but there were difficulties.

'I believe your story,' she said, 'but my father, the rajah, will not let me marry you, unless you can prove you are a rich prince.'

It was agreed that the prince should go to Persia and return with rich gifts and a marriage contract for the princess, but at the last they could not bear to be parted and early one morning, Prince Firoze and the princess flew away on the magic horse and in secret.

Two hours later they saw the town of Persia beneath them. The prince guided the horse down to land at a small palace outside the city.

'You wait here,' he said to the princess. 'I will tell my father of our arrival and he will prepare a welcome worthy of your high rank.'

He left the princess and rode to see his father, who was overjoyed at his son's safe return after so long an absence.

The emperor ordered a feast to be prepared and also released the unfortunate Hindu from prison.

However the Hindu's heart was filled with hatred and a longing for revenge. He had been imprisoned for months, when he had done no wrong. He hurried towards the palace where the princess was waiting.

6
August

The Magic Horse

The Hindu learned that the magic horse and Prince Firoze's intended bride were at a palace outside town. He hurried to the gates of this palace and told the guard he had been sent by the emperor to carry the princess on the magic horse to the great palace in town. Knowing that the Hindu was the inventor of the horse, the guard believed his story. The man was taken before the princess, who also believed him and willingly mounted the magic horse behind him and flew up into the sky.

As the Emperor of Persia, his son Prince Firoze and the courtiers rode in rich robes along the highway from town, they were horrified to see the Hindu flying over their heads with the princess sitting behind him.

They shouted and waved their fists in anger and called all sorts of threats to the

Hindu, if he did not restore the princess to them. But the Hindu merely jeered at their helplessness and flew on his way.

The unfortunate princess now realized she was being kidnapped, but could do nothing for fear of falling to her death from the sky.

The magic horse flew through the sky all night and in the morning landed in a forest in the kingdom of Kashmir. The Hindu tied the princess to a tree to prevent her from escaping and then went to look for food of which they were greatly in need.

7
August

The Magic Horse

The princess shouted and screamed for help and attracted the attention of the Sultan of Kashmir, who was out hunting. The sultan and his men rode towards the princess, but before she could tell her story, the Hindu returned and said that she was his wife and that the sultan had no right to interfere in their affairs.

However the princess screamed out that the man was not her husband, but that she was really meant to be the bride of the Prince of Persia and she begged the Sultan of Kashmir to rescue her.

Seeing that the girl was richly dressed and spoke like a princess, the sultan believed her. He ordered his men to cut off the Hindu's head, and he took the princess back to his palace. He also took the magic horse and stored it in his treasure house.

The princess was happy, thinking that she would soon return to Persia and be married to Prince Firoze. However, the days went by and the Sultan of Kashmir seemed in no hurry to provide her with escorts for the journey. Finally he admitted that he was planning to marry the beautiful princess himself.

'You are the Princess of Bengal,' he said.
'That is a rich country, with which I should
like to be in alliance. We shall marry as
soon as I can arrange the marriage feast.'

Again the poor princess was plunged
into despair. The only plan she could think
of was to pretend to be mad.

The Sultan of Kashmir promised a rich
reward to anyone who could cure the
princess of her madness. This special
announcement was spread to all the towns
and villages.

8
August

The Magic Horse

Meanwhile Prince Firoze of Persia was
searching far and wide for the princess, his
lost bride. At last in a town of Hindustan,
he heard tales of a princess of Bengal, who
had arrived in Kashmir on a flying horse
and was now sick with madness. He hurried
to the palace of the Sultan of Kashmir and
pretending to be a doctor, was allowed to
see the princess. They recognized each
other and hastily planned their escape.

Prince Firoze told the Sultan of Kashmir
that the flight on the magic horse had so
shocked the princess, that only sitting on
the horse once more and seeing that it
could not harm her, would restore her to a
normal state of mind.

He told the sultan to put the horse in the
courtyard of the palace and let the princess
sit upon it. Then the prince placed incense
all around the horse. He chanted magic
sounding words and set light to the incense.
At once dense smoke blew up and swirled
round the courtyard. The prince then
leaped on to the horse's back, turned the
knob on its neck and together they flew
high in the air. To the fury of the sultan,
watching helplessly from below, they flew
out of his kingdom, out of his power and
safe home to Persia.

The princess's father, who had travelled
from Bengal, was waiting for her in Persia.

How happy the princess was to be free at
last and together with her beloved Prince
Firoze. Her father agreed to their marriage
and a great wedding was held. From that
day on the Princess of Bengal lived with her
prince in happiness and contentment. They
never rode the horse again.

9
August

The Not So Silly Cockerel

Once upon a time there was a vain and proud cockerel. However, he was a good-hearted fellow, in spite of his silly vanity. He became friendly with a dog and they agreed to travel together.

One evening, they found themselves in a forest and as usual the cockerel flew into the branches of a tree to roost while the dog settled down in the hollow trunk of the same tree. After chatting for a while, when the cockerel told some of his funny stories, for he was an amusing fellow, they both fell asleep.

In the morning the cockerel woke at dawn, as cockerels do, and crowed and preened his feathers and crowed some more and made a big silly show of himself.

A passing fox thought he would eat the cockerel for his breakfast.

'Do come down and talk to me,' he called. 'I should so like to shake the hand of a creature with a beautiful voice like yours.'

'Certainly,' beamed the cockerel, 'knock at the door and ask my butler to let you in.'

Suspecting no trickery from the silly, vain cockerel, the fox banged at the foot of the tree and the dog rushed out and ate him.

The lesson of this story is that people are not always as silly as they look.

10
August

Soldier Teddy

Soldier Teddy had been all around the world. In his youth, he had belonged to an army family. He had travelled to hot countries and to cold countries, to wet countries and to dry countries, to windy countries and to quiet countries. He had climbed mountains and forded rivers. He had travelled by plane, and jeep and ship and horse. He had been to big cities and lonely deserts.

Soldier Teddy had been everywhere and seen everything.

'What was the food like?' the other toys would ask him.

'Oh, usually ghastly,' he would reply, 'all grease and garlic, or all pasta and no meat, or raw fish and seaweed. We had to carry cabinets full of medicine with us to settle our poor tummies.'

'What about seasickness? Or airsickness? Or travelling on camel-back sickness in the desert?' a blue rabbit asked.

'The first year was the worst,' Soldier Teddy said, with a brave smile. 'After that you got used to it or else you were sent home as a failure.'

There was a little silence at such a terrible thought.

'Of course, that never happened to me,' said Soldier Teddy.

'Of course not,' agreed the others.

'One teddy who joined the teddy army because he wanted to see the world, was always sick.' Soldier Teddy remembered. 'He didn't last even six months.'

11
August

Soldier Teddy

Then one day, a young teddy bear with light golden fur came in all a-twitter with excitement. He was going to join an army

family and set off round the world, just as Soldier Teddy had done so many years before.

'Please give me some advice,' he said. 'Tell me what medicines to take against all that foreign food. What should I do about sunburn? What is best to take into the desert, water or orange juice? Is one thick coat better in the cold weather or two thin ones?'

Soldier Teddy held up a paw.

'A sensible young fellow like you will learn all that as you go along,' he said. 'I will now give you the advice an old soldier gave me when I was young. Following it brought me home safely from many far lands.'

'What is it?' asked the young bear eagerly. 'Carry plenty of money? Learn lots of foreign languages?'

'No,' said Soldier Teddy. 'The advice is: "Never go out alone and always carry a big stick".'

'Thank you,' smiled the young bear. 'I will remember that.'

And he never came to any harm the wide world over.

12
August

The One Bite

The old bull stood munching the grass and buttercups in the meadow and chatting over the hedge to the donkey in the next field.

Suddenly up ran a fine young dog, newly come to the farm and scarcely more than a puppy. The young dog wanted to prove what a brave fellow he was. He ran into the meadow, wanting to show the bull he was a hound to be reckoned with. First he ran round and round him in circles, barking ferociously. Then he began snapping at his heels, till finally he bit the bull's leg.

Naturally, the bull could not let the dog

get away with this. He chased him and gave him a little kick and a prod with his horns, just enough to teach him to treat the bull with respect from then on, but not enough to harm him.

The donkey was amazed.

'You could easily have killed the dog,' he said. 'Why didn't you?'

'Oh,' said the old bull, 'he is young and inexperienced. Every dog is allowed one bite, but if he tries again, then I will really punish him.'

The lesson of this story is that the young are allowed one foolish act, but they should learn from experience. Like the dog, they will be allowed no more than one bite.

13
August

The Twelve Dancing Princesses

Once upon a time there was a king who had twelve beautiful daughters. They all slept together in a hall. Every night the king locked the door, but every morning, when he unlocked it, he found that the princesses' shoes had been danced to pieces. No one could explain this, least of all the princesses.

The king sent out a proclamation saying whoever could discover how the shoes became worn could choose one of the princesses as his wife and inherit the kingdom; but if after three nights, he had not discovered the secret, he would be executed.

A noble prince came forward to try to solve the mystery. He was given a bed in the room outside the princesses' hall and the door to the hall was left open so the princesses could not dance nor leave without being seen. The prince tried to keep watch, but soon his eyelids drooped and he fell asleep. In the morning the shoes were worn out, as usual, but the prince could not say why. The same thing happened three nights running and after the third night, the unfortunate young man lost his head.

Many other noblemen tried their luck too, but they all failed and lost their heads.

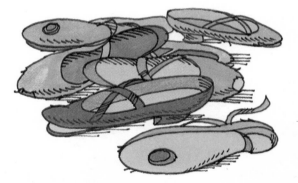

The Twelve Dancing Princesses

A poor soldier happened to be walking through this same kingdom, when he fell in with an old woman. They chatted as they walked and the soldier said that he would like to find out how the princesses wore out their shoes, so he could be king.

'That is not so difficult,' replied the old woman. 'All you need do is to avoid drinking the wine given to you at bedtime, and take this cloak.'

So saying, she gave the soldier a short cloak, which she said would make him invisible when he put it on.

All this gave the poor soldier the courage to go to the palace and offer to solve the mystery. He was well received and given a bed outside the princesses' room. At bedtime, the eldest princess arrived and gave the soldier a glass of wine. However,

he only pretended to drink it. Then he settled down in his bed and presently started to snore, but all the while he was watching the princesses through half closed eyes.

When they heard the soldier snoring, they laughed and said:

'He is as stupid as the others.'

Then they took their lovely dresses from their cupboards, put them on together with their finest jewellery and of course their shoes. Then the eldest princess tapped a flagstone in the floor of the room. It opened to reveal a staircase down which the laughing girls went.

However, the youngest princess paused.

'You may laugh,' she said, 'but I feel strange. Something is wrong.'

'You are just being silly,' replied the others and hurried on down the steps.

The Twelve Dancing Princesses

As soon as the girls were out of sight, the soldier put on the short cloak given to him by the old woman, and became invisible. He hurried down the steps after the princesses, not wishing to lose them in the dim light, and accidentally trod on the cloak of the youngest princess.

She was frightened and asked who was holding on to her dress.

'Oh, no-one,' called her sisters. 'Your clothes must have caught on a nail. Do not make such a fuss.'

On they all went until they reached the foot of the steps and stood in an avenue of trees, whose leaves were made of silver.

'I must pick one of these leaves to prove I have been here,' thought the soldier.

As he picked a leaf, its stalk snapped loudly and again the youngest princess

heard the noise and said that something was wrong. Once more her sisters laughed at her and they went on their way.

With the soldier close behind them, the princesses walked along the avenue of silver trees, to another of golden trees and a third avenue hung with diamonds. In each avenue the soldier broke a twig from a tree, but although the youngest princess heard him and warned the other princesses of trouble, no one would believe her.

16
August

The Twelve Dancing Princesses

The princesses came to a lake and by the shore of the lake twelve handsome princes in twelve small boats were waiting. Each princess greeted a prince, then climbed into a boat and set off across the lake. The soldier, made invisible by his cloak, managed to scramble into the last boat before it pulled away from the shore.

'This boat is heavy tonight,' groaned the prince in the last boat. 'I am having to use all my strength to pull it along.'

'The hot weather must be making you tired,' said the youngest princess, who sat in the boat with him and with the soldier.

On the other side of the lake all the princes and princesses went into a beautiful palace and danced till dawn. They danced so much the princesses' shoes were in tatters.

When the princesses returned to their room at dawn, the soldier hurried ahead of them, lay down in his bed and started to snore. As the girls, worn out with dancing, climbed into their own beds, they glanced at the soldier and said:

'We are quite safe. He saw nothing.'

Their beautiful dresses were back in the cupboards and their worn-out shoes were under their beds.

17
August

The Twelve Dancing Princesses

The next day the soldier said nothing of what he had learned. He wanted to go again to the strange kingdom at the foot of the steps. That night he again followed the princesses into the beautiful palace where they danced with the handsome princes. This time, when the youngest princess went to drink from a glass of wine, the soldier drank from it himself before it could reach her lips. She was frightened and called to her sisters:

'Some unseen person is drinking my wine!'

'Rubbish! You have drunk it without noticing,' they laughed.

When the youngest princess complained that someone was snatching the food from her plate, the eldest princess told her to be silent and make no more trouble.

After the third night, on which the soldier had kept watch outside the princesses' room, the king sent for him and asked:

'Can you tell me how my daughters wear out their dancing shoes?'

'Yes, Your Majesty,' replied the soldier. 'They go to an underground palace and dance the night away with twelve princes.'

Then he showed the king the leaves of silver and gold and the diamonds he had picked from the underground avenues. The youngest princess called to her sisters:

'I heard the picking of the leaves. I told you something was wrong, but you would not believe me. We are betrayed.'

18
August

The Twelve Dancing Princesses

Then the princesses, seeing there was no help for it, admitted everything to their father. The king sent a magician to the underground palace, where he discovered that the princes were under a spell and were only too eager to be released and allowed to go back to their own lands. This was done. Then the king turned to the soldier.

'As I promised, you may choose one of my daughters for your wife,' he said.

'Oh well,' said the soldier. 'I am no longer young. I will marry the eldest.'

At this the court exclaimed in admiration and pleasure, as the eldest daughter was supposed to marry first.

There was a great wedding party and the kingdom was promised to the soldier, when the king should die. Good husbands were also found for the other princesses.

And all the husbands kept a close watch on the dancing shoes of their wives.

The Old Woman and her Pig

Long ago, out in the country, a woman found a penny. She was pleased with her good luck and went to market and used the penny to buy a pig. She tied some string to the leg of the pig and led it towards her home. However, on the way they came to a stile, over which the pig refused to jump. The old lady called to a dog:

'Dog, dog, bite my pig! The pig won't jump over the stile and I shall never get home tonight.'

The dog refused, so the woman looked for a stick and said to it:

'Stick, stick, beat the dog! The dog will not bite the pig. The pig will not jump over the stile and I shall never get home tonight.'

The stick refused, so the woman found a fire and called to it:

'Fire, fire, burn the stick! The stick will not beat the dog. The dog will not bite the pig. The pig will not jump over the stile and I shall not get home tonight.'

The fire would not, so the woman looked for some water and called to it:

'Water, water, put out the fire! The fire will not burn the stick. The stick will not beat the dog. The dog will not bite the pig. The pig will not jump over the stile and I shall not get home tonight.'

The water refused, so the woman looked for an ox and called:

'Ox, ox, drink the water! The water will not put out the fire. The fire will not burn the stick. The stick will not hit the dog. The dog will not bite the pig. The pig will not jump over the stile and I shall never get home tonight.'

'Give me an apple, first,' said the ox.

The woman did. The ox drank the water. The water put out the fire. The fire burnt the stick. The stick beat the dog. The dog bit the pig. The pig jumped over the stile and the woman got home that night.

20
August

If I Had a Donkey

Long ago, there lived a little boy who liked to sit at the front window of his home, watching the world go by.

In those days loads were not carried in trucks, but on the backs of donkeys. The boy used to watch well-fed donkeys trotting strongly by, and thin, starved donkeys dragging sadly along the road.

He reckoned he learned all about the right way to treat donkeys, just by watching from the front window.

He made up a rhyme about it and it goes like this:

'If I had a donkey that wouldn't go,
Would I beat him? Oh no, no.
I'd put him in the barn and give him some corn,
The best little donkey that ever was born.'

21
August

The Oak and the Reeds

Once a tall oak tree grew on the banks of a river. The tree was strong and proud and it stood firm against any wind which blew. It was always jeering at the reeds on the riverbank, which bowed and yielded to the slightest breeze.

'It must be terrible to be weak and feeble like you! How much better to be big and strong like me,' he would laugh.

Then one day a mighty hurricane blew and uprooted the tall oak tree and flung it on its side amongst the reeds.

The tree was furious that it was wrecked, while the reeds were living as happily as ever.

'How is it that I, who am so strong, have been thrown over, while you still stand upright?' it asked.

'You were stubborn and fought against something which proved stronger than you,' said the reeds. 'We bent and gave way and the wind passed harmlessly over our heads. Sometimes it is better to bend before the wind than to oppose it.'

Alas, the tall oak tree had learned his lesson too late. He had no choice but to stay there and wait to be chopped up for firewood.

22
August

Sailor Teddy

Sailor Teddy Bear had been round the world several times.

'Oh yes, I've been around,' he would say, smiling pityingly at the other toys, most of whom had not been further than the swings in the park at the end of the road.

'Did you ever meet Sinbad the Sailor?' Dolly asked one day. 'I understand he had a lot of exciting adventures.'

'So he said,' replied Teddy. 'Personally I think he told some very tall stories. I mean take that business about the whale. I could scarcely believe a word of it, but see what you think. Sinbad tried to make me believe that he went aboard a ship with a lot of goods, which he intended to sell in India. While he was sailing down the Gulf, the ship was becalmed and, seeing a little island, the captain said they could go ashore for a picnic.'

Teddy sniffed.

'Pretty slack discipline it all sounded to me. In my day, when we were becalmed, the captain always found plenty of work for us to do, cleaning out below decks and mending the sails and so on. None of this going soft with fancy picnics. However, row ashore on this little island they did – and how they wished they hadn't! It was a very strange island. Nothing grew on it. That should have warned them.'

23
August

Sailor Teddy

'They had not been long on this island,' said Teddy, 'when it started to heave and roll and it turned out it was not an island at all, but a whale.'

Teddy stopped for a little laugh.

'I don't know where those sailors got their training,' he said, 'but if they couldn't tell the difference between an island and a whale, I'm glad I didn't go to their naval academy! Anyway, when the whale dived under the sea, some of the men were saved and went back to their ship, but Sinbad was overlooked and left clinging to a spar of wood. At that moment the wind got up and the captain hauled up his sails.'

Here Teddy had another sly laugh.

'He had been taught enough to trim his sails to a good wind, so that was something to be grateful for. However, it was bad luck for Sinbad, who was left all on his little own, floating in the Gulf of Arabia. The poor fellow swam all day and all night and at dawn stumbled ashore on a real island. I did ask him,' said Teddy, 'why he had not been eaten by sharks, as had most unfortunate people, who had fallen overboard in those seas and he said he supposed he was lucky. I gave him a hard look and said it was so lucky almost to pass belief, but he said that was the way it had happened and then went on with his story without a blush.'

24
August

Sailor Teddy

'Sinbad told me,' said Sailor Teddy, 'that the people on this island were very kind to him and fed him and gave him clothes and took him to see the king, who made a big

fuss of him and let him live at the palace all for nothing. I did venture to mention to Sinbad,' said Sailor Teddy, 'that when I had landed on islands in the Gulf, the folk there had wanted paying for food and clothes and a night's lodging, just like they do everywhere else in the world. And how was it he had not been sold as a slave or set to work sweeping the streets, as would any other penniless drifter? But he shrugged and said Allah was watching over him. And I said, "indeed he must have been", and on the story went.

'One day, when Sinbad was strolling round the docks, not having to soil his hands with work like the rest of us, you understand, whom should he meet but the captain of the ship on which he had set sail for India in the first place. The captain had landed on the island to trade and there, standing on the docks were the crates of goods which actually belonged to Sinbad. The captain had just sold them and was putting the money into his pocket.

'Sinbad had to pinch himself to make sure he wasn't dreaming. He wasn't prepared to watch someone else pocket his money.'

Sailor Teddy

'Sinbad rushed up to the captain and said that he was Sinbad, not drowned at all, but alive and well, and how about giving him the money he had just obtained from selling Sinbad's goods.'

Here Teddy paused and looked at Dolly and said:

'When Sinbad told me this last part of the story, I did say to him that if he thought I would believe that, then he must think I would believe anything, but he swore it was true. He said that when the captain saw him he said:

' "Sinbad! How wonderful to see you! I am so pleased you are safe. I am delighted to give you the money I just got for selling your goods and I will not deduct a penny for transporting the goods or unloading them or selling them. All the money is yours." So Sinbad became a rich man and paid for a passage home and lived in luxury for many years.'

Teddy smiled. 'I thanked Sinbad very much for telling me his story, but I did venture to add that they had some very unusual sea captains in those parts.'

Dolly smiled. 'That was a lovely story,' she said. 'You must tell us about Sinbad again.'

On the back of the Tiger

Once there was a big, fierce tiger living near a rajah's palace in India. The rajah was cruel and greedy and ruled his people badly.

At last the rajah's subjects could stand his rule no longer and asked the Wise Man in the mountains how they could get rid of

Man's advice had been no use. Then the tiger decided to run away into the forest and there was nothing the rajah could do to stop him. His subjects wondered why the rajah did not jump from the tiger's back and come home. Then they realized that if the rajah dismounted from the tiger's back, the tiger would be able to attack him. Only while he stayed on the tiger's back was the rajah safe.

So the tiger ran away with the rajah and neither of them was ever seen again. And from that day on, the subjects of the rajah lived happily.

From that tale comes the saying: He who rides on the back of the tiger can never dismount.

27
August

Diddle, Diddle, Dumpling

Not long ago, there was a mother who was busy getting the food ready for some visitors who were coming to dinner.

She said to her son, John:

'John, just for once, could you get yourself ready for bed? Take off your clothes, have a good wash, clean your teeth,

the rajah with no danger to themselves.

'That is easy,' replied the Wise Man. 'Say to him, that powerful and brave and clever as he is, yet there is one creature stronger and more clever than he and that is the tiger who prowls round his palace.

'When the rajah says he is as clever and brave as the tiger, tell him that the only way he can prove it, is to ride on the tiger's back. That will show that he is master of the tiger.'

The subjects did as the Wise Man said. The rajah laughed and said:

'I can easily ride on the back of the tiger. That is no problem to a brave, clever man like me.'

He climbed into a tree above a path where the tiger often prowled. When the tiger walked beneath, the rajah dropped on to his back and rode him up and down for everyone to see. He seemed to be coming to no harm, for the tiger could not reach the rajah with either his teeth or his claws.

For a while it seemed that the Wise

put on your nightclothes and go to bed. It's easy really and you can leave the lights on and your bedroom door open. You will hear me about downstairs and there will be no need to feel lonely.'

John was a good boy so he agreed.

But whilst he was getting undressed, he kept popping downstairs to taste the soup, try the fish sauce, bite into a dumpling and, of course, to lick the chocolate sauce spoon clean! In fact, John paid such poor attention to what he was supposed to be doing, that he went to bed half-dressed.

How his mother did laugh when she saw him in the morning! She made up a rhyme about it and here it is:

'Diddle, diddle, dumpling, my son, John,
Went to bed with his stockings on,
One shoe off and one shoe on,
Diddle, diddle, dumpling, my son, John!'

28
August

The Town Mouse
and the
Country Mouse

One summer evening, a Town Mouse took a stroll in the country and met a Country Mouse at the edge of a wood. The Country Mouse was eating nuts from a hazel thicket and fine fat nuts they were.

'I must say it seems pleasant in the country,' said the Town Mouse. 'Do you enjoy life here?'

'Yes, indeed,' replied the Country Mouse. 'We have fresh air and sunshine, beautiful trees and bushes laden with berries and nuts, and streams of clear water. What is it like in town?'

'Oh, very nice,' replied the Town Mouse. 'It is all elegance and delicate living in town.'

The two mice chatted for a while and it was arranged that the Town Mouse should visit the Country Mouse for Christmas and that the Country Mouse should visit the Town Mouse at the New Year.

29
August

The Town Mouse
and the
Country Mouse

When Christmas came, the Town Mouse set out for the burrow of the Country Mouse. The lanes were not filled with warm sunshine and no soft breezes blew. Snow lay thick upon the ground and the wind was bitter.

The Town Mouse had to struggle hard to reach the Country Mouse's hole and arrived wet and exhausted.

The Country Mouse had done her best to prepare a welcome for her friend. She fetched out her store of nuts and dried roots which she had saved from summertime, and she showed the Town Mouse the underground stream which flowed damply at one end of the burrow.

The Town Mouse felt cold and wet for the whole of her visit. She thought the food was nothing but poor scraps. She was glad when it was time to take the Country Mouse back for a stay in town.

The Town Mouse
and the
Country Mouse

The house in which the Town Mouse lived was warm from the fires which the lady of the house kept burning in the grate.

The Town Mouse's larder was full of cheese and butter and pieces of cherry cake and candle ends and pastry and many more good things which she took from the larder and the kitchen floor.

As for drinking water, the Town Mouse would not dream of it. She drank the drippings from the barrels of beer and the spillings from the wine bottles.

At first the Country Mouse thought that life in town was marvellous. However, one evening, the cat came stalking across the cellar floor.

The Country Mouse was too full of good food and drink to run away and the cat caught her.

The Town Mouse
and the
Country Mouse

Hearing the squeals of the Country Mouse, the Town Mouse, who was used to dodging the cat, hid in her hole and kept quiet.

The Country Mouse looked into the cat's yellow eyes and pleaded:

'Do not eat me and I will tell you a story.'

'Make it a good one, then,' purred the cat.

'Once upon a time there were two mice,' said the Country Mouse.

'Good,' purred the cat. 'When I have eaten you, I will catch the other one.'

'But one was a Country Mouse and thin and not worth eating,' went on the Country Mouse desperately.

'I'm not snobbish,' smiled the cat. 'I don't look down on folk from the country.'

The cat was opening its mouth to eat the Country Mouse, when the lady of the house called and the cat had to go running. Thankfully the Country Mouse scurried into the Town Mouse's hole.

'I'm not staying in town another moment,' shivered the Country Mouse. 'The living may be fine, but I almost lost my life.'

She hurried home and the lesson of that story is that folk are safer in their own familiar surroundings.

September

1
September

Wee Willie Winkie

Long ago a Mr. Wilbur Winkie was mayor of a town. Mr. Winkie had a son named William.

'What does a mayor do?' William asked his father.

'He has to see that everything in town is managed correctly and that everyone does as they should,' replied Mr. Wilbur Winkie.

'I should like to be mayor when I grow up,' smiled Master William Winkie.

'Then you must start practising now,' said his father, meaning that William should behave himself and keep his room tidy and things of that sort.

However, as we always believe what we want to believe, William thought his father meant him to run round telling folk what they should or should not do. He did not dare to tell the grown-ups what to do, so he thought he would tell the children when they ought to be in bed.

That evening, as soon as William had been put to bed, he jumped up again and ran round the town telling the other children they ought to be in bed. Evening after evening he ran round the town, until his mother found out and put a stop to it.

Some folk made up a rhyme about William which went like this:

'Wee Willie Winkie runs through the town,
Upstairs and downstairs, in his nightgown;
Rapping at the window, crying through the lock,
"Are the children in their beds? It's past eight o'clock".'

2
September

The Fairy Cup

One night, a blacksmith had been visiting his friend in the next village. He stayed longer than he should and it was night-time when he rode home on his good horse.

Suddenly, to his surprise, he heard the sound of laughter and merry voices and the clinking of cups and knives on plates.

He dismounted and crept from the road to where a door stood open in the side of a

large, grassy mound. A brilliant light shone from inside the mound and looking in, the blacksmith saw the Fairy Folk feasting and dancing.

He was frightened and would have run away, but the fairies saw him and invited him to join them. He dared not refuse.

One of the fairy men handed him a golden cup and told him to drink. Instead of drinking, the blacksmith turned and ran away with the cup, because he knew it was very valuable. All the Fairy Folk ran shouting after him, but the blacksmith's horse was swift and no one caught him.

The blacksmith reached home and set the cup on his table. Whenever he looked into it he found money and he became a rich man. But he was not happy. He knew he had done wrong and he was afraid to step outside his house in case the Fairy Folk were waiting to catch him. He stayed indoors for the rest of his life and was miserable, which proves it is wrong to steal, especially from Fairy Folk.

3
September

The Magic Mill

Once there were two brothers. One, Richard, was rich and the other, Thomas, was poor. Thomas was always begging from Richard and Richard became tired of it. One Christmas he gave Thomas a fine leg of ham on condition that he walked to Timbuctoo with it.

'Timbuctoo is a long way away,' he smiled. 'I shall not see Thomas again for many weeks.'

Thomas took the ham and walked to Timbuctoo, where, as it happened, ham was rare and highly valued. He exchanged the leg of ham for a mill, which would grind forth anything he wanted. He learned the words to control the mill and went home.

Thomas soon became rich. Anything he wanted from food to money to clothes, he asked the mill to grind for him, and it did.

Richard became jealous and said Thomas should give the mill to him, as it had been obtained in return for his ham.

'Very well,' agreed Thomas and gave the mill to his brother.

Richard hurried home to his wife feeling highly pleased.

'Now we can have anything we want,' he smiled.

'Then let us start by asking for herrings and bread and broth for lunch. That will

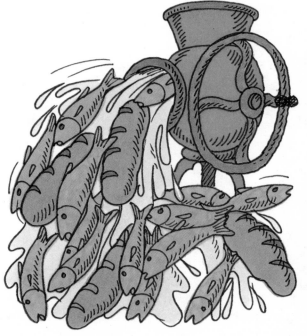

save me having to do any work,' said his wife.

Richard agreed and setting the mill on the table, he ordered it to grind herrings and bread and broth. In a moment the food came spilling out on to the table.

It covered the table and the floor and poured out of the windows. It covered the yard and went in a tide to meet the workers coming in from the fields.

No matter what Richard said, the mill would not stop grinding. For Richard had forgotten to ask the correct words to stop the mill. He had to run to Thomas's house and beg him to halt the mill and take it back.

Thomas agreed in return for three hundred golden crowns, which Richard gladly gave him.

4

September

The Magic Mill

Thomas became so rich that he put tiles of gold on his house. The gold shone so brightly in the sunshine that a sea captain saw them gleaming as he sailed by and came ashore to admire such an unusual sight.

When he heard about the mill, he begged to buy it and Thomas sold it to him for many hundreds of gold coins.

'He will soon bring it back when he finds he cannot stop it,' thought Thomas, not telling the unfortunate captain that the mill would stop only at the command of certain magic words.

The captain took the mill and put to sea. Hardly was the ship in deep water than the ship's cook came on deck and said he had forgotten to bring cooking salt with him.

'No matter,' smiled the captain.

He set the mill on the deck of the ship and ordered it to grind salt.

This the mill did and went on grinding, grinding and grinding. No matter how much the captain shouted at it to stop, the mill went on grinding salt until the ship sank under the weight and went to the bottom of the sea. Even there the mill went on grinding salt. Indeed, it is grinding to this day. And that is why the sea is salty.

5

September

Teddy's Biscuit Tale

It was four o'clock and the toys were sitting cosily in front of the fire while Dolly poured tea and handed round a plate of biscuits.

'I wonder where that saying "dry as a biscuit" comes from,' she said. 'I know biscuits need to be crisp, but these chocolate and jam sandwich biscuits are not really dry. I think they are delicious.'

Sailor Teddy looked up from putting a third lump of sugar into his tea and said:

'Ah – only we old sailors know the true meaning of "dry as a biscuit". Ah – the weeks of hardship and brave suffering there are in that simple remark.'

'Tell us about it then,' said Dolly, 'and

you can miss out the bit where you suffer terrible hardships sailing round Cape Horn. You have told us about that over and over again. We know that. Get straight to the part about the dry biscuits.'

'Well,' said Sailor Teddy, 'in those far off days, when we were coming back from Cape Horn.' He paused for a moment to glare at Dolly and then went on:

'It was a long haul up from the South Atlantic and we were running short on rations.'

6
September

Teddy's Biscuit Tale

'There was not much of anything left,' said Sailor Teddy, 'but ship's biscuits and some stale water at the bottom of a barrel. Two sips of water in the morning and two sips of water in the evening were all we were allowed. Our mouths became dry and our lips cracked. Imagine trying to eat hard ship's biscuits in a state like that. Why, the biscuits seemed like the hardest things we had ever had to eat. And of course at the end of the voyage, as we were, the biscuits were the hardest they had ever been because they were so old and stale. I tell you, we were so desperate that if we found weevils in the biscuits we were quite pleased. At least they were soft.

'So,' said Sailor Teddy, 'the saying really was "Dry as a ship's biscuit at the end of a voyage". However, we old sailors remember all about it. We are not likely to forget hardships like that. Did I ever tell you about the second time I was sailing round Cape Horn before the mast. . .'

'Thank you, Teddy, that is enough, very interesting, but enough,' smiled Dolly. 'Would you like another chocolate biscuit?'

'Yes, please,' said Sailor Teddy.

7
September

The Barking Dog

Once there was a dog who always barked when he travelled in the back seat of a car.

'I wish I knew how to stop that dog from barking in the back seat of the car,' said his owner.

He tried playing soft music as they drove along. That did not work.

He tried talking to the dog as they drove along. That did not work.

He tried singing to the dog. He even gave him a bone to chew and a dog biscuit. But nothing worked.

'Will you give me a chocolate cake if I tell you how to stop the dog from barking in the back seat of the car?' said the owner's little boy.

'Yes! Yes!' replied his father eagerly.

'Put him in the front seat,' said the boy.

The owner did as his son said, but the dog barked just the same.

'The dog is barking in the front seat,' complained the man.

'Yes, but he isn't barking in the back seat, is he?' smiled the boy, 'so I deserve my chocolate cake.'

8
September

Arthur
in the Cave

Many years ago, a Welshman drove his
sheep to London to sell at a good price.
When this was done, he brought a present
for his wife and then went to look at the
famous London Bridge, which in those
days had shops and houses all across it.

In his hand he held a good hazel staff,
which he had cut in the Welsh mountains
and which he needed to defend himself on
the journey. A man caught sight of the stick
and stood staring. At last he came up and
asked the Welshman where he came from.

'As good a country as this,' snapped the
Welshman, thinking he was going to be
mocked as a country boy.

'Do not take offence,' said the man. 'If
you can only remember where you cut that
stick and take my advice, you will reap
much benefit.'

Then the Welshman realized he was

talking to a sorcerer and was in two minds
what he should do. On one hand, he wished
to gain benefit, on the other, he feared to be
mixed up in magic. At last greed won and
he took the man back to Wales with him
and showed him the bush from which he
had cut the hazel stick.

9
September

Arthur
in the Cave

'This is a magic spot, as I could tell from
the hazel stick,' said the sorcerer. 'We must
dig here.'

They dug until they came to a broad, flat
stone. Prising this up, they found a
staircase. They went down the stairs and
along a narrow passage until they came to a
door.

'Are you brave?' asked the sorcerer. 'Will
you come through the door with me?'

'I will,' answered the Welshman, who
was very frightened, but very curious.

They opened the door and entered a great cave. A faint red light lit the cave and the first thing the Welshman saw was a large bell.

'Do not touch that bell,' said the sorcerer, 'or it will be the end of us.'

They walked further into the cavern and all around him the Welshman saw armed men lying asleep. They all wore shining armour with not a trace of rust. Their shields were over one arm, their swords held in the other and their spears were stuck in the ground at their sides. In the centre of the cave was a round table at which sat the leaders of the soldiers, all with their heads bent in sleep and on a golden throne at the head of the cave sat a crowned king.

10
September

Arthur in the Cave

'These men have been asleep for a thousand years,' said the sorcerer. 'They are King Arthur and his knights of the Round Table together with their men. They are waiting till the day shall come when they must rise and rescue Britain from her enemies. That sword in Arthur's hand is Excalibur.'

The sorcerer suddenly stopped talking as he caught sight of what he was really seeking – a heap of yellow gold on the floor of the cave. He hurried forward and put as much of it as he could into his pockets. He told the Welshman to take what he wanted of the gold so they could both be off. However, the Welshman was fascinated by the soldiers.

'What will awake them?' he asked.

'The ringing of the bell,' replied the sorcerer, 'but do not rouse them. Let them sleep and let us be on our way.'

He hurried the Welshman towards the door leading from the cave, but as they passed the bell, the shepherd could not resist striking it.

The noise rang through the whole cave. The hundreds of warriors leapt to their feet.

11
September

Arthur in the Cave

The sorcerer shook with terror.

'No, no! It is all a mistake,' he shouted. 'Do not awake! Go on sleeping!'

It was too late. The mighty host stirred and dazzled the shepherd with the brightness of its armour.

A voice echoed through the cave: 'Arthur awake! The day is come!'

'No, no! It hasn't! It is still night,' shrieked the desperate sorcerer.

Arthur stood up from his golden throne.

'The day has not come. The time is not yet,' he said. 'Sleep on, my warriors. Only a stealer of gold comes to disturb us. We are not yet needed to save our country.'

A sound like the distant sigh of the sea filled the cave and once more all the warriors slept.

The sorcerer and the Welshman hurried, shaking, from the cave and never dared to return. Be sure that Arthur still sleeps there, waiting for the bell to sound again.

12
September

The Miller and his Donkey

Once a miller and his son were taking a donkey to market. They had not gone far when they passed a group of women who laughed at them.

'Fancy walking, when they could ride on the donkey. What a silly pair they are!' the women laughed.

At once the miller told his son to mount the donkey and they went on along the road to market. A little way further, they met a group of old men.

'Fancy that strong young fellow riding and letting his poor old father walk!' they said. 'That is not right.'

At once the man told his son to dismount and rode the donkey himself. Further along the road they came upon a group of women and children.

'For shame, letting your son walk, when he could ride on the donkey behind you,' called one of the mothers.

Not wishing to appear unkind, the father pulled his son up behind him on the donkey's back. By this time they were almost at the market place. They saw a shopkeeper who called to them:

'You cruel men! How could two of you ride on the back of that poor little donkey! You are more fit to carry him that he is to carry the two of you.'

Not wishing to appear cruel, the miller and his son dismounted and, tying the donkey's legs to a stick, carried it over their shoulders to market.

People laughed more than ever to see a fine donkey being carried when it could easily walk. The donkey became upset at all the noise and struggling free, ran away and never came back.

The miller and his son trudged home, sadder and wiser men. In trying to please everyone, they had succeeded in pleasing no one, not even themselves.

13
September

The Biscuit Jar

A jar of tasty biscuits was standing on the table. A boy thrust in his hand, grasped as many of them as he could and then tried to pull his hand out again. However, he could not, because the neck of the jar was too narrow to let out so large a handful.

The boy's uncle was watching and gave the boy this advice:

'Don't be greedy. Let half the biscuits go, then you will easily get your hand out. It is better to be content with what you can get, than to struggle for what is impossible!'

14
September

The New Puppy

Everyone was very pleased. A new puppy had come to live in the house. However, after a few days nobody was pleased.

The puppy missed its mother and brothers and sisters. Every night it howled and cried. The miserable noise kept the whole family awake.

'Let the puppy come and sleep on my bed,' said the little girl, Sally.

'Certainly not,' snapped her father. 'The dog must learn to sleep downstairs and guard the house.'

'Perhaps we should buy another puppy to keep it company,' suggested Mother.

'Certainly not,' snapped Father again. 'One dog is expensive enough without buying two.'

Then little Jack, the youngest in the family, spoke up. He said:

'I have heard that if you put a warm hot water bottle in with a puppy, it will sleep close to it, thinking it is his warm mother and brothers and sisters and that then it sleeps quietly through the night.'

'We will try that,' smiled Father.

That very evening Mother put a warm, but not too hot, hot water bottle in with the puppy. The puppy snuggled close and slept the night through.

'Jack is the cleverest one in the family,' smiled Father.

15
September

Hansel and Gretel

Close to a large forest there once lived a woodcutter and his wife and their two children, a boy called Hansel and a girl called Gretel.

Times were hard. The whole family was hungry. One day Hansel and Gretel were sent into the forest to gather berries. They wandered too far and became lost and had to spend the night sleeping amongst the dead leaves at the foot of a tree.

In the morning they were cold and more

hungry than ever. They wandered on until they came to the strangest little cottage. The walls were made of bread, the roof of cake and the windows of transparent sugar.

Hansel was delighted. He broke a piece of cake from the roof to eat himself and cracked a window and gave some sugar to Gretel. The children sat down and ate greedily. Then they were startled to hear a voice calling from inside the house:

'Who is nibbling at my house?'

'Only the wind. Only the wind,' replied Hansel quickly, taking more cake for himself and more sugar for Gretel, for both children were very hungry. Suddenly the door of the house opened and an old woman came hobbling out, leaning on a stick. Hansel and Gretel were frightened, but the woman did not seem angry. Instead she spoke kindly and invited the children in to rest.

16
September

Hansel and Gretel

At first the old woman was kind to the two children. She cooked them a tasty dinner of pancakes and then let them sleep in two pretty white beds. However, the woman was really a witch. While Hansel was asleep, she carried him to the stable and

locked him behind a barred door. In the morning she woke Gretel and said:

'Get up, you little lazybones! From now on you will be my servant. You will bake the bread and fetch the water and clean the house. Most of all, you will cook fine meals for your brother, Hansel. I am fattening him up to eat for my dinner. He must have the best food, but you can live on scraps.'

Gretel was very upset and cried bitterly, but she could do nothing except obey the witch's orders. She worked from morning till night and took good food to Hansel, as the witch commanded. However, she also gave him a thin bone.

Every morning the witch who had poor eyesight went to visit Hansel and told him to stick his finger out between the bars of the door, so that she could feel it and see if he was getting fat. Every morning Hansel pushed the bone through the bars. The witch thought he was still thin and so he was not eaten.

After some weeks the witch said as usual: 'Stick out your finger, Hansel that I may feel whether you are getting fat.'

The boy again pushed out the bone and this time the witch grew impatient.

17
September

Hansel and Gretel

The next morning she said to Gretel:

'I can wait no longer for Hansel to become fat. Fat or thin, I will eat him for my dinner today. Boil some water and make some bread.'

Gretel wept and begged the witch to let her and her brother go, but the witch refused.

'You should not have eaten the cake and sugar from my house,' she said. 'I will have no mercy.'

Poor Gretel kneaded the dough for the bread and when it was ready, the witch told her to put it in the oven.

'Get right in with it yourself to make sure you push it well to the back,' screeched the witch.

'I cannot, I cannot! There is no room,' replied Gretel.

'Of course there is, you stupid girl. Look! I will show you,' snapped the witch, eager for the bread to be baked, so that she could get on with her dinner. She pushed Gretel

aside and climbed into the oven herself. At once Gretel slammed the door and ran to release Hansel. The witch shouted and banged on the oven door, but she could not get out.

18
September

Hansel and Gretel

Gretel unlocked the barred door, which kept her brother a prisoner. He rushed out, overjoyed to be free, hugged and kissed Gretel and the two children danced for joy.

They searched the witch's cottage and found drawers full of precious stones.

'The witch will need them no more,' said Hansel, 'let us take some to our poor father.'

He filled his pockets with pearls and rubies and diamonds and Gretel tied some up in her apron.

'Now,' said Hansel, 'we must try to find our way through this terrible forest to our own home.'

The children set out, but had not gone

far when they came to a great stretch of water. A big swan came swimming towards them. Gretel begged its help and one at a time the swan carried the children on its back to the opposite bank of the lake.

At once the children found themselves in familiar surroundings. They hurried home and threw their arms around their father's neck. He had not known a happy moment since they had been lost and was overjoyed to hold them in his arms again. The children gave him the jewels and they lived happily for the rest of their lives.

19
September

The Spotted Dog and the Pink Rabbit

Once a toy pink rabbit lived with the same family as a toy spotted dog. They were not the best of friends.

If the spotted dog was allowed to sleep on the boy of the family's bed, the pink rabbit would be jealous and say that Spotty was being spoiled and that dogs should be trained more strictly, even toy ones.

If the pink rabbit was allowed to play at schools with the girl of the house and her dolls, the spotted dog would be jealous and say that Pinky was being given big ideas

about how clever she was and that no good would come of it.

Then one day the girl went to stay with her grandmother and took Pinky, the pink rabbit with her.

At first Spotty, the spotted dog, was pleased. Then he found he was lonely without Pinky. There was no one to chat to while the boy was out swimming; no one to watch television with, while the boy was showing the baby-sitter how the washing-up machine worked. By the time the girl and Pinky came back from the visit to Grandma, Spotty was waiting on the doorstep and calling:

'Pinky! How lovely to see you. I have missed you.'

Pinky, the pink rabbit smiled and said:

'I have missed you too.'

Then they both understood how true the saying is that, absence makes the heart grow fonder.

20
September

The Lion's Share

Once an ass agreed to go hunting with a lion. The ass worked hard, spying out the land and running after their prey, till at last they had caught a nice dinner.

'Now is the time to share out our spoil,' smiled the lion. 'We will divide it into three equal portions. I will take the first because I am the King of the Beasts. I will also take the second portion, because as your partner I am entitled to half of what remains.'

Then he stretched out his paw and rested it on the third portion.

'And I will also take this,' he growled.

'What about my share?' asked the bewildered ass.

The lion bared his sharp yellow teeth and raised his long claws.

'Do you want to argue with me?' he

roared in a terrifying voice.

But the ass ran away. He had learned that it was unwise to go into partnership with someone a lot stronger than himself. The lion will always take the lion's share.

21
September

Sailor Teddy
Meets Sinbad Again

The toys were sitting chatting one wet afternoon, when Dolly said to Sailor Teddy Bear:

'Did you ever meet Sinbad the Sailor again? I should like to hear more about his adventures.'

'I certainly did,' smiled Sailor Teddy. 'Sinbad's home was in Baghdad, you know, and we had stopped there for a few days to take on water and fresh food, when who should we meet strolling round the docks, but Sinbad.

' "Come round to dinner tonight," he invited, "and I will tell you some more about my voyages."

' "Oh yes, more tall stories," we thought to ourselves, but we smiled politely and accepted his invitation, because it was very

kind of him to offer us dinner. We couldn't help suspecting that all the local people had heard his stories too many times already and he was looking for new faces to talk to. However, be that as it may, a kind invitation was a kind invitation and round we went that evening with a nice present of tea from India, which pleased him greatly.

'He said that the tea reminded him of the time he had been sailing back from India himself and had endured the frightful adventure with the Giant Roc.'

22
September

Sailor Teddy
Meets Sinbad Again

'Sinbad served us a really delicious dinner,' said Sailor Teddy, 'then he told us that he and some companions had been sailing back from India up the Arabian Gulf, when they had landed on an island to pick fresh fruit and restock with water.'

Teddy grinned: 'I could not resist asking if this island turned out to be a whale, like that other island he landed on, but he gave me quite a cool look and said one did not make that sort of mistake twice. I refrained from saying that in Her Majesty's Navy one was not allowed to make that sort of mistake once. We were his guests, after all. Anyway, Sinbad went on to say that after picking a lot of fruit he lay down for a doze

in the sun, only to wake up and find that the others had sailed away without him. Pretty careless both of him and his companions, I thought, but perhaps they had been quarrelling. No one ever tells you the full story, do they? Quite naturally, feeling very upset, poor old Sinbad looked round the island. He found no sign of human habitation, but far inland, he caught sight of something huge and white gleaming in the sun. He had nothing else to do, so he walked towards this white object which turned out to be an egg fifty paces round.'

23
September

Sailor Teddy
Meets Sinbad Again

'So,' said Sailor Teddy, 'Sinbad said he stood in the middle of the uninhabited island staring at this simply enormous egg, when the sky above him darkened and looking up he saw a gigantic bird coming down to land. At once he realized this bird must be the Giant Roc, of which he had often heard tell, and that it was coming down to sit on the egg for the night. This proved to be true and while the bird was sitting on the egg, Sinbad crept close to it, took off his turban and using the length of cloth which made the turban, tied himself to the Giant Roc's leg. Thus they both slept all night.'

Teddy sighed. 'I suppose it was wrong of me, as I was a guest, but I could not help asking Sinbad why the Giant Roc did not notice that someone was tied to its leg. I am quite sure I should have noticed if anyone had tied himself to my leg for the night, and so I think would most people. Sinbad replied that I was not a Giant Roc with a leg as thick as a treetrunk, a fact which I could not deny, and on with the story he went. Apparently, the next dawn, the Giant Roc rose into the air, taking Sinbad with it and flew to a neighbouring island for food. This was most fortunate for Sinbad, as the second island was inhabited.'

24
September

Sailor Teddy
Meets Sinbad Again

'As the Giant Roc landed on the second island, Sinbad untied himself from its leg

and jumped to safety,' Sailor Teddy went on. 'They were high up in the mountains and at first Sinbad was delighted, because strewn on the ground around him were diamonds. He filled his pockets with the stones, enough to make him rich for life, but then he became more and more worried. He could find no way to get out of the high valley in which the Giant Roc had left him. It seemed that poor Sinbad was doomed to stay there and starve, with a fortune in diamonds in his pockets. He wandered round for hours, amongst horrible serpents and eagles which swooped to and fro, and at last lay down to sleep completely exhausted. He had not slept for long when he was woken by a large steak of best beef landing on his face. He looked round and saw lots of chunks of meat being tossed into the valley by unseen people. The pieces of meat were being picked up by the eagles and carried off. Sinbad realized he had found a way of escape.'

25
September

Sailor Teddy Meets Sinbad Again

'Well,' said Sailor Teddy, 'Sinbad told me he was trapped in this high mountain valley, when he had the idea of tying a large piece of raw meat to himself – some people were conveniently throwing raw meat into the valley you remember – then the eagles who were swooping about would pick up the raw meat, carry it out of the valley and take Sinbad with it.'

Teddy sighed: 'It did not sound like the sort of plan I should care to try, but Sinbad vowed that that was what he did. An eagle picked him up and carried him to its nest lower down the mountain. By this nest some merchants were waiting, who, it turned out, were the people who had been throwing the raw meat into the high valley. Their plan was for the raw meat to land on the diamonds in the valley; the diamonds would stick to the meat; the eagles would pick up the meat, carry it to their nests to feed their young and then the merchants would leap out and snatch the diamonds!'

Teddy shook his head and went on:

'I couldn't help saying to Sinbad that he and those merchants thought up some very risky plans. He simply replied that it was necessary to have Faith in Good Fortune.'

26
September

Sailor Teddy
Meets Sinbad Again

'Anyway,' Teddy Bear went on, 'Sinbad told me that he was standing on this mountain with his pockets full of diamonds and that these merchants he had met took even more diamonds from the nests of some eagles. Then, all feeling well pleased with themselves, they went down to the lowlands and the merchants showed Sinbad the way to the seaport, where he could pick up a ship to take him back to his home port of Baghdad.

'I did ask Sinbad,' said Teddy, 'whether he saw any more of the Giant Roc and he replied that of course he did. Rhinos and elephants were living on the island and on any day of the week you could see the Giant Roc swooping down and picking up the rhinos and the elephants or sometimes both at once and taking them home to feed their young ones in the nest.'

Teddy smiled and looked round at the other toys: 'So Sinbad went home a rich man and that was the end of that adventure.'

'How much of it did you believe?' asked Dolly.

'Well,' replied Teddy, 'Sinbad was living in a big house and was obviously rich. He must have found some diamonds somewhere, but whether it was in the way he said, or some other way he wanted to keep secret, we shall never know.'

27
September

The Yellow
Legged Cockerel

Once upon a time there was a young lad who was always boasting and talking in a loud voice. At last his grandfather said to him:

'Do not talk so loud my lad, or the same thing will happen to you as happened to the yellow legged cockerel.'

'And what did happen to that silly old cockerel?' enquired the boy in a loud voice.

166

'Well,' replied his grandfather, 'once there was a farmyard with a big full grown red cockerel and some hens and some young half grown cockerels and one of them had yellow legs. This yellow legged cockerel kept strutting about and crowing and making a big noise just as if he were the big full grown red cockerel, which he wasn't. This annoyed the big red cockerel, who cuffed the yellow legged cockerel and told him to be quiet until he was fully grown and had a farmyard of his own. However, the yellow legged cockerel had a big opinion of himself and every time the big red cockerel's back was turned, he would perch up on the farm gate and crow and strut and make a big show of himself, while the other half grown cockerels stayed quiet down in the farmyard with the hens. Now, it so happened that one day the big red cockerel was busy along the lane looking at a new nest one of the hens had made. The yellow legged cockerel seized his chance and leapt on to an upturned bucket and crowed at the top of his voice. A passing fox heard him and slipped under the farm gate and seized the yellow legged cockerel and ate him for dinner.

'Dear me!' sighed the big red cockerel. 'I feared it would come to this. I tried to warn the yellow legged cockerel, but he would not listen. It is no use crowing and strutting like a big fellow, until you are big enough to defend yourself.'

The grandfather looked at the young lad.

'So, take heed,' he said. 'Do not make a loud noise and draw attention to yourself until you are big enough to fight your enemies.'

After that the boy was always quiet, until he became a man.

28
September

The Wise Old Owl

Once upon a time there lived a farmer whose farm was overrun by mice. They ate his corn and nibbled his cheese and kept him awake at night as they scampered from attic to cellar eating anything they chose.

'We should keep a cat,' said the farmer's wife.

'No,' replied the farmer. 'I do not like cats. Their fur makes me come up in a red rash and itch all over.'

The mice heard this talk and scampered about the farm more than ever. They were quite sure the farmer could never do anything to harm them.

At last the farmer's wife said:

'I think we should ask advice from the Wise Old Owl. Folk say he is the wisest creature in the forest.'

The farmer shook his head.

'The Wise Old Owl will offer to come here and eat the mice for me,' he replied, 'but I am too kind-hearted for that. The mice are naughty, but I do not want to see them all killed.'

Nevertheless the farmer's wife did go to see the Wise Old Owl.

'There is no need for your husband to be upset,' said the Wise Old Owl. 'Tell him to make a home for me in his barn. A hole where I can fly in and out will do. Then all his problems will be over.'

The farmer followed the advice of the Wise Old Owl and the owl came to live in the barn. The night he arrived, he flew across the farmyard in the moonlight, and every creature saw his shadow. The Wise Old Owl hooted as he flew and every creature on the farm heard his too-whit, too-whoo.

At once every mouse packed its bags and left. By morning there was not a mouse on the farm. There had been no need for the Wise Old Owl to eat them. They had run away before he had the chance.

The farmer was pleased and ever since farmers and owls have been friends.

29
September

The Clever Teddy Bear

Once there was a clever teddy bear, who liked reading. He used to read all the children's books, especially the bedtime stories. He read those so often he knew them off by heart.

He used to correct Mother, when she was reading.

'No, the old lady was dressed in a red jacket, not a bed jacket,' he would say to Mother.

Then he would add:

'I do not wish to be rude, but do you think you should get some reading glasses? That is the third mistake you have made this evening.'

'Thank you, Teddy,' Mother would reply, 'My eyesight is perfect.'

Sometimes, if Mother was in a hurry, she would leave parts of the story out and

Teddy always told her about it.

'You've missed a bit,' he would say. 'Jack climbed the beanstalk three times you know, not twice.'

'Thank you, Teddy,' Mother would say with a freezing smile, wishing that Teddy was not so clever.

Then, one evening, Mother said to Teddy:

'You are so very clever, Teddy, I think you should study and take exams and become a professor.'

'I agree,' beamed Teddy, 'brains like mine should not be wasted.'

Mother bought some school books and every evening, instead of listening to bedtime stories, Teddy studied and learned a lot of important things and passed many hard exams. It took several years, but in the end he did become Professor Bear and was very happy.

In the meantime, Mother went on reading bedtime stories just as she wished and without any interference from Teddy!

30
September

The Fine Hen

Once upon a time there was a little girl who lived on a farm. She was not old enough to go to work, but she wished to earn some money to buy a pretty doll she had seen in the village shop.

'Please give me one of the new hatched chicks,' she said to her mother. 'I will look after it and feed it well and then I will sell the eggs and earn some money.'

The mother agreed and gave her daughter a chick. For weeks the little girl took the greatest care of the chick. She gave it the best food, kept it warm by night, took it out for walks in the fresh air by day. It was the healthiest hen which ever lived.

Naturally, when the hen came to lay eggs, it laid the biggest, finest tasting eggs anyone had ever seen. Word went round the village that anyone who wanted a tasty egg for tea should buy one from the little girl at the farm. The finest folk from the biggest houses came for the eggs and soon the little girl had enough money to buy her doll. The girl was so pleased, she made up this rhyme about her hen:

'Hickety, pickety, my fine hen,
She lays eggs for gentlemen;
Gentlemen come every day
To see what my fine hen doth lay.
Sometimes nine and sometimes ten,
Hickety, pickety, my fine hen.'

And the hen still lays the finest eggs.

October

The Beaten Track

A little while ago and not very far away, two boys set out to go to town. They each came from different farms, but they walked together when they met in the forest.

One wide beaten track led through the forest, but going off to the side of it were several pretty little paths lined with bushes laden with berries and with mushrooms growing in the shade.

'My father says one should always keep to the beaten track, because it is safer,' said one of the boys called John.

'You may stick to the beaten track, if you like,' said Jimmy, the other boy, 'but I am going to walk along those little paths. The grass will be nice to walk on and I shall pick berries and eat them. I can't see any berries on the side of the beaten track and all the mushrooms have been picked. I'll pick mushrooms from the sides of the little paths and meet you on the other side of the forest.'

John walked easily along the beaten track and reached the other side of the forest first. How he laughed when two hours later Jimmy came limping through the trees!

'No wonder those paths are little trodden,' gasped Jimmy. 'No sooner was I away from the beaten track than the ground became boggy and my shoes filled with water. The bushes were laden with berries because everyone else has better sense than

to tread there. The brambles met across my path and the thorns scratched me as I pushed through. A nest of bees hung in a tree I climbed to see my way and the bees came out and stung me. A fierce dog guarded a woodchopper's hut and nipped at my heels as I ran through the clearing. I stopped to pick some mushrooms, but they were swarming with ants, which bit me until I dived into a stream to wash them off. Now I am soaked to the skin and tired out and I have made up my mind: In future I

shall stick to the beaten track. It is well beaten because everyone knows it is the best route to walk.'

2
October

Snow White and the Seven Dwarfs

Long ago and far away, when the snow lay deep upon the ground, a queen sat by her window, working at her embroidery. In a careless moment, she pricked her finger and some drops of red blood fell on to the snow.

'How I wish I could have a baby daughter with skin as white as snow, lips as red as blood and hair as fine as the finest silk in my embroidery,' she said.

Her wish was granted and in the spring she held a baby girl in her arms and named the child Snow White.

Unluckily for Snow White, her mother died when she was a baby and after a year the king remarried. The new queen was beautiful, but cruel. She could not bear to be surpassed in beauty by anyone. She owned a magic mirror and she would stand in front of it and ask:

'Mirror, mirror, on the wall,
Who is the fairest one of all?'
The mirror would always answer:
'You are the fairest one of all.'

With this answer the queen was well satisfied and went about her affairs, taking no notice of the child, Snow White, who was left to be brought up by her serving women.

3
October

Snow White and the Seven Dwarfs

The years went by and at last Snow White grew into a lovely young woman. She was no longer a child.

One day, when the queen stood before her magic mirror and asked:
'Mirror, mirror, on the wall,
Who is the fairest one of all?'
The mirror replied:
'Queen, you are full fair, 'tis true,
But Snow White is fairer still than you.'
The queen was astonished, then furious, then she turned green with envy. From that moment on her heart was filled with hatred for Snow White. Her hurt pride gave her peace neither by day nor by night.

At last she sent for a huntsman and told

him to take Snow White far into the forest and kill her.

'Be sure you do as I command,' she hissed. 'I never want to hear of Snow White again.'

The huntsman was afraid to disobey the queen and the next day he took Snow White into the forest. However, he could not bring himself to kill the pretty girl and told her to run away into the forest and never return to the castle. Then he returned himself and told the queen that Snow White was dead.

4
October

Snow White and the Seven Dwarfs

Poor Snow White, left all alone in the wild forest was afraid, and did not know where to look for shelter. She ran over the rough ground and through the thorn bushes. The wild beasts prowled around her, although they did not hurt her. She found nothing to eat and not even a stream of water from which she could drink. Then, at last, in the evening when she was exhausted with hunger and thirst, Snow White stumbled into a clearing where she saw a pretty little cottage.

She knocked at the door, but no one answered. She went in and found a little table laid for supper with seven small plates, seven sets of knives and forks and seven mugs. She ate some of the food and drank some of the milk, for she was weak with hunger. Then she found seven small beds and lay down on one of them to sleep.

Darkness fell and there was the sound of footsteps. The masters of the house were returning. They were seven dwarfs who worked in their mine in the mountains by day and by night returned to their cottage to eat and sleep.

They hurried into their home and lit their seven candles. At once they noticed their food had been touched. They looked into the bedroom and were astonished to see Snow White, asleep. They crowded round the bed, and smiled.

'Look at her lovely white skin and beautiful hair as fine as silk,' they said admiringly.

5
October

Snow White and the Seven Dwarfs

'That pretty little thing can do us no harm,' said one of the dwarfs. 'Let her sleep till morning and then she can tell us how she came here.'

The dwarfs ate their supper as quietly as they could and left Snow White till she awoke in the morning.

She was terrified when she sat up and found herself not in her familiar room in her father's castle, but in a cottage with seven strange dwarfs. However, the dwarfs spoke to her kindly and she told them how her stepmother, the queen, wished to be rid of her and how she dared not return to her home.

The dwarfs felt sorry for Snow White. They said that if she would do the housework and the cooking, she could stay in their cottage for as long as she wished and they would give her food and see she lacked for nothing.

Snow White agreed, only too pleased to have found shelter and kindness. For many months, the dwarfs went to dig in their mine in the daytime, while Snow White cleaned the house and in the evening the dwarfs came back and found a hot supper on the table.

All seemed well, but the dwarfs warned Snow White to be on her guard against the day when the queen would discover that she was still alive.

6
October

Snow White and the Seven Dwarfs

Snow White was living safely in the cottage owned by the seven dwarfs. In the castle, the wicked queen was happy, because she believed herself to be the most beautiful woman in the kingdom.

At last one day, wishing to hear words of praise, she stood before her magic mirror and asked:
'Mirror, mirror, on the wall,
Who is the fairest one of all?'
To her astonishment, the mirror replied:
'Queen, thou art of beauty rare,
But Snow White living in the glen,
With the seven little men,
Is a thousand times more fair.'
The queen knew that the mirror never lied and that the huntsman must have deceived her. She burned with jealousy and vowed that she would make an end of Snow White, so that she herself would again be the fairest in the land.

She disguised herself as an old pedlar woman and walked across the mountains to the dwarfs' cottage. Waiting until the little men had left for their work in the mine, the queen knocked at the door and called out to Snow White that she had pretty laces and ribbons to sell.

173

Snow White peeped from the window and thinking she had nothing to fear from a little old woman, let the queen into the cottage!

Snow White and the Seven Dwarfs

In her disguise as an old pedlar woman, the queen pretended to make friends with Snow White.

'Goodness! What a sight you are!' laughed the pedlar woman. 'You need someone to help you brush your hair and lace your bodice. Let me assist you. Look! I will give you this pretty new lace.'

Before Snow White realized what was happening, the queen laced her so tightly in her bodice that she could not breathe and fell down in a faint. The queen hurried away and Snow White was left lying on the floor until the dwarfs returned in the evening.

At once the little men cut the tight laces. Snow White started to breathe again and was soon returned to life. When she told the dwarfs about the pedlar woman, they guessed at once that she had been the wicked queen.

'You must never let anyone into the cottage while we are away,' they said to Snow White and she promised to obey them.

Meanwhile the queen had returned happily to the castle and asked her mirror who was the fairest in the land. She fell into a rage when the mirror told her that Snow White still lived.

Snow White and the Seven Dwarfs

Again the queen disguised herself and visited Snow White in the pretty little cottage in the woods. This time she put a poisoned comb into Snow White's hair, but again the dwarfs returned in time to pull out the comb and save Snow White.

The third time the queen went to the cottage, she took with her an apple, which was poisoned one side, but safe to eat on the other. She tricked the innocent girl into taking a bite from the poisoned side of the apple and Snow White fell to the ground with the piece of apple stuck in her throat. The queen fled back to the castle and the

dwarfs returned from their work in the mine in the mountains.

They were heartbroken to find Snow White lying as if dead. They did everything they could think of to revive her. Nothing was any use. For days the dwarfs sat weeping. Then they put Snow White in a glass coffin and laid her on the mountainside. Although she did not breathe her cheeks were still rosy and her skin fresh, as if she were alive.

'We cannot bury her in the dark ground,' they said. 'We will take it in turns to guard her here on the mountain.'

Round the side of the glass coffin, the dwarfs wrote Snow White's name in letters of gold and words saying that she was a king's daughter.

So matters stayed for a long while.

9
October

Snow White and the Seven Dwarfs

One sunny, springtime day, a prince came riding by. He saw the glass coffin with Snow White lying as if dead, but with her skin still as white as snow, her lips as red as blood and her hair as fine as silk.

He asked the dwarfs to tell him the story of such a strange thing and then begged them to let him take the coffin back to his father's palace. In the end they agreed.

Joyfully, the prince ordered his men to pick up the coffin and carry it away through the forest. As the men walked, they tripped and let the coffin fall with a bump to the ground. At once the piece of apple was dislodged from Snow White's throat. She started to breathe again and sat up and asked in amazement where she was.

The prince explained what had happened and, as Snow White was so beautiful, he asked her to marry him. She agreed and with the seven dwarfs went to the prince's home where his father, the king, arranged a great wedding feast. One of the people invited was Snow White's stepmother, the wicked queen.

175

10
October

Snow White and the Seven Dwarfs

When the wicked queen read her invitation to the wedding, she smiled and said:

'How nice! I will wear my grandest gown and be the most beautiful woman at the ceremony.'

She looked into her mirror and asked:

'Mirror, mirror, on the wall,
Who is the fairest one of all?'

Instead of replying that the queen was the fairest one of all, the mirror told her that the bride at the wedding would be more lovely. The queen stamped and screamed with rage, but she decided to go to the wedding just the same, hoping she would find a way of doing some mischief.

All this time, the queen had thought that Snow White was dead. When she saw that the lovely bride was Snow White herself, her fury knew no bounds.

'Shall I never be rid of this wretched girl?' she screeched.

'Maybe not, but we shall certainly be rid of you,' said the prince's father. He ordered the wicked queen to be put into magic shoes, which danced her so far away, that she could never find her way back again. And Snow White and her prince were left to live happily and in peace for ever after.

11
October

The Disappointed Wolf

Once upon a time a little lamb was being naughty.

'You behave yourself,' said his mother sternly, 'or I will let Big Bad Wolf get you.'

Of course, she did not mean it. She was only teasing the cheeky little lamb.

However, it happened that at the same moment Big Bad Wolf was trotting by their field and he heard what mother lamb had said.

'Oh goody and yum, yum, yum!' he thought. 'If I wait here, I shall get a tasty meal.' So he lay down very quietly and he waited and he waited and he waited, but the tasty meal did not come his way.

Bedtime arrived and the little lamb had a nightmare. He dreamt that Big Bad Wolf caught him. The little lamb called out to his mother and told her about the dream.

'Don't worry about dreams,' smiled the mother, 'dreams cannot hurt you. In any case, if Big Bad Wolf did come here, I would not let him catch you. I should set father on to him and he would soon be chased away.'

When he heard that Big Bad Wolf was most indignant and got up and trotted off.

'I'm not staying here trying to help a mother who keeps changing her mind,' he said.

12
October

The Tale of Telly Bear

Not long ago and only as far away as the next street, there lived a teddy bear who liked watching television.

Telly Bear the other toys called him, but they never had much to do with him, because he was always too busy watching television to have time to chat.

The thing Telly Bear could not understand was how all the people got inside the television set and where they all went to when their story was finished.

One day he asked Dolly about it.

'That's easy,' smiled Dolly. 'The people you see on the television screen are really hundreds of miles away in a television studio. A camera takes photographs of them and sends the pictures through the air and they come down a wire into the television set and then you see them.'

Telly Bear laughed until the tears ran down his cheeks.

'Really, Dolly!' he gasped. 'I did not come down with the last shower of rain, you know. Fancy expecting me to believe a story like that.'

At that moment Elizabeth, the little girl to whom Dolly belonged, joined in the conversation.

'Telly Bear,' she said. 'The people you see on the television screen are under the spell of a wicked fairy, who only sets them free when the people watching have seen enough of them.'

'Thank you,' smiled Telly Bear. 'That is a much more likely story. I can believe that.'

Elizabeth thought it was very funny that Telly Bear believed such a ridiculous explanation. However, Dolly was worried about Telly Bear and made him go to evening classes to find out how television really did work. Soon Telly understood it all and what is more, he made some nice new friends at the classes. They came round to supper one evening and did nothing but fiddle with the television set, saying the contrast needed darkening and the colour was too blue and the vertical hold was out of true. Dolly was not able to watch a programme in peace for five minutes together.

She looked at Elizabeth.

'I wish we had stuck with the story about the wicked fairy,' she said.

13
October

Too Many Cooks

Not long ago, nor far away, there was a young man living away from home for the first time.

'I think I will cook soup for my supper,' he said on his first evening alone.

He put some potatoes and water and salt into a saucepan and set it to simmer.

Just then a friend called to see how he

was getting along. He said:

'Potato soup is rather plain. Add some carrots and a knob of butter and some pepper.'

The young man did as his friend said. Then his cousin called and said:

'Carrots taste horrid. Add some onions and garlic and sage to hide the taste of the carrots.'

The young man did as his cousin advised. Then his brother called. He said:

'What a wretched soup! Add some lamb bones and a pinch of curry powder and mint. And what about a chopped apple and some raisins? Be a little adventurous!'

The young man did as his brother suggested. Then his uncle called. He said:

'I always think soup is nice with cream and grated cheese scattered over the top.'

When at last he was alone, the boy gave himself a plateful of the soup, not forgetting the cream and the grated cheese.

'Ugh!' gasped the poor fellow. 'This is terrible! I wish I had stuck to my potatoes and water and salt. I have taken the advice of too many cooks and my soup is spoilt.'

Now, when someone says:

'Too many cooks spoil the broth,' you will understand what they mean. Soup is another word for broth. Soup or broth, that particular one was horrid!

Jimmy MacBear

Jimmy MacBear was a Scottish teddy bear from Edinburgh. He wore a tartan kilt with a sporran at the front. He wore a tweed jacket and a Tam o' Shanter on his head.

'Och aye, lads and lassies,' he said when he met the other toys in the mornings. If, as always happened, he was given porridge for breakfast and haggis for dinner, he ate it up and said:

'Och aye! That was delicious the noo!'

When anyone called: 'Hey, Scotty!', Jimmy MacBear turned and smiled and waved.

'How I do admire Jimmy! He is a wonderful person!' said Dolly, as she saw Jimmy eating his third bowl of porridge that day and smiling and waving at some little visitors to the house, who were calling: 'Hey, Scotty!'

'What is so wonderful about Jimmy?' asked a woolly lamb, who had come for the afternoon with the little visitors.

'Well,' explained Dolly, 'Jimmy doesn't really like wearing tartan and eating porridge and haggis. Any more than people in America like going round in fur skin caps and eating squirrel stew, just because Davy Crockett used to do it. But Jimmy knows that people expect him to say "Och aye!" and answer when they call him "Scotty", so he does it to please them. He chokes down plateful after plateful of porridge, when he would much rather be eating pancakes and maple syrup. And although he does like haggis, he often sighs for a doughnut and coffee for lunch instead.'

The woolly lamb looked across at Jimmy MacBear.

'What should I call him, if I don't call him Scotty?' he asked.

'In Scotland,' said Dolly, 'they call each other Jimmy, whatever their names happen to be. However, if I were you and as you haven't been introduced, I should stick to calling him Mr. MacBear.'

15
October

The
Story of Aladdin

Long ago, in one of the great cities of China, there lived a poor tailor named Mustapha. He worked hard from dawn till dusk to earn a living for himself, and his wife and his son. Unfortunately the son, Aladdin, did not take after his father. He was a wild and idle fellow, more interested in playing in the street with wastrels than in learning his father's trade.

The heartbreak of such a son sent Mustapha to an early grave and then without the restraint of a father upon him, Aladdin ran wild competely. He was in the streets day and night. His poor mother never knew where he was.

One day, when Aladdin was swaggering round the market with his cronies, a stranger stopped to watch him. The man was a sorcerer from Africa and had been in China but two days. Thinking that Aladdin was exactly the boy he was seeking, the African asked the stallholders the boy's name and something of his history. When he had learned all he needed to know, he approached Aladdin and told him that he was his long lost uncle. He gave Aladdin some money to take as a present to his mother.

'Tell your mother I will visit her tomorrow evening,' said the African sorcerer.

16
October

The
Story of Aladdin

Full of curiosity, Aladdin ran home and asked his mother if he had an uncle, for he had never heard of one before.

'Your father had no brother, neither did I,' replied Aladdin's mother. 'You have no uncle.'

Then Aladdin gave his mother the money and said the man claiming to be his uncle was going to visit them for supper the next evening.

Aladdin's mother thought this was a strange matter, but the next day she prepared a good meal and at supper time the sorcerer arrived laden with gifts of money and fruit for the meal. He talked with many kind words of the dead Mustapha, Aladdin's father, saying the things about him, which he had learned from his enquiries in the market place. Then he explained that he himself had been out of the country for forty years, which was why Aladdin's mother had never met him before. He said he was heartbroken that he would never see Mustapha again, but that in memory of his brother he wished to do everything he could to help Aladdin.

Aladdin's mother began to believe that the sorcerer was her brother-in-law. Why else should he help them?

17
October

The Story of Aladdin

The sorcerer said he would buy Aladdin a shop and stock it with goods, so that he might become a merchant. He took the boy to a tailor and bought him fine clothes. Then he showed him round the inns and the mosques where he would meet other merchants with whom he could do business.

Aladdin's mother was delighted that her idle son was being taken in hand and taught to behave properly. When the sorcerer asked her permission to take Aladdin out of the city in order to choose a country house in which they all might live, she gave her consent gladly.

The sorcerer enticed Aladdin far from the city gates, past all the fine houses and into a valley in the mountains.

'Aladdin,' he said, 'here I will show you some extraordinary things, which may frighten you, but for which you will thank me later. First you must gather dry wood to make a fire.'

Aladdin gathered together a great pile of sticks to which the sorcerer set light. Then he threw incense on to the flames and said magic words which Aladdin did not understand.

At once the earth opened before them.

18
October

The Story of Aladdin

In the opening in the ground Aladdin saw a great stone with a brass ring attached to it. He was frightened and would have run away, but his so-called uncle held him back and said:

'Hidden under this stone is a treasure destined to be yours, which will make you rich beyond your dreams. Only you may lift the stone and go into the palace beyond, and there are great dangers there, but if you do exactly as I say, you will come to no harm. First take hold of the ring and lift the stone.'

'You must help me,' said Aladdin. 'The stone is too heavy for me.'

The sorcerer shook his head.

'No one may help you,' he said. 'You will lift the stone easily enough.'

Aladdin pulled at the ring and to his surprise the heavy stone rose up to show some steps leading down to a door.

The sorcerer said:

'That door leads to a palace. You must walk through three rooms filled with gold and silver, which you must not touch. Open a door and walk into a garden. You may touch what you wish there, but take my advice and do not bother with anything except a lamp which you will see in a niche in the far wall. Tuck the lamp in your waistband and bring it back to me.'

Then a sorcerer gave a ring for Aladdin to wear on his finger and told him it would keep him from harm.

Aladdin stepped down into the earth and pushed open the door.

19
October

The Story of Aladdin

The palace was as his uncle had described it. Aladdin hastened through the rooms, filled with gold and silver, into the garden. Growing in the garden were trees loaded with strange, hard looking fruit coloured red, green and silver. He picked a handful of the jewels and filled his pockets and crammed the front of his vest full of the strange fruit. Then, remembering his uncle's words, he picked up the lamp from the niche and hurried back to the steps leading out of the palace.

As soon as he reached them, he called:

'Uncle, please lend me your hand to help me out!'

'Give me the lamp first,' replied the sorcerer.

'I cannot reach it now,' replied Aladdin, for the lamp was mixed up with the jewels he had picked in the garden. 'I will give it to you when I am at the top of the steps.'

However, the sorcerer was determined to have the lamp before he let Aladdin back into the fresh air.

'Give me the lamp,' he shouted.

'Not until I am out of here,' replied Aladdin.

At once the sorcerer flew into a rage. He

stamped his feet, and then he threw incense on to the fire and said two magic words. The stone went back over the hole leading to the palace. The sorcerer spread earth over the stone, as it had been before. Then he went back to Africa from where he had come.

The Story of Aladdin

The truth was that the sorcerer had learned of the lamp's existence from his books of magic, but the lamp would only serve him, if it was handed to him willingly by a young person. He had picked out Aladdin as a boy he could train for this purpose. When Aladdin had refused to hand the lamp to the sorcerer, he knew his plans had come to nothing and he had no further use for the boy.

Meanwhile, Aladdin was in despair. He tried to go back into the underground palace, but the door was fast shut. Aladdin was trapped on the steps between the palace door and the stone. He clasped his hands together to pray for help and in so doing rubbed the ring which the sorcerer had given to him. At once a huge genie appeared before him and said:

'What wouldst thou have, o master? I am

the slave of the ring and will obey thy commands.'

'Save me from this place,' begged Aladdin.

Immediately he found himself standing in the fresh air above the stone. He hurried as fast as he could to his mother's house and arrived hungry and exhausted. He told his mother all that had happened, ate a meal and then fell into a deep sleep.

The Story of Aladdin

When Aladdin awoke the next morning, he asked his mother for a meal.

'Alas,' she replied, 'I have no food nor money with which to buy it.'

Aladdin felt amongst the clothes he had taken off the night before and lifted up the old lamp he had taken from the underground garden.

'I will sell this for a few pieces of silver,' he said. 'That will buy us food for several days.'

'It is dirty and old,' replied his mother. 'Let me clean it before you take it to the market place.'

Hardly had she commenced to rub the lamp, than a huge genie appeared. The poor woman dropped the lamp in fear, but Aladdin picked it up. At once the genie looked at him and said:

'I am the slave of whoever holds the lamp. Your wish is my command.'

'I am hungry. Bring me something to eat,' ordered Aladdin.

The genie disappeared and in a few moments returned with a delicious meal in silver dishes on a silver tray. Aladdin and his mother enjoyed the meal, and sold the silver in the market place. They lived modestly on this money for several months.

The Story of Aladdin

Several years passed in happiness for the mother and son. Aladdin rubbed the lamp and used the services of the genie very rarely. They were content with living in quiet comfort.

Then one day everything changed. Aladdin saw Princess Buddir, the daughter of the king, and fell in love with her.

At once Aladdin asked his mother to go to the palace and arrange with the king that he should marry Princess Buddir. Aladdin's mother burst out laughing.

'The king will never let a poor boy like you marry his daughter,' she said. 'Forget such nonsense.'

Then Aladdin took out the strange fruit he had picked in the underground garden so many years before. By now he realized that the stones were precious jewels.

'Give these as a present to the king,' he said. 'They will persuade him to let me marry his daughter. He will be sure to think I am a rich nobleman.'

Aladdin's mother went to the palace and after she had given the king the jewels and many more presents beside, the marriage was arranged. With the help of the genie of the lamp, Aladdin built a beautiful palace in which he and the princess lived for several happy years after the wedding. However their happiness was not to last.

The Story of Aladdin

The sorcerer, who had shown Aladdin how to find the lamp, had decided to try once more to get it for his own. He left his home in Africa and went again to China where he learned of Aladdin's marriage and his favour with the king.

The African sorcerer stood outside the magical palace in which Aladdin lived with Princess Buddir and plotted to gain possession of the magic lamp.

From speaking to the palace servants, the sorcerer learned that Aladdin was setting off that very day on a hunting expedition and would not be back for a week.

The sorcerer smiled. Now he knew what to do. He walked into the shop of a lamp maker and ordered him to make twelve fine copper lamps to be ready the next day. The following morning, the sorcerer collected the lamps and stood outside Aladdin's palace shouting:

'New lamps for old! Who wants new lamps in exchange for old ones?'

At once a crowd gathered around him either jeering at his silliness or asking what the trick was and what else he wanted for his fine new lamps.

Aladdin's wife, Princess Buddir, heard the noise and sent a servant to enquire the cause. The girl came back laughing.

'There is a crazy old man outside offering new lamps in exchange for old ones,' she said. 'No one believes he means it. He must be mad.'

24
October

The
Story of Aladdin

Then another servant spoke up and said there was an old lamp on a shelf in Prince Aladdin's dressing room and should she take it and see if the old man really meant what he said. Princess Buddir agreed and watched from the window, as the servant took the old lamp to the man in the street.

The sorcerer knew at once this was the lamp he wanted. Everything else in the palace was made of gold or silver. This old lamp could have been kept for no other reason than that it was magic. Smiling at the servant girl, he gave her a shining new

lamp in exchange for the old one. Then, when she went laughing back to her mistress, the sorcerer hurried out of the city.

Now he was master of the magic lamp.

In the darkness of evening, he rubbed it and immediately the huge genie stood before him and said:

'I am the slave of whoever holds the lamp. Your wish is my command.'

The sorcerer smiled a cruel smile. Now he would be able to punish Aladdin for not giving him the lamp all those years ago. He looked at the genie and ordered:

'This very night take me and Aladdin's palace and everyone in it back to my home in Africa.'

The command was obeyed.

25
October

The
Story of Aladdin

The next morning, the king, Princess Buddir's father, looked as usual from his window, expecting to see Aladdin's palace. To his amazement, it was not there. He sent for the grand vizier and asked his opinion of what could have happened. The grand vizier said it was his belief that Aladdin had built the palace by magic in the first place and that now for some wicked purpose of his own, he had had it taken away by magic.

The king sent a band of soldiers to fetch Aladdin from his hunting expedition and told him if he did not bring back the princess and the palace within forty days, he would lose his life.

As can be imagined, Aladdin was distraught and could not think what he should do. Then he remembered the magic ring, which he had not used for years, preferring to rub the magic lamp and give his orders to that genie. Standing alone and deserted by his friends, Aladdin rubbed the ring. To his great relief, it still worked and a huge genie came to stand before him and obey his commands.

At first Aladdin ordered the genie to bring the Princess Buddir and the palace back to China. However, the genie of the ring said this was not within his power. He was not as clever as the genie of the lamp. Instead he took Aladdin to Africa and stood him outside the palace, beneath the window of the princess.

26
October

The Story of Aladdin

The sad and lonely princess, looking from her window, was overjoyed to see Aladdin and she sent a servant to let him secretly into the palace.

'Where is the old lamp?' asked Aladdin.

By now Princess Buddir knew the importance of the lamp and begged Aladdin's forgiveness for giving it to the sorcerer.

'He keeps it always in his pocket,' she sighed. 'No one else may touch it.'

Aladdin hurried to the nearest town and brought a sleeping potion which he put into the sorcerer's wine. That evening at supper, the sorcerer fell into a deep sleep. Aladdin took back the lamp and at once transported himself, and his wife, the palace and all his servants back to their home town in China. The sorcerer was left in Africa under a spell never to bother Aladdin or his family again. Thus Aladdin lived with the princess in wealth and splendour for the rest of their lives.

27
October

The Hare and the Tortoise

One day a hare was making fun of a tortoise for being slow on his feet.

'Do not be so sure of yourself,' replied the tortoise. 'Let us run a race and I am certain that I shall win.'

The hare agreed, still laughing heartily.

The time and course of the race was set by a fox and at the appointed hour the hare and the tortoise started off.

The hare ran swiftly and was soon far ahead. However, the sun was hot and the hare lay down to rest. Soon he was fast asleep.

Meanwhile the tortoise kept plodding on and in good time reached the winning post. Suddenly the hare woke up and raced as fast as he could to the end of the course, only to find that the tortoise was already the winner.

The fox, who was judging the race, smiled.

'Slow and steady wins the race,' he said.

28
October

Birds of a Feather

There was once a boy who came of age and for the first time was able to go out with whom he liked without asking his father's permission. He fell to roaming round town with some young thieves, who did wrong, but were handsome and fashionably dressed and amusing in their talk.

Gradually the boy found that his old friends wished to have nothing more to do with him. He received no invitations to dinner, nor to visit his cousins for the weekend in their nice houses.

He asked his father why this could be.

'It is because you are mixing with thieves,' replied his father.

'But I am not a thief,' protested the boy. 'I am as honest as ever.'

'No one will believe you,' said his father. He pointed up at the birds in the sky. The swallows were flocking with other swallows. The starlings were flocking with starlings. Each bird kept with its own kind.

'Birds of a feather flock together,' said the father. 'If you are seen with thieves, people will think you have sympathy with stealing and that you are probably a thief yourself. That is the way of the world, like it or not.'

After that, the boy chose his friends more carefully.

29
October

Twinkle, Twinkle, Little Star

Some folks, when they go to bed, like to draw the curtains fast across the windows to shut out the dark and keep everything cosy.

There are other folk who fling the curtains apart, switch off the lights and lie in bed looking out at the stars.

Many years ago there was a little boy who loved watching the stars. He would lie in bed whispering:

'*Twinkle, twinkle, little star,*
How I wonder what you are!
Up above the world so high,
Like a diamond in the sky.'

The little boy's name was Galileo and he became famous for studying the stars and finding out how they moved.

The trouble with star gazing is that it is very chilly work on cold winter nights. Galileo's mother had to make him a warm dressing-gown and knit him thick bedsocks, so that he would not catch cold as he sat at the window staring up at the night sky.

When Galileo grew up and youngsters came to him and asked what they needed to buy to become good star gazers, he did not say they needed a telescope. He would laugh and say:

'The most important things for a star gazer to have are – a warm dressing-gown and thick bedsocks.'

30
October

The Brave Teddy Bear

Once there was a teddy bear who was very brave. Brave Teddy the other toys called

him and he was much respected.

Nothing frightened Brave Teddy, not witches nor bad fairies, nor things which went bump in the night. If a goblin or a naughty elf came poking his nose into the room, Brave Teddy would say:

'Now look here, my good fellow, it's no use trying your tricks in this house. I'm sure you can find some work to do at home. When did you last tidy your bedroom or weed the garden? Not recently, I'll wager. Now cut along about some honest business.'

'You only have to speak to these chaps firmly,' Brave Teddy would say to the other toys, 'and they soon know who is boss.'

It was true. No naughty mischief-makers from Fairyland dared go into a room when Brave Teddy was there. He became so famous he was asked to go back to Teddy Bear Land to train all the young teddies to be as brave as he was. He did a fine job and that is why so many children like to take teddy bears to bed with them. While Teddy is there, no wicked fairies nor naughty elves dare come near. It is Teddy's job to keep them away. That is why wicked fairies and naughty elves hate teddy bears, and why we love them!

31
October

The Old Lion

Once an old lion became too feeble to hunt his prey. Instead he had to catch his dinner by trickery. He lay in a cave and said he was ill. When the other animals came in to enquire how he was getting along, he seized them and ate them.

However, a wise old goat could never be caught. He always stood at the cave entrance to ask after the lion's health.

'Why don't you step inside?' asked the lion. 'Surely a sick old thing like me cannot hurt you!'

'Indeed not,' agreed the wise old goat, 'but I would rather keep my distance. I can talk to you perfectly well from here. You see I cannot help noticing all the footprints of your other visitors lead into the cave and none lead out. I would rather be safe than sorry.'

November

1
November

Ali Baba and the Forty Thieves

Long ago in a town in Persia, there lived two brothers, one named Cassim and the other Ali Baba. Cassim was married to a rich wife, but Ali Baba and his wife were poor. Ali earned a living by cutting wood in the forest and bringing it back to sell in town.

One day Ali Baba was working in the forest. He had cut enough wood to load his three asses and was preparing to return to town, when he saw a cloud of dust far along the forest road. He watched it and as it drew closer, he observed that it was being thrown up by a large body of horsemen. Not knowing whether they were friend or foe, he tied his asses to a tree away from the road and hid himself on a high rock from which he could watch, unseen.

Presently the men arrived at the rock and Ali Baba was able to see that they were forty well mounted, armed men. They dismounted under the rock, tethered their horses and hung a bag of corn round the horses' necks so that they might rest and feed.

2
November

Ali Baba and the Forty Thieves

As Ali Baba watched, each rider took a saddlebag from his horse and walked behind the man who seemed to be the leader. This man pushed his way through some bushes until he came to a rock face. Raising his arms and looking at the smooth, apparently solid rock, the leader of the men said:

'Open, Sesame!'

Immediately a door opened in the rock. Making the men go in first, the leader followed and the door closed behind him.

The men, whom Ali Baba assumed to be robbers, stayed some time in the rock and Ali Baba stayed in his hiding place. He was

afraid to come down and fetch his asses in case the men came out and caught him before he could ride far enough away.

After a long time of waiting, Ali Baba saw the door in the rock open. First the leader came out then his men. He counted the men as they came out, then, satisfied they were all there, he ordered them to prepare their horses for another journey.

Turning back to the door, the man said: 'Shut, Sesame!'

The door shut and the men rode off.

3
November

Ali Baba and the Forty Thieves

Ali Baba watched the men until they were out of sight. Then he waited a while longer. So fierce had the men looked, he was afraid of what they might do to him if they returned and caught him.

When he was quite sure they were gone, he descended from the rock, stood in front of the smooth rock face, held up his arms and said:

'Open, Sesame!'

The door instantly flew open and taking his courage in his hands, Ali Baba stepped into the cavern. To his surprise, it was not dark and damp, but dry and well lit and spacious. On shelves round the walls were all sorts of provisions as well as sacks of gold and silver, bales of silk, valuable carpets and jars of jewels. Clearly this was the hoard of a robber band.

Ali Baba fetched his asses, threw away the wood he had been chopping, loaded the animals with as much gold as they could carry, stood outside the cave and said:

'Shut, Sesame!'

The door of the cave slammed shut and Ali Baba hurried back to town with the gold.

4
November

Ali Baba and the Forty Thieves

When Ali Baba arrived home, he drove the asses into his little yard, unloaded them with great secrecy and poured the gold on

to a table in front of his wife.

'Tell no one about this,' he warned her.

However, the wife was eager to weigh the gold and see exactly how rich they were. She ran to the house of her brother-in-law, Cassim, and asked to borrow some scales. Cassim's wife knew that Ali Baba was poor and wondered what he and his wife could have that needed weighing. She spread a little suet at the bottom of the pan on the scales, so that traces of whatever was weighed would stick to it.

Ali Baba's wife took home the scales and weighed the gold. Well pleased with the new riches, she hurried back to Cassim's home without noticing a small piece of gold sticking to the suet.

'Thank you for the loan of the scales,' she smiled.

As soon as she was gone Cassim's wife saw the gold and immediately told her husband that Ali Baba and his wife had so much gold they needed scales to weigh it.

Ali Baba and the Forty Thieves

Cassim was amazed and angry to think that his brother was rich. He could hardly sleep for brooding over the matter. The next day at dawn he hurried to Ali Baba's house.

'I am surprised at you, Ali Baba,' he said. 'You pretend to be poor, yet you have so much wealth you need to borrow my scales to weigh it.'

Then he showed Ali Baba the piece of gold his wife had found the night before. Ali Baba was not pleased that his secret was known, but what was done could not be undone. He told his brother the whole story of how he had found the gold in the robbers' cave and offered to share the riches with him, if only he would keep the secret.

The brother agreed, but only on condition that Ali Baba told him exactly where the cave was so that Cassim could help himself to the riches whenever he desired. So it was done.

The next morning, long before dawn, Cassim set out along the road into the forest with ten strong mules, each laden with empty chests. He easily found the rock from Ali Baba's description and standing in front of it, he called:

'Open, Sesame!'

At once the door in the rock flew open and Cassim stepped inside.

Ali Baba and the Forty Thieves

Cassim went forward deep into the robbers' cave, scarcely noticing that the door was closing behind him. He was astounded at the treasures he beheld, they were so much greater than Ali Baba had related.

He dragged as many bags of gold as he could to the mouth of the cave and then tried to re-open the door, so that he might go out to load his mules. However, all the excitement of finding so great a treasure had confused his brain and he could not remember the magic words. He fell into a panic, shouting every word he could think of, but none was the right one.

At noon the robbers rode back towards their cave. From a distance they saw Cassim's mules and were much alarmed.

Galloping at full speed towards the cave, they drove away the mules, then drew their sabres and stood before the rock while their leader pronounced the words:

'Open, Sesame!'

At once the door flew open and Cassim rushed out. He tried to escape, but he could not elude forty men and he was soon beaten unconscious and dumped in the cave for dead. The robbers looked round the cave and saw the disturbance Cassim had made, but did not realize that another man, Ali Baba, had been there also. Thinking that they had killed their only enemy, they rode away.

Ali Baba and the Forty Thieves

Night fell and when Cassim did not return home, his wife became alarmed. She ran to Ali Baba and confessed that his brother had gone to the forest to plunder the treasure cave. At this Ali Baba became concerned for the safety of even so treacherous a brother. As soon as there was enough light, he saddled two asses and rode towards the cave. Standing before the entrance, he called:

'Open, Sesame!'

When the door opened, he hurried in and found his brother injured and scarcely alive. At once Ali Baba realized the robbers knew that their hiding place was no longer a secret and he was frightened. However, he was not too frightened to load his asses with gold before he put his poor brother on to the back of one of the beasts. He covered him with sacks to disguise his wounds and then went and hid in the forest near to town. As soon as it was dark, Ali Baba led his asses along the deserted streets. First he unloaded the gold at his own home and then took Cassim to his own wife. The wife sent Morgiana, a slave girl, to fetch a doctor in secret and Cassim's wounds were tended. Neither of the brothers wanted anyone to know of the gold they had found.

8
November

Ali Baba and
the Forty Thieves

So Cassim lay in his house recovering
secretly from his wounds and Ali Baba
enjoyed his wealth, but visited the cave no
more for fear of the robbers.

When the robbers next visited the cave
and found Cassim gone, they were
astounded. For sure, someone in town must
know their secret. The leader sent one of
his men to ask in the market place if anyone
had recently died and his family become
suddenly wealthy.

In town this man was recognized as a
robber and thrown into prison. When he
did not return, the robber chief sent a

second man, who was also imprisoned.
Then the robber chief decided to go into
town himself and being more clever than
the others, he was not caught, but found
out that Cassim had not been seen for
many days and that his brother, Ali Baba,
was spending much gold.

Correctly believing that these two
brothers were the ones who knew the secret
of the cave and that Ali Baba had taken the
gold from the cave, the robber chief devised
a plan. He bought nineteen mules and
loaded them with thirty-eight jars. Into one
jar he put oil. He ordered his remaining
thirty seven men to climb into the other
jars.

9
November

Ali Baba and
the Forty Thieves

As darkness fell, the robber chief, with his
train of mules, went knocking at the door of
Ali Baba's home.

'I am an oil merchant, lost before I can
reach my destination,' pleaded the robber
chief. 'Will you take me in and shelter me
for the night? The roads are full of thieves
and I am afraid.'

Ali Baba willingly agreed and the robber and the mules with their load of thirty eight jars went into the courtyard of Ali Baba's home. The merchant, as Ali Baba thought him to be, was invited to eat and sleep in the house, the mules were unloaded and fed and the jars left in the yard.

The robber chief had arranged with his men that when the household was safely asleep, he would throw stones from his window. Then the robbers would spring from the jars, kill everyone in the house, find their gold and hasten back to the forest before any of the neighbours could guess what was happening.

However, the best laid plans often go awry. Morgiana, the slave girl, had gone to live in Ali Baba's household and it happened that with the extra guest, she ran out of oil. It was late and she did not wish to go into the streets.

'I will get some oil from the merchant's jars,' she thought.

10
November

Ali Baba and the Forty Thieves

As by this time most of the household was asleep and Morgiana required the oil only for her own lamp, she crept quietly into the courtyard and up to one of the jars. As she touched the fastening at the top of the jar, her amazement can be imagined when she heard a man's voice whisper:

'Is it time, master?'

Morgiana almost fainted with fear, but keeping her presence of mind, answered in a gruff voice:

'The time is not yet.'

The brave girl went along the line of jars, tapping at them to see how many contained men instead of oil and whenever a voice asked:

'Is it time, master?' she replied in a deep man's voice:

'The time is not yet.'

When she had found out that thirty-seven men were hidden in the courtyard

and that only one of the jars contained oil, she filled her lamp and then roused Ali Baba and told him the dreadful news.

Thanking the girl for her bravery, Ali Baba crept round the yard, securing the lids of the jars with strong ropes, so that the men could not get out. Then he went into the shadows and watched.

11
November

Ali Baba and the Forty Thieves

Later on in the night, when the robber chief thought that everyone was asleep, he threw stones from his bedroom window. The stones rattled against the sides of the jars, but no men leapt out. Again the robber threw stones, harder this time. They made a great clatter against the sides of the jars, but still no men clambered forth.

The robber chief crept from his room and down into the courtyard. Then Ali Baba called his servants and leaped upon the man and seized him. With his merchant's disguise pulled from his head, Ali Baba recognized the robber chief for who he was.

'Neither I nor my family will ever be safe now that these brigands know who we are and where we live,' gasped Ali Baba.

Hastily he took the robber chief and the mules and the jars to the dockside. He sold them to a merchant to be taken to a far country from which they could never return.

Then, with peace of mind at last, Ali Baba returned home, where, with the help of the treasure in the cave, he lived in luxury for the rest of his life. Morgiana, the brave slave girl, lived happily too. She married one of Ali Baba's sons and became a rich woman. And the robber chief and his men were never heard of again.

12
November

The Witch and the Cat

Once upon a time a cat fell in love with a handsome young man. The cat went to a witch and asked her to change her into a pretty young woman, so that she might marry the young man.

The witch agreed, for she cared nothing for the young man, nor whom he married.

The cat, who was now a pretty girl, moved into the cottage next to the young man's home and soon they were engaged to be married.

However, the boy's mother, who knew something of witchcraft, did not like the girl. She did not like her green eyes which had black slits like cat's eyes, instead of round pupils as ordinary humans have.

The mother suspected that the girl was really a cat and told her son. However, he would hear nothing against his sweetheart and said his mother was merely jealous.

Determined that her son should not marry a cat, the mother waited until the whole family was seated in the parlour, then she let loose a mouse to run across the room. Immediately the girl, forgetting she was a young lady and only remembering her cat's feelings, pounced on the mouse and shook it in her mouth.

Then the young man believed the girl was a cat and the marriage did not take place; and the girl went back to being a cat and took up all her old ways.

13
November

The Six Sillies

Once upon a time there was a young woman who had reached the age of thirty-seven without finding a husband. She was a foolish young woman and no one wished to marry her.

However, one fine day, a young man did come to pay court to her. Feeling very pleased, the mother sent her daughter down to the cellar to fetch a jug of beer to offer to the visitor.

The young woman was gone for a long

time and wondering what was detaining her, the mother went to the cellar herself.

To her amazement, she saw her daughter sitting on the steps with her head in her hands, the empty jug at her side, the tap of the barrel turned on and beer running all over the floor.

'What is the matter?' gasped the mother.

'Well,' replied the young woman, 'I am so worried. Suppose I marry that young man upstairs and we have a child. What shall I call it? Names are so important and all the best names are taken already.'

'Dear me! I must think about that with you,' said the mother and sat on the steps with her daughter and with the beer still running all over the floor.

The father, who had been sitting upstairs chatting to the young man, could not understand why his wife and daughter were so long. He went down to the cellar to look for them.

14
November

The Six Sillies

He was surprised to find them both sitting on the stairs with the beer running all over the floor beside them.

'What are you thinking of to let the beer run all over the cellar?' he asked.

'We are worried about what to call the children that our daughter will have if she marries that young man upstairs,' said the mother.

'I will sit down and think about it with you,' said the father and down he sat while the beer continued to run all over the floor.

Meanwhile the young man sat upstairs alone. Eventually he decided he should go down to the cellar in search of the young woman, her mother and her father. He could not understand what was taking them so long.

He found all three of them sitting on the cellar steps while the beer ran all over the floor.

'What are you doing sitting there and letting the beer run to waste?' he gasped.

'Never mind about the beer,' replied the father. 'We have more important things to worry about than that. If you marry our daughter and have children, what names shall we give them? All the best names are taken already.'

The young man could not believe his ears. 'I don't think I want to marry into such a silly family,' he said to himself. 'Now that will give them something to worry about!'

15
November

The Six Sillies

He looked at the family and the beer on the floor.

'I have never heard such nonsense,' he said. 'I am going away. However if I ever find three people sillier than you are, then I will come back and marry your daughter.'

The young man left the house and set off for a walk. Before long he came to an orchard, where a man was knocking walnuts from a tree and then trying to load them into a cart with a fork.

'What are you doing?' asked the young man.

'I am trying to load this cart with walnuts,' was the reply, 'but I am not getting on very fast with this fork.'

'Try putting the walnuts into a basket and then tipping the basketful into the cart,' advised the young man going on his way.

'Well,' he thought, 'I have already found one person more foolish than those other three.'

A little further on the young man saw a man who was trying to make his pig climb an oak tree.

'What are you doing, my good man?' asked the young fellow. He could not figure out what the man was doing. Whoever heard of a climbing pig?

16
November

The Six Sillies

The man who was trying to make his pig climb the tree turned and replied:

'I want my pig to feed on the acorns, but he will not go up the tree, the silly creature.'

'It is you who are silly,' replied the young man. 'Pigs cannot climb trees. It would be better if you climbed the tree, knocked down the acorns and let the pig eat them on the ground underneath.'

'I never thought of that,' replied the man. 'I will do it straight away.'

'Well, here is the second person I have met who is more foolish than those other three,' thought the young man and went on his way.

Further along the highway, the young man saw the strangest sight he had ever beheld. A man had tied a pair of trousers

'Yes, indeed,' replied the strange fellow 'and it takes me ages. Do you know a better way?'

between two trees and was now jumping high in the air, trying to come down with his legs in the trouser legs! It seemed more likely he would break his legs.

'Surely that is not the way you try to get into a pair of trousers?' gasped the young man.

17
November

The Six Sillies

The young man spoke kindly to the fellow who had tied his trousers between two trees and who was obviously a very foolish person.

'Untie your trousers,' he said. 'Hold them in your hands. Stand on one leg while you slip the other leg into the trousers, then stand on that leg while you put the second leg into the trousers.'

'How clever,' smiled the man. 'I will do that in future.'

'Well,' thought the young man. 'I have now met three people more silly than the daughter and her mother and her father who let the beer run over the cellar floor, so I had better keep my word and go back and marry her. The world seems to be full of sillies.'

So the young man and the foolish young woman were married and were quite happy, so folk say.

18
November

Mr. and Mrs. Sprat

Once upon a time there lived a couple who were always wasting food. No sooner would Mrs. Sprat come home with a bag of sugar than Mr. Sprat would say that he had read in the papers that sugar was bad for your teeth and it would have to be thrown away.

No sooner would Mr. Sprat come home with a loaf of fresh baked bread than Mrs. Sprat would say that bread was fattening and it had to be thrown away.

So it went on with everything they bought. In the end, their dustbin was full and their stomachs were empty. Their friends became worried about them.

Then one fortunate day Mr. Sprat read that lean meat was good for you and Mrs. Sprat read that fat meat was good for you. They bought some meat and between them ate all of it.

Mr. Sprat so enjoyed the lean meat and Mrs. Sprat so enjoyed the fat meat that they bought some for every day of the week.

Their friends were very pleased and advised them not to read anything more about eating, but to carry on enjoying their food. They took this good advice and lived happily ever after.

Their friends wrote a rhyme about them. It went:

'Jack Sprat could eat no fat,
His wife could eat no lean,
And so between them both, you see,
They licked the platter clean.'

19
November

The Fairy Wife

Many years ago, up in the mountains, the fairies used to come out and dance in a ring in the evenings. The son of a farmer often used to hide and watch them because the dancing was so pretty.

One evening, Thomas, the farmer's son, fell in love with one of the pretty fairy girls he saw dancing in the fairy ring. Although

The Fairy Wife

Thomas was very much in love with the fairy girl and after months of pleading, she agreed to marry him.

'But remember,' she said, 'never touch me with anything made of iron. Iron is hateful to fairies. If iron touches me, I shall have to go straight back to living with the fairy folk and you will never see me again.'

Thomas was pleased. It seemed to him that keeping iron away from his wife would be easy. They were married and lived happily for several years. They had two children, whom they both loved. Then one day Thomas could not catch the horse to ride to market. He called his wife to help him and in the flurry and the struggle some of the iron work on the saddle struck the fairy wife on the cheek. Immediately she disappeared. She had gone back to fairyland and poor Thomas thought he would never see her again.

he knew it was forbidden for humans and fairy folk to mix, he ran forward and snatched up the girl and took her back to his farmhouse.

The other fairy folk ran after him, but he slammed the farmhouse door in their faces and bolted it with a bolt of iron. He knew that iron was hateful to fairy folk. Thomas locked the fairy girl in a room and begged her to marry him. She refused and said she longed only to return to her own people. However, she did say, after a while, that if Thomas could find out her name she would become his servant and work on the farm.

That evening, Thomas crept back to the fairy ring. Although the fairy folk were not dancing, Thomas saw them holding a meeting on a hillock surrounded by a ditch. He crawled along the ditch until he could hear what was being said.

'How shall we ever rescue our sister, Penelope?' the fairies were saying.

Then Thomas knew the name of the girl he loved. He went back to the farm, told the fairy girl her name and she became a servant at the farm.

Thomas was heartbroken and the two children wept for their mother. Then one night, weeks later, Thomas heard tapping at his window and the faint voice of his wife calling to him.

'I miss my children,' she said. 'The fairy law forbids that I should ever set foot on earth again, but tomorrow evening, come down to the lake and you will see me.'

The next evening Thomas took the two children down to the lake. Floating on the water was a turf of grass and standing on the grass was the fairy wife.

'I cannot come closer,' she said, 'but we can talk to each other.'

For the rest of their lives Thomas and the children went to the lake to talk to the fairy wife and to tell her their news. They had to be content to see her and talk to her from a distance. The fairy wife could never again kiss her husband, nor her children.

But since those days, she has never been seen again.

21
November

The Ass and the River Trick

Back in the old days, a farmer went to market with his ass and loaded it with sacks of salt to take back to the farm. On the way home, the ass stumbled and fell in the stream. Some of the salt was dissolved and carried away in the water.

When the ass stood up and resumed its journey, it found the load lighter, and it was pleased.

Next time the ass was used to carry a load home from town, it deliberately fell in the stream and when it stood up, its load was again lighter, as once more the ass was carrying salt.

The ass was very pleased at this trick it had learned to lighten its workload.

Next time it went to town, it again fell into the water on its way home. However, this time the load was a sack of sponges. They soaked up the water from the stream and when the ass rose to its feet, its burden was ten times heavier than before and walking home was a hard struggle.

The load was so heavy that the ass fell again and again on the stony path, and each time it fell, it was harder to get back on its feet. The ass vowed it could never play such a trick again.

That day the ass learned a lesson. It is possible to play a good trick once too often.

22
November

Early to Bed

Once there were two brothers. One went to bed early, got plenty of sleep, woke early in the morning and went to the market place and bought all the best bargains. He became wealthy and enjoyed good health.

His brother sat up late chatting with his friends, then slept late and woke up tired with red-rimmed eyes and did not bother to go to market, because he knew his brother would have snapped up all the best bargains anyway.

This brother never became rich and was unhealthy, with dark shadows under his eyes from all the late nights and pale cheeks from lack of fresh air.

Folks looked at the two brothers and made up a rhyme:

'Early to bed and early to rise,
Makes a man healthy, wealthy and wise.'

However, the second brother managed quite well in life. He heard so many funny stories from sitting up every evening, chatting with friends, that he was always being asked out to free dinners. Folks were willing to give him dinner, because in return he made them laugh.

23
November

The Parrot

Just a little way away and only a few weeks ago, there was an old lady who kept a parrot as a pet.

The old lady trained the parrot to say things like 'Pretty Polly' and 'Good

morning' but the old lady did not know that the parrot was also learning to imitate the sound of the front door-bell.

The old lady would be busy in the kitchen or the bedroom when she would hear – or think she heard – the front door-bell ringing. She would leave her cooking, or her dusting and hurry to the door, only to find that there was no one there.

The parrot was very amused, but the old lady was cross. She blamed the children next-door and said they rang the bell and ran away. She went to see the doctor to check if there was anything wrong with her ears. She called in the electrician to see if there was anything wrong with the bell.

Then the parrot grew careless and imitated the front door-bell when the old lady was standing in the hall and could hear that the sound came from the parrot's cage.

'I will outwit you, you naughty parrot,' she said and she had the bell taken away and a door knocker put in its place. The parrot could not imitate the sound of a door knocker and for a while it sulked and felt that all its fun was over.

Then it had an idea.

It learned to imitate the sound of the telephone bell and to this day it is still tricking the old lady into thinking the telephone is ringing when it is not.

The old lady was no match for the parrot!

24
November

The Sword in the Stone

Long, long ago when knights in armour rode the land and there was much fighting, a baby son was born to King Uther Pendragon.

King Uther knew that he had not long to live and that he had many enemies, so he gave the baby into the care of the magician Merlin. Merlin in turn took the baby to a good man known as Sir Ector, who already had a small son, called Sir Kay.

The baby, Arthur, was brought up well and kindly by Sir Ector, who did not know that the boy was the son of a king.

The years went by and the kingdom fell into lawlessness and danger. At last, on the advice of Merlin, all the great lords met together at Christmas time to see if God would give them a sign to show who should be king and save the land from ruin.

A great mass was held in the cathedral and when it was finished, a wonderful sight awaited the knights out in the courtyard.

A huge marble stone had appeared and set on this stone was a heavy anvil. Deeply

embedded in the anvil was a fair sword. Written in letters of gold on the anvil were the words:

'Whosoever pulls out this sword from this stone and anvil is rightful King of England.'

25
November

The Sword in the Stone

This seemed to be the sign from God for which everyone had been waiting. A huge crowd gathered about the sword in the stone, but although many knights tried to pull it out, none succeeded.

'Our future king is not yet here,' said Merlin. 'Let us set ten good knights to guard the sword and wait here until New Year's Day. Then let us hold a tournament and invite all the fine knights of the realm to take part. Surely one of them will be able to pull the sword from the stone.'

This was agreed and messengers were sent out to call all knights of any importance to come and take part in the tournament.

It so happened that Sir Kay, Sir Ector's son and the foster brother of Arthur, had that year come of age. He was of course very eager to take part in his first tournament and urged his father to take the family to the great meeting.

So, Sir Ector, who did not often leave home, took Sir Kay, with young Arthur as his squire, to compete in the tournament.

The family had to take lodgings quite a long way outside the city, for many hundreds of people had come to watch the show and rooms were scarce.

26
November

The Sword in the Stone

On New Year's Day another service was held in the cathedral asking God to help find a king for the troubled land.

Then all the knights went to the tournament field, including Sir Ector and Sir Kay. Just as they arrived, Sir Kay realized that he had left his sword behind at their lodgings.

'Please ride back and fetch it for me, Arthur,' he said. 'If I go it will tire my horse and me and I shall not be fit to ride in the tournament.'

Arthur agreed willingly to ride back. He wanted to see his brother fight in the tournament with a good sword.

Arthur had no idea that he was adopted and thought that Sir Kay was his brother.

It was a long ride back to the lodging house and Arthur urged his horse on with a will, in order to get back to the tournament on time.

However, when he reached the house, it was locked up and the windows shuttered. The landlady had gone to watch the tournament and there was no way Arthur could get in to fetch the sword.

He rode back to town feeling upset and not knowing what to say to Sir Kay. Then as he was passing the cathedral courtyard, he saw a fair sword sticking from an anvil set in a stone.

27
November

The Sword in the Stone

The sword in the stone was quite unguarded, as all the knights had been called to the tournament.

Arthur walked in and looked at the huge square of marble set with an anvil, in which was thrust a sword.

'No one can care much about so fair a sword to have left it stuck in that stone,' thought Arthur. 'I will take it to my brother, Sir Kay. He will make good use of it, I know.'

Arthur scrambled up on to the slab of marble, took hold of the sword, pulled it from the anvil, then took it to the tournament field and gave it to Sir Kay.

Sir Kay, who had been at the meeting of the knights and knew all about the sword, recognized it at once.

Sir Kay was a good young man, but the temptation of the chance of becoming king was too great for him to resist. He took the sword to his father, Sir Ector, and said:

'Father. I have the sword from the stone, therefore I must become the king.'

Sir Ector was amazed and puzzled. He knew neither he nor Sir Kay had the slightest claim to the throne.

He took Sir Kay back to the courtyard outside the cathedral where the anvil still stood on the stone.

'Tell me again, son,' he said. 'Where did you get this sword?'

28
November

The Sword in the Stone

Faced with the stone and anvil and his father and with Arthur looking on, Sir Kay could not tell a lie.

'I did not pull the sword from the stone,' he said. 'Arthur gave it to me.'

Sir Ector turned to Arthur.

'Tell me truthfully,' he said. 'Where did you get this sword, Arthur?'

'Well,' replied Arthur, beginning to feel guilty, 'I rode all the way back to our lodgings, but the lady had gone out and the house was locked. I could not get in to fetch Kay's sword. I did my best, really I did, but

the house was locked and that was that. On my way back to the jousting field, I looked in here and saw this sword sticking into the anvil on the stone. Well, no one seemed to want it, so I thought Kay might as well have it, but if I did wrong to take it, I will put it back.'

And taking the sword from Kay's hands, to the utter astonishment of Sir Ector and Sir Kay, Arthur pushed the sword back into the anvil with no trouble at all.

Sir Ector swallowed hard and to make sure that this was not all a simple trick, tried to pull the sword from the stone himself. He could not move it.

Then he ordered Sir Kay to try to pull the sword from the stone. He could not move it, even though he was a strong young man.

Turning again to Arthur, Sir Kay said:

'Arthur, let me see you pull the sword from the stone.'

Arthur climbed back on to the slab.

29
November

The Sword in the Stone

With Sir Ector and Sir Kay watching, Arthur pulled the sword from the stone.

At once Sir Ector and Sir Kay knelt before him and Sir Ector said:

'Arthur, my lord, you are the rightful king.'

Arthur was puzzled and upset.

'My dear father and brother, why are you kneeling before me?' he asked.

Then Sir Ector explained that he was not Arthur's father and that Kay was not his brother, but that Arthur had been brought to them by Merlin when he had been a baby.

Arthur wept at such unwelcome news, for he loved his father and brother dearly.

'If I am to be king, you will not leave me,' he said to Sir Ector. 'You and Kay will be my faithful lords.'

'Gladly,' smiled Sir Ector. 'We will never be parted from you.'

So then the three of them sought out Merlin, who called the other knights together and many times Arthur showed them how he could pull the sword from the stone.

Young Arthur became King Arthur and had many a dreadful battle to fight and many a struggle to win, but always Kay and Ector were at his side in true friendship.

30
November

Burying the Hatchet

Once, out in the West, there used to be a tribe of Indians which fought with hatchets. It was the duty of young braves to keep a hatchet, polished and sharp, ready to be snatched up if an enemy should come near.

After years of war, several chiefs met and decided they would be happier if their tribes were at peace.

They agreed to take turns in fishing the rivers and hunting the buffalo and taking the honey of the wild bees, instead of quarrelling about it.

The tribes put away their fighting weapons, all except the tribe which fought with hatchets. The braves of that tribe continued to sharpen their hatchets and keep them ready for use.

The other chiefs said:

'We do not believe you mean to keep the peace. We think you are waiting until we have forgotten how to fight and then you are going to take your hatchets down and drive us all away from our lands.'

'What can we do to make you believe we mean to keep our word?' asked the tribe which fought with hatchets.

'Bury your hatchets in the ground where you cannot reach them quickly,' replied the other Indians.

So it was done and there was peace between the tribes for many years.

Now, when folks say they are 'burying the hatchet', everyone knows they mean they intend to keep the peace for a long time.

206

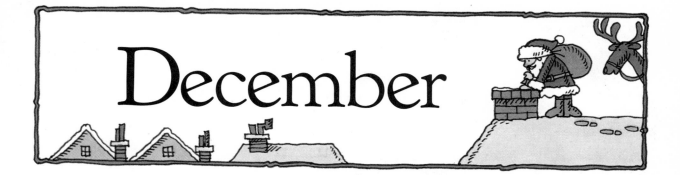

1
December

Beauty and the Beast

Many years ago, in the lovely country of France, there lived a rich merchant with many handsome children. However, the youngest daughter was his favourite and he called her Beauty, because she reminded him of his beloved and alas, dead, wife.

As is the way with the world, the fortunes of the merchant changed. He had to sell his fine house and take his children to live in a small farmhouse. Life was hard and dull for them all, after the fine clothes and parties to which they had been accustomed but which were now no more.

The merchant's last hope for wealth was the one ship he had left. After trading on the high seas, it was due home the next month. The merchant saddled up his horse, packed some food, took the small amount of money he could spare and set off for the seaport to see if his ship would come in. Before he left home, he asked his daughters if there was anything he could buy for them in town.

The two eldest daughters asked for expensive presents which the merchant could scarcely afford. Beauty asked for a white rose.

2
December

Beauty and the Beast

Luck was not riding with the merchant on that journey. At the seaport he learned that his ship had sunk and that all his remaining wealth was at the bottom of the sea. After a night's sleep, he turned his horse towards home with a heavy heart.

It was a long, long journey and with so many troubles to occupy his mind, the merchant did not pay proper attention to where he was going. Clouds gathered, snow fell, a cold wind howled and suddenly the

merchant found that night was falling and he was lost and alone in bitter weather.

How pleased he was, when suddenly shining through the falling darkness and glittering amongst the whirling snowflakes, he saw the lights of a castle set on a hill! He urged his tired horse towards the tall stone walls which surrounded the castle and soon they came to huge wrought iron gates, which swung open as he approached.

'How strange!' thought the merchant. 'But perhaps the gate keeper opened the gates and then hurried back indoors because of the bitter wind.'

3
December

Beauty and the Beast

The merchant could see no sign of a gatekeeper and no one replied to his shouts, so he rode on up the driveway towards the castle doorway. How puzzled he was to find that within the walls of the castle grounds no snow fell and no cold wind blew. The air was as warm as in summertime. Flowers

bloomed and fruit hung on the trees.

The door to the castle stood open and dismounting, the merchant left his horse at the foot of the steps and walked into the huge building. He found a fire blazing in a large hall, but although he called, no one came to speak to him. Feeling weary and seeing a chair by the fire, he could not refrain from sitting down to rest. At once, unseen hands brought a meal and set it on the table beside him.

Again the merchant called and no one replied. Although he was frightened, he ate the meal, for he was hungry and there was no other shelter for miles around. After the meal he remembered his horse. It had vanished from the foot of the steps, but when the merchant explored further, he found the horse in a warm stable. The merchant went back inside the castle and finding a bedroom, fell into a deep sleep.

4
December

Beauty and the Beast

The next morning the merchant awoke and again searched the castle, looking for the unseen strangers who were making him so welcome. He found no one.

However, again invisible hands set a meal for him on the table. He ate with a good appetite, for by then he had lost his fear. It seemed that no one in the strange castle intended him any harm.

He went outside and looked in the stable for his horse. There it was, saddled and bridled ready for his departure, but with no sign of the groom, who must have done the work.

The merchant led the horse through the lovely flower gardens towards the wrought iron gates, which opened to the outside world.

Suddenly he remembered the request of his favourite daughter, Beauty. She had asked that he should take her a white rose.

'I have lost all my wealth,' thought the merchant, 'but at least I can take a white rose to Beauty. There are plenty growing in this garden. Surely one will not be missed.'

He stretched out his hand to pick a rose. As he touched the bush a terrible ROOOOAAAR echoed through the castle grounds.

5
December

Beauty and the Beast

The merchant looked up. Standing at the top of a flight of stone steps and glaring down at him was a terrifying beast. It had the body of a man, but the head and paws of a lion.

'Ungrateful wretch!' it roared at the merchant. 'I treat you with the utmost kindness and you repay me with robbery.'

The merchant was amazed.

'I was taking only one rose from amongst many,' he said, 'and I am quite willing to pay for it. Surely we can settle a little thing like this without quarrelling.'

'I will throw you into a dungeon and keep you there for life, you wicked thief!' the beast roared.

The merchant went down on his knees and begged for mercy, saying he had a family which depended on him for their support. At last the Beast agreed to let the man go, on condition that he sent to live with the Beast the first living thing to greet him on his return home.

'That will be the old dog,' thought the merchant and agreed to the condition.

6
December

Beauty and the Beast

The journey to the merchant's home was long and he was half asleep as he rode up the path to the front door. Looking up, expecting to see his old dog running towards him, the merchant was horrified when his favourite daughter, Beauty,

stepped from the door and took the bridle of the horse.

'Where is Bran?' asked the merchant.

'Why, he has a thorn in his paw and is resting in the stable,' replied Beauty, surprised that her father should enquire after the dog, instead of greeting her.

In great distress the merchant explained that now Beauty must go to live with the terrible Beast in his castle.

'Why do you bother to keep such a silly promise?' asked the other children.

However, Beauty could see that her father was in great fear of the Beast and she agreed to go back to the strange castle.

After a night's rest, the father and daughter rode out together, the merchant sunk in gloom and Beauty fearful of what lay ahead. They came to the castle in the afternoon.

7
December

Beauty and the Beast

Everything happened as when the merchant had been there before. The gardens bloomed under a warm sun. Unseen hands stabled the horses. A fire blazed a welcome in the empty hall. A delicious meal was set on the table.

Then, as Beauty and her father sat down to eat, a roaring echoed through the passages of the castle. Doors opened and slammed shut. Scratching, heavy footsteps thudded over the floors. The Beast burst into the room. He looked at Beauty.

To Beauty's surprise, the Beast spoke to her kindly. He showed her to the most magnificent room she had ever seen and said that it was hers. The cupboards were full of lovely clothes. The shelves were full of books. The furniture was elegant and comfortable.

Beauty could not help being pleased.

Her father stayed one night at the castle with Beauty and then left with tears in his eyes.

'Do not cry, father,' said Beauty. 'I shall be happy here.'

8
December

Beauty and the Beast

In fact Beauty was happy at the castle. She scarcely saw the Beast, except at meal-times and then he hardly said a word. There was no hard work to do, for the unseen hands prepared the food, did the cleaning and washed Beauty's clothes. She enjoyed reading the books and playing in the lovely gardens. Every day she found new and pretty clothes in her room. Life was even better than in the days when her father had been rich.

Then one evening at dinner the Beast said:

'You seem to be so happy here, Beauty,

would you consider marrying me?'

Beauty burst out laughing, although she was sorry when she saw the hurt look on the Beast's face.

'You have been kind, dear Beast,' she said, 'and I like you, but how could I marry a monster? It is out of the question.'

The Beast ate the rest of his meal in silence.

A few days later Beauty was looking in the mirror in her room when her reflection faded and in its place she saw her father in his home. He was pale and ill and the house looked dirty and neglected.

'I must go to my father,' thought Beauty.

9
December

Beauty and the Beast

Beauty ran through the long corridors of the castle, until she found the Beast. Then she begged him to let her return to her father to nurse him through his illness. The

Beast was reluctant to let Beauty go and said that he would die without her. At last he agreed she could go, if she promised to return in eight days. He gave her a ring and told her that when it was time for her to return to the castle, she should put the ring on the table, lie down on her bed and when she awoke, she would find herself once more at the Beast's home.

Then by magic, the Beast transported Beauty to her father's house. She found that her brothers had gone away to join the army, that her sisters were married and that her father was living with only a few old servants to take care of him.

Beauty nursed her father with all the care of a loving daughter and gradually he became well again. However, the days flew by so quickly that before she realized it, Beauty had been away from the Beast for much longer than the eight days she had been allowed. One night she dreamed that she saw the Beast lying, as if dead, near the white rose bush in the castle gardens.

Then Beauty realized how much she loved the kind Beast and how heartbroken she would be if she never saw him again.

Next morning, she told her father she must return to the castle where the Beast lived.

10
December

Beauty and the Beast

Beauty said goodbye to her father and placed the ring given to her by the Beast on the table at the side of her bed. She lay down on the bed and closed her eyes. When she awoke, she was in her room in the Beast's magic castle.

At once she searched through the long corridors and through the warm, sunny gardens, calling the Beast's name.

On she ran, until, as in her dream, she saw the Beast lying under the bush of white roses. In spite of the summer weather, the creature lay cold and still. It seemed to Beauty that he was dead. She kneeled down and put her arms round him and said:

'Oh, dear Beast. How can I live without you? I love you.'

Beauty had scarcely uttered those words than the sound of music and laughing voices came from the castle behind her. The Beast disappeared and in his place knelt a young man more handsome than the sun. He smiled at Beauty and thanked her for releasing him from a terrible enchantment.

He told her that a wicked fairy had condemned him to live in the shape of a beast until a beautiful young woman should fall in love with him. Now that had happened, he was free.

Beauty and the handsome youth walked back to the castle, which was now filled with servants and friends, who too had been put under a spell. It was their invisible hands which had done the work and waited on Beauty and her father.

So Beauty and the young man were married and lived happily ever after. And Beauty, who was now rich, was able to help her father and her brothers and sisters.

11
December

The Little Fir Tree

There was once a pretty little fir tree growing in a fine spot in the forest. It enjoyed plenty of sun and air and had many tall companions growing nearby, pines as well as firs.

The fir tree longed to be grown up and tall. When the peasant children came to picnic and gather wild strawberries, they looked at the little fir tree and said:

'How sweet! What a lovely baby tree!' The fir tree was not pleased. It longed to be big and strong and useful.

Every year the tree grew a ring wider and felt proud and stretched up to try to be like the other trees.

'How I wish I could stretch my branches wide and look out upon the great big world! How I wish the birds could build nests in my branches and I could stretch my head up to sway in the wind,' it sighed.

In the winter the snow fell and made the branches of the little fir tree white. The snow hare came and jumped right over the top of the tree, which annoyed it very much. How it longed to be taller!

The Little Fir Tree

In the autumn, woodcutters would come to the forest and fell the tallest trees. The young fir tree would watch while the great trees crashed to the ground and their branches were hewn off and the trunks left bare. They were loaded on to wagons and dragged out of the forest by horses.

'Where are they going? What will happen to them?' asked the little fir tree.

The swallows who flew into the forest in the springtime, said they did not know what happened to the trees, but a stork said that as he had been flying from Egypt, he had seen some fine wooden ships which smelt of pine.

'They looked grand as they sailed over the sea,' said the stork. 'I think your friends must have been made into ships.'

'Oh, how wonderful,' thought the little fir tree. 'How I should like to be a ship sailing on the sea! But what is the sea? What is a ship? How I wish I knew these things.'

'The sea is like a never-ending puddle and a ship sails on it,' the stork replied.

The Little Fir Tree

One year, near Christmas time, the woodcutters came to the forest and cut down quite a number of the smaller trees. The branches were not lopped off and they were carried carefully out of the forest on carts.

'Where are they going?' asked the little fir tree. 'They are not big like the other trees which were taken to make ships.'

'We know! We know!' twittered the sparrows. 'We have seen them down in the city. They are taken into warm shops and houses and set up in the most magnificent splendour. They are hung with sweets and toys and golden apples and candles. They look wonderful.'

The little fir tree was very excited.

'Does such a splendid future await me?' it

wondered. 'That is better than being a ship. Oh, I am sick with longing for next Christmas to come.'

For the rest of that year the little fir tree grew with all its strength until it became

green and beautiful. When next Christmas came, it was the first tree to be chosen by the woodcutters.

14
December

The Little Fir Tree

The little fir tree was taken down to town and sold to a man from a grand house. Two footmen in livery carried the tree into a big warm room with pictures on the wall and silk covered chairs and sofas.

The tree was planted in a tub of sand and stood on a carpet. Children ran round it saying how beautiful it was.

The tree trembled with excitement.

Then young ladies and men servants began to decorate the tree. They decorated it with baskets of sweets, golden apples, dolls, candles, chocolate figures, little presents and on top, a gold star. The tree looked truly beautiful.

On Christmas Eve presents were put all round the foot of the little fir tree. Then on Christmas day, in the afternoon, when a fine fire crackled in the grate, the candles on the tree were lit. Two double doors were opened. A crowd of children came running into the room.

'Now you may find your presents and take what you want from the tree,' said the lady of the house.

The children were so happy. The tree stood up so proud. It was the most wonderful Christmas tree that had ever been seen.

The little fir tree was happy at last.

When Christmas was over the tree went to live in a pretty garden, till the next year, when it went indoors to be a Christmas tree again, and so it lived for many contented years.

15
December

Father Christmas and the Reindeer

Up near the North Pole a little hut stood in a clearing. It was the home of Father Christmas and Mrs. Christmas. The elves lived in a log cabin, and at this time of the year, they all worked very hard in the big workshop at the side of the clearing, making toys for children all round the world. There was some talk that when the Christmas deliveries were over, they all went for a holiday down Florida way, or on some hot islands in the Pacific, or that those who were good at languages went to the south of France, but no one was sure.

Anyway, one morning, as they were walking across to the workshop after breakfast, Father Christmas looked into the stables to make sure the reindeer were being brought into a good condition ready for their long journey round the world on Christmas Eve.

'Rudolph!' he said, looking at one of the reindeer, which had a red nose. 'Have you got a cold?'

'Just a liddle one,' snuffled Rudolph, 'but don't worry. I'll hab id fixed by Christmas!'

16
December

Father Christmas and the Missing Elf

December was a very busy time for Father Christmas. When he had had a word with his reindeer, he hurried into the workshop. All the elves were hard at work making the usual toys which children had been

enjoying for years. Things like dolls and railway engines and cuddly toys and cars and pushalong horses and pullalong carts were scattered everywhere.

Father Christmas glanced round anxiously.

'Isn't he back yet?' he asked. 'He should have been here by December 1st.'

The elves nearest to Father Christmas shook their heads and looked sympathetic. They knew he was worried.

Father Christmas went into the crisp cold frosty air and stared hopefully into the sky. At last, far in the distance he saw a dot. The dot grew bigger and Father Christmas heaved a sigh of relief as Brainbox Elf made a safe landing in his little flying shuttle.

'You took your time,' said Father Christmas. 'I sent you on that course to find out how to make computer toys, so that none of the modern little children would be disappointed if they wanted a computer for Christmas.'

'Don't panic,' grinned Brainbox Elf. 'I have learned everything. I must just set up the program and we'll have them made like shelling peas.'

'Oh yes,' said Father Christmas. 'I've heard that before. Anyway, why are you late back? You were due here days ago.'

'Sorry about that,' said Brainbox Elf. 'There was trouble in the transport schedule computer. A rubber band broke.'

Then they hurried into the workshop.

Father Christmas and the Pink Rabbit

Father Christmas and all the elves, including Brainbox Elf, were hard at work in their workshop near the North Pole. Things were going well and it looked as if all the toys would be ready on time.

Then, suddenly, there was trouble in the packing and labelling department.

'It is this cuddly pink rabbit,' said Packer Elf. 'He says he won't be sent as a present to 12, Cosy Crescent, because that is where Dolly Dimple lives and she is very bossy and makes all the other toys keep going to her tea parties and mind their manners. Or else she is always the school teacher when they play schools and makes the other toys do hard sums. He says he can do without all that and wants to go somewhere else.'

Father Christmas sighed and took the pink rabbit on his knee.

'Listen, son,' he said. 'Don't believe everything you hear. I happen to know that Dolly Dimple has a heart of gold. Why, if you fall and graze your knee, no one will come to your aid faster than Dolly.'

'Yes,' said the pink rabbit stubbornly, 'with salt water medicine and scratchy bandages. I've heard all about Dolly.'

Father Christmas sighed again and said:

'Don't you think you are being a bit selfish? This isn't the spirit that keeps the toys flying, you know. There is a nice little boy of three years old waiting at 12, Cosy Crescent, to receive you as a Christmas present. Now, you aren't going to disappoint him because you are afraid of Dolly Dimple, are you?'

The pink rabbit shifted uncomfortably.

'All right then, I'll go,' he said.

'That's my brave lad,' smiled Father Christmas, giving the pink rabbit back to Packer Elf.

'You just have to know how to handle them,' smiled Father Christmas, as everyone went back to work.

Father Christmas and the Missing Maps

After working frantically for days, Father Christmas and his elves had finished making all the Christmas toys. Brainbox Elf had even managed to complete all the computer toys, although there had been a terrible panic when one of the reindeer chewed through the electricity cable one morning and cut off the power for three or four hours. Father Christmas had had to send for the Fairy Queen and ask her to plug her magic wand into the power socket of the computer, until the electricity cable was mended.

'You can't beat old fashioned methods,'

everyone agreed. But then the cable was mended and everything went back to normal.

Anyway, all the toys were finished and packed at last. The reindeer were fighting fit. The sleigh was cleaned and polished.

Everyone was taking a well deserved rest, when Pathfinder Elf said:

'Has anyone seen the maps recently? I can remember my way to most places, but I do need a map for some of the new towns.'

At once there was a terrible panic.

19
December

Father Christmas and the Missing Maps

'I know I put the maps away on the usual shelf after last Christmas,' said Pathfinder Elf. 'It isn't my fault if they aren't there any more. Perhaps Mrs. Christmas threw them away when she was spring cleaning.'

'Isn't that typical,' snapped Mrs.

Christmas. 'You boys lose something and then blame it on to the poor old housewife.'

She was feeling rather tired after all the Christmas work. There were so many more mouths to feed in December, to say nothing of the extra washing up.

Then Brainbox Elf spoke up:

'You don't mean these things I'm using to prop up one of the legs of the computer, do you?' he asked. 'They were covered in dust and I thought no one wanted them and the computer only seems to work when one side is higher than the other. You know how it is with these temperamental high tech products.'

With a sigh of relief Pathfinder Elf pulled the wad of maps up from the floor.

'Can you imagine how terrible it would be if I missed out some boys and girls this Christmas? They would be so sad! But now I shall be able to find our way to every little boy and girl in the world,' he smiled. 'All the presents are ready, so there is no need for anyone to worry about a single thing. Christmas will be wonderful.'

20
December

Christmas is Coming

Quite a long time ago, when folk used to eat goose for their Christmas dinner, there was a rhyme which went:

'Christmas is coming, the geese are getting fat.
Please put a penny in the old man's hat.
If you haven't got a penny, a ha'penny will do.
If you haven't got a ha'penny, God bless you.'

Now a naughty fox knew this rhyme and used to say it to a family of geese which lived on a pond in the woods. This made the geese very annoyed.

'I will have you know, young fellow,' said the mother goose, 'that no one is fattening us for Christmas. We are wild geese and belong to no one but ourselves.'

However, the naughty fox went on laughing at the side of the pond and saying the rhyme. He was really saying it for a good reason. He wanted to make the geese so cross, that they would come out of the pond to chase him and then he could catch one of them for his dinner. Foxes are cunning creatures.

21
December

Christmas is Coming

However, this family of geese was quite clever. They saw through the fox's plan. They were wise enough not to get out of the pond to chase him, but they still wanted to stop him from chanting the annoying rhyme. They thought of a plan of their own.

At the bottom of the pond was an old saucepan which someone had thrown away. Very early one morning, before the fox was awake, two of the geese flew up on to the branch of a tree with the saucepan full of pond water. The branch of the tree was near the edge of the pond.

Later on in the morning, when the fox arrived and started chanting:

'Christmas is coming and the geese are getting fat,' one of the geese swam to the edge of the pond immediately under the branch where the other two geese were hidden with the saucepan full of water.

'Do you really think I am getting fat?' the goose called to the fox. 'I do worry about my figure and perhaps I am not as slim as I was when I was young. Now tell me honestly whether I am too plump or not.'

Scarcely able to believe his luck, the fox hurried close to the goose, meaning to gobble it up. However, at the last moment, the goose dived back into the pond and the geese in the tree poured the water all over the naughty fox. He was upset!

The geese were not upset one little bit. They cackled and flapped their wings with glee at the sight of the dripping fox.

'What unfriendly geese you are!' he gasped and he ran away and never bothered them again.

22 December

Once a Year

Mrs. Brown liked to prepare everything well before Christmas. Already the Christmas puddings were made. The cake was made too and was covered with marzipan icing. It was now waiting for the sugar frosting to be put on.

The turkey and the stuffing and the sausages and the mince pies were all in the deep freeze. The Christmas cards were written and addressed.

Mrs. Brown was tired.

She said to her father, who had dropped in for a chat:

'Making an old fashioned Christmas is such a lot of work. I sometimes wonder why I bother.'

'Ah,' said her father, remembering Christmasses long past. 'It is worth it. Who knows what the rest of the year, or the years ahead may bring? Let us be happy together while we can. Remember the old saying:

"At Christmas play and make good cheer,
For Christmas comes but once a year".'

23 December

A Mince Pie for Santa

A little boy was going to bed on Christmas Eve.

'Santa Claus works very hard at Christmas time,' said the boy. 'I should like to leave a little snack for him to eat when he comes to deliver the presents.'

'Very well,' smiled the boy's mother.

Downstairs, between the Christmas tree and the chimney, on a little table, they put a small glass of sherry and a mince pie and of course some carrots for the reindeer.

However, as the little boy was going to bed, he said:

'Someone ought to keep guard over the snack, until Santa Claus arrives.'

'But no one is supposed to wait up to see Santa Claus,' said mother. Then she added: 'But I suppose Teddy Bear could sit on guard. It doesn't matter if teddies see Santa, I'm sure.'

So Teddy was left on guard. He felt terribly important. After all, there can't be many teddies guarding Santa's snack.

In the morning the snack was gone and in its place was a thank you note from Santa saying how much the reindeer had appreciated the carrots.

'Did Santa really eat the snack?' the boy asked Teddy.

Teddy stared straight ahead without replying.

'Teddy is not allowed to discuss Santa's affairs with unauthorised persons,' mother explained.

24 December

The Night Before Christmas

As we all know, people are supposed to get to bed early on Christmas Eve, so that Father Christmas can deliver the Christmas presents without being seen.

One Christmas, in one house, everything was as it should have been. Just as the old rhyme said:

"Twas the night before Christmas,
When all through the house,
Not a creature was stirring,
Not even a mouse.'

Father Christmas had parked his sleigh on the roof and was about to descend the chimney with a sack of presents, when he heard a squeaking. A naughty, greedy mouse had decided to get up and eat some of the nice Christmas food, which had been prepared for the great day.

It ran squeaking up the side of the dining room table, and licking its lips was about to take a bite out of the Christmas cake, which stood there, delicious and untouched, when an elf barred its way.

'Stop that at once!' ordered the elf.

The mouse was indignant.

'Mind your own business!' it said rudely.

'This is my business,' replied the elf. 'Father Christmas is waiting on the roof to deliver the Christmas presents. You know quite well that no one is supposed to see him. How can he come down here with you running about all over the place? And,' added the elf, 'you should not be eating the Christmas cake. Christmas cake should not be touched until Christmas day.'

The mouse hung its head.

'I'm sorry,' it said, 'I did not mean to interfere with Father Christmas. It is just that I am so hungry. But I will come back tomorrow night. There are sure to be a lot of crumbs then.'

It slunk back into its hole, but when it woke in the morning, amongst its presents it found a little Christmas cake from Father Christmas with a note saying: 'Thank you!'

25
December

On Christmas Day

Christmas Day is always full of excitement, with so many presents to open, so much food to eat, so many visitors to talk to.

There is very little time to read books, or even play with presents properly.

Once there was a little boy, who was old enough to remember several Christmasses quite well. He knew that he would enjoy playing with his presents much better when the fuss and frolics were over. So, on Christmas Day, he put his presents somewhere very safe and he appointed himself paper monitor.

He trotted round with a waste paper basket and whenever anyone had unwrapped a present, the boy took the wrapping paper. First he checked to see that no part of the present was still left inside. That was very important. Then he put the paper tidily into the waste paper basket. When the basket filled up, he emptied it outside and came back for more. That way the house was kept tidy, nothing was thrown away which should not have

been, the boy was kept busy and Mummy was pleased.

'How should we ever manage without our paper monitor!' the grown ups said.

26
December

The North Wind Doth Blow

The day after Christmas, a little girl looked out of the window and saw a wind blowing the dead leaves across the garden. The sky was grey and heavy clouds were blowing from the north.

Her grandmother looked over the girl's shoulder and said:

'The north wind doth blow,
And we shall have snow,
And what will the robin do then, poor
thing?
He'll sit in the barn,
To keep himself warm,
And hide his head under his wing, poor
thing.'

Grandmother had scarcely finished speaking when the first flurry of snow flakes blew against the window. Soon the garden was full of leaping, dancing snow and the lawn became whiter and whiter, until no green grass could be seen at all.

The little girl stared out rather anxiously.

'There are no barns round about here,' she said. 'What will the robin do here, poor thing?'

'I'm sure he will be fine,' smiled Grandma. 'Robins are clever birds. I'm sure he will find a hedge tucked away behind a shed somewhere, where he can shelter from the wind.'

At that moment a robin came and perched outside the window, his red breast showing up brightly against the snow and his black eyes gleaming. He hopped about on the window sill.

'Do you think he knows we are talking about him?' asked the girl.

'Maybe,' smiled Grandma. 'I know he will be grateful if we put out some bacon scraps.'

The little girl hung some food scraps in a tree and watched while the robin ate. Then he flew in amongst some bushes and found a cosy shelter from the wind, just as Grandma had said he would.

27
December

Rain, Rain, Go Away

Billy had a new tricycle. He wanted to go outside and ride it round and round the yard, but the rain was falling.

For a moment the sun would shine and Billy would put on his outdoor shoes and his jacket and warm gloves, but when he reached the door, the rain would be falling again.

Grandpa said to Billy:

'Why don't you try saying the rhyme I used to say when I was a little boy and it would not stop raining? It goes:

"Rain, rain, go away,
Come again some other day,
Little Billy wants to play".'

Billy stood at the door and shouted up at the clouds:

'Rain, rain, go away,
Come again some other day,
Little Billy wants to play.'

After a few minutes all the clouds blew away and Billy went out and rode his new tricycle.

'The rhyme doesn't always work,' said Grandpa, 'but it is worth a try.'

28
December

Mr. Scrooge

Once upon a time, down in the greenwood, there lived an elf named Mr. Cuthbert.

The thing which puzzled Mr. Cuthbert was that the little elf urchins used to run after him, as he walked along the woodland pathways, calling:

'Mr. Scrooge! Mr. Scrooge!'

'My name is not Scrooge,' he would say, turning to the little elves. 'If you want Mr. Scrooge, I suggest you ask Mr. Pat the Policeman elf. He knows everyone.'

The elf urchins would run away, but the next day they would be back again, calling:

'Mr. Scrooge! Mr. Scrooge!'

Eventually Mr. Cuthbert went to see Mr. Pat the Policeman elf himself.

'Do you know where a Mr. Scrooge lives?' he asked. 'There are some urchins

running through the woods, who seem to be looking for him. They also seem to have the mistaken idea that I am Mr. Scrooge. I keep telling them that I am not, but it makes no difference.'

Mr. Pat the Policeman elf could not help smiling.

'Have you never heard of Mr. Scrooge?' he asked. 'I can see I shall have to tell you about him.'

29 December

Mr. Scrooge

'Mr. Scrooge was a rather mean man,' explained Mr. Pat the Policeman elf. 'He made the people who worked for him stay in the office for very long hours. He did not believe in holidays for himself, let alone anyone else. He paid the lowest wages possible. At Christmas time he bought in no special food, gave no presents, sent no cards and certainly did not waste money on decorations. The only way he noticed it was Christmas at all was because for once he had to give his employees a day off. That made him cross.

'Then, one night before Christmas, when he was in bed, Mr. Scrooge had some horrid dreams, in which he saw himself as others saw him and had a glimpse of the lonely Christmasses he would spend in future years, because no one would love

him. All that upset him so much that the next day he got up, bought some presents, purchased a turkey and other nice things and went to see a poor young man who worked for him. Mr. Scrooge gave presents to the young man's children and then stayed and shared a turkey dinner with them. After that he was never mean again.'

'What a nice story,' smiled Mr. Cuthbert. 'I suppose the urchins call me Mr. Scrooge because I am so kind and generous, as Mr. Scrooge became.'

Mr. Pat the Policeman elf shifted his feet and looked uncomfortable, because actually Mr. Cuthbert was very mean and that was why the urchins called him Mr. Scrooge.

'Maybe they think you are generous,' said Mr. Pat the Policeman elf, 'but just in case they think you are mean, why don't you try being a little more generous in future? Just to be on the safe side.'

'I will,' smiled Mr. Cuthbert – and he was.

30 December

A Treat for Father Christmas

Christmas had been over for several days. All the Christmas presents had been delivered on time and Father Christmas and Mrs. Christmas and the elves and the reindeer were all exhausted.

They sat about in their home near the North Pole, dozing and eating biscuits or sandwiches, too tired to get a proper meal, too tired even to get ready and fly away on holiday.

Suddenly there was a tapping on the front door.

'Oh no! Not visitors!' groaned Father Christmas. 'I am too tired to talk to anyone.'

However, the person knocking at the

door did not go away. Instead, the door flew open to show the Fairy Queen and a troupe of her little baby fairies fluttering on the doorstep.

'I'm sorry,' gasped Father Christmas, 'I did not mean to be rude, but you know how it is after Christmas. We're all so tired.'

'I know,' smiled the Fairy Queen. 'That is why we are here. You did such a fine job of making everyone happy at Christmas, that we have come to do all the housework and cooking until you feel fit again and then we will take you on holiday to the Enchanted Land where the sun always shines.'

How pleased the elves and reindeer and Father and Mrs. Christmas were!

'This is a thank you present on behalf of all the little boys and girls in the world,' said the Fairy Queen.

Wasn't that nice?

31
December

The Old Year and the New

It was New Year's Eve. Teddy Bear was sitting on top of the toy cupboard, kept awake by the noise from the New Year's Eve party.

He had thought of knocking on the floor and complaining, but he did not want to be a spoilsport.

At last the clock started to chime midnight.

'Soon be over now,' thought Teddy.

Then, he rubbed his eyes and stared. Shuffling along the road was a very old man in long robes and with a scythe over his shoulder and, running along behind him, almost catching him up, was a jolly, bouncy, healthy, golden haired toddler.

Teddy leaned out of the window. 'You poor old man! Are you lost? And what is that baby doing out alone?'

The old man looked up wearily.

'I am the Old Year on my way out,' he sighed. 'I shall be glad to go and rest my weary head.'

The toddler laughed up at Teddy.

'I am the New Year, starting life,' he called in a clear, young voice. 'Show me the happy days and the beautiful people.'

Teddy sat back and gasped.

'Well, I never did!' he said. 'I don't suppose there are any other teddies who have seen the Old Year out and the New Year in. Wait till I tell the other toys in the nursery!'